THROUGH A DRAGON'S EYES: BOOK 1

CHRONICLES OF THE FOUR

MARISSA FARRAR

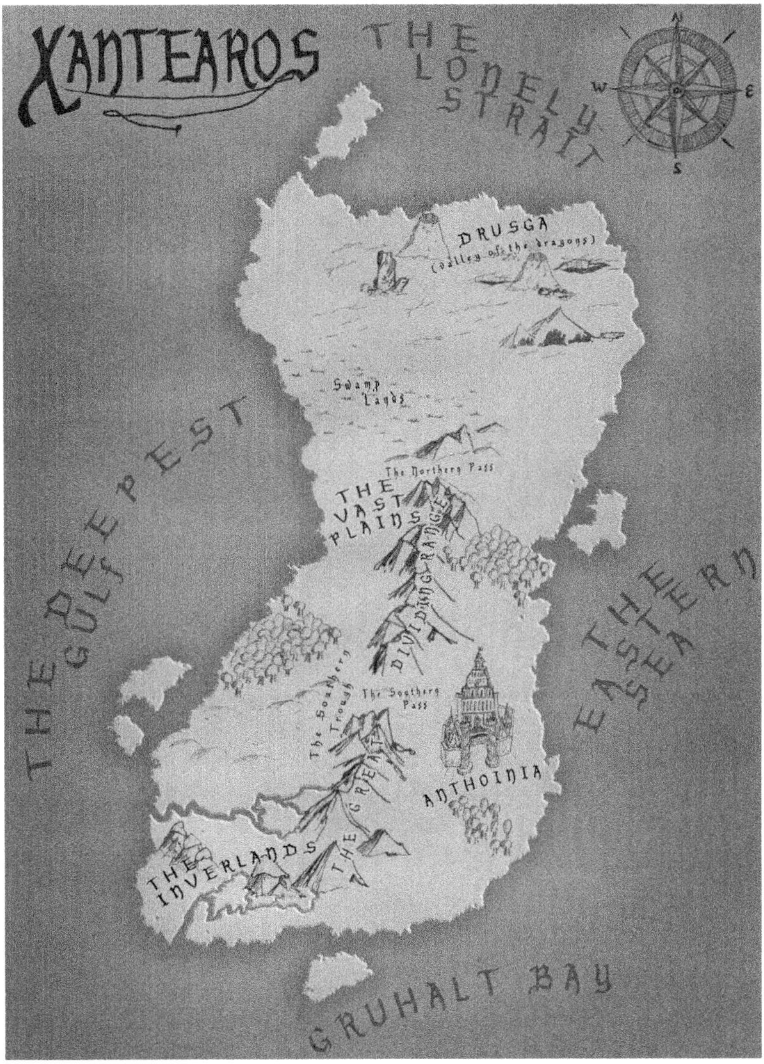
XANTEAROS
THE LONELY STRAIT
N
W
E
S
DRUSGA
(valley of the dragons)
Swamp Lands
The Northern Pass
THE VAST PLAINS
DIVIDING RANGE
THE DEEPEST GULF
THE EASTERN SEA
The Southern Trough
The Southern Pass
THE GREAT
ANTHOINIA
THE INVERLANDS
GRUHALT BAY

CHARACTERS

Information on the cast of characters and the different races and their homelands can be found after the final chapter.

CHAPTER 1

DELA

Dela Stonebridge couldn't take any more of her mother's tears. Maybe she could have handled it if either of them had gotten any rest, but morning had taken forever to arrive.

No one slept the night before The Choosing.

Her fingers automatically went to the ring held on a string of leather at her throat, and she bit down on her irritation. She understood her mother's sorrow. She'd already lost her son—Dela's older brother, Ridley—three years ago, and now every six months, on the day of The Choosing, she was terrified she'd lose her remaining daughter, too.

It was highly unlikely Dela's name would be called to go on the journey. The population of the capital city of Anthoinia was several thousand, and though those of a higher class were not entered, that still left plenty of others. Her mother or father was as likely to end up traveling through the Southern Pass as she was. Besides, for the most part, people came back safe and well. It had only been bad luck that meant they'd lost Ridley.

The thought of her older brother caused her heart to tighten with grief. She tried not to think about him—how he'd shared her coloring, with their strawberry blonde hair and golden brown eyes—knowing it would only bring her pain. They had been three years apart in age, but people always commented on how they could have been twins, had they been closer together. He would be twenty-three, had he lived, and she was now the same age he'd been when he'd been killed on the journey.

Dela slipped out of bed and quickly pulled her short tunic over her head, covering the vest she'd slept in. Most women wore their tunics longer, but Dela found it wasn't practical, especially when she was trying to work. She pulled on her soft leather pants, tugging the belt tight around her waist, and shoved her feet into her boots. Finally, she tied her long hair into a knot at her nape.

Her mother and father's bed was across the room from her own. The house wasn't big enough for separate bedrooms. They had one living area, where they lived and slept, and a bathroom out back. It was barely a house, really, more of a shack, but even the presence of a bathroom was considered luxury to some.

Most young women her age would have left home by now, but she hadn't wanted to leave her parents alone. It was hard enough getting by in this city, especially during the time approaching The Choosing when food was stored up to exchange with the population on the Western coast. They needed her income to get by, and she wasn't about to just up and leave them. Besides, since losing Ridley, she'd known her mother, Johanna, had needed her in more than just a practical way. The hole he'd left in all their hearts was an impossible one to fill, but that didn't stop Dela from trying.

She went to her mother's bedside and crouched next to where she lay. Her mother's eyes opened as she sensed Dela approach, and Dela covered her hand with her own. The back was crepe-papery with age, though her mother was only in her forties. But a hard life had caused her to age fast.

"It'll be okay, Mama. Just like it has been for the last five Choosings."

Johanna sniffed and sat up in bed. Beside her, Dela's father, Godfrey, grunted and rolled over.

"You don't know that, Dela, darling. And I know you're trying to be kind, but until this day is over and I can be sure you're not one of the people going, I'm going to stay upset, okay?"

Her mother once had the same strawberry blonde hair as Dela, but now the tresses were streaked with white. She wore it long, like Dela, but Johanna's was caught up in a thick braid which fell down her back.

"I know, but it doesn't stop me from wanting to make you feel better."

"You're a good girl."

Dela leaned in and kissed her mother's cheek. "The Choosing isn't for a few hours yet, anyway. I'm going to go out and fetch us some breakfast."

"Okay. Be careful."

"I will."

Dela crossed back to her side of the room and bent to slide her hand beneath the thin mattress. Her fingertips met with cool steel, and she pulled the dagger out from where she'd hidden it, its weight solid in her palm. There were times when her job came in useful, and getting her hands on this dagger of Elvish steel for a fraction of what it was worth was one of those times. She pushed the blade into her belt, and then pulled the bottom of her tunic over the hilt, hiding the weapon from prying eyes. If someone tried to steal the blade, they'd find themselves sorry. It might not be a full-sized sword, but Dela was skilled with the dagger.

She didn't have work today. Normally, she assisted the blacksmith, forging various tools, household goods, and weapons, but today was a special day, and unless you were one of the market stall holders, or one of the taverners, hoping to make some extra money, it wasn't worth working over.

Dela opened the front door and stepped out onto the street. Already, the city was busy, people rushing about, getting ready for The Choosing. She walked the narrow winding streets, stepping over puddles and dodging small children playing chasing games.

The little ones didn't really understand the importance of the day. Anyone under the age of sixteen wasn't eligible, and only when children approached their teenage years did they consider this to be something that would affect them. Parents sometimes went away, but for the most part, they came back. Pregnant or nursing mothers were also exempt from The Choosing, and often families had many children in order to prevent the mother of the family ever being entered. Unfortunately for her own mother, nature hadn't been kind, and Johanna had been unable to have a big family. And when their family's name had come up in The Choosing, it had been the youngest male of the family who'd gone and never returned.

As Dela approached the market square, she sensed the atmosphere building. There was understandable tension in the air, but also excitement. There were some who wanted to be part of the Chosen, who looked forward to an opportunity to escape the confines of the city and prove themselves.

Food stalls were already crowded with people, and the scent of spices filled the air. Small buns filled with fried vegetable patties, crispy pastry containing raisins and spices, flatbreads stuffed with spiced potatoes and chickpeas. Prices had begun to rise as the City Guards started to store grains for the Passover. Once the Chosen had returned from their mission, however, they would have several months of opulence before things started to get expensive again in time for the next Choosing.

Located behind the market square, the intimidating fortress of the castle rose into the sky. Its splendor was a contrast to the poor slums of the rest of the city. There were a few areas where wealthier folk lived, but most of Anthoinia were like her family, or even poorer. Officially, King and Queen Crowmere ruled over the whole of the lands of Xantearos, but each of the races had their own region, which the humans stayed well away from. During the forging of the Treaty, one hundred and fifty years ago, Xantearos was divided up so each of the races no longer needed to mix. The only time they did was during the Passover, when commodities were exchanged to ensure each race was able to survive comfortably, and even then, it was only for a short while.

Knowing her mother loved the raisin pastries, Dela headed over to that stall.

Suddenly, hands grabbed at her waist from behind, and her stomach lurched. Dela reached for her dagger and spun around at the same time.

When she saw who had grabbed her, she exhaled a sigh. "By the Gods, Layla, I almost stabbed you!"

Her friend took a couple of dancing steps back, her dark hair flying around her face. "Only if you were fast enough."

She rolled her eyes. "Don't tempt me!"

Layla Buckley laughed. "I've always been quicker than you. Even when we were at school together."

"Things can change, you know."

Layla grinned, not taking her threats seriously. "You getting something for Johanna?"

"Yeah, she's worrying herself sick again. Just like every Choosing. I thought a decent breakfast would make her feel better."

Her friend appraised her. "And how are you feeling?"

She shrugged. "Okay. Same as every Choosing. How about you?"

"I'm fine, but I'm not the one who lost my big brother through this process. You're allowed to be a bit freaked out by it all, Dela. I know you want to stay strong for your mother, but this affects you, too."

"Like I said, I'm fine. In a few hours, this will all be over, and we can get back to our normal lives."

"For the next six months, at least," Layla pointed out.

"True."

She'd reached the front of the line, and so ordered three of the pastries. "Do you want one?" she offered her friend as she was ordering.

"Nah, I'm fine. I ate already. Save them for your family. We can all barely afford to feed ourselves, never mind other people's families."

"Your family is a lot bigger than mine," she said. "And anyway, you're practically family, Layla. We've known each other since we were in diapers."

Layla nudged her in the side. "We certainly fight like sisters!"

It was true, but they looked after each other like sisters, too.

The stall holder handed Dela a paper bag containing the warm pastries, and she paid him the money in return, not getting anything like the sort of change she had for exactly the same thing only a matter of weeks ago.

Dela nodded to the castle overlooking them. "I bet *they* don't have to pay double for everything this close to The Choosing."

Layla snorted. "Even if they did, it's not as though they couldn't afford it. They're probably sitting on more money than either of us will see in our lives. Queen Crowmere probably wipes her backside with bills."

"Layla, hush!"

She glanced around, making sure none of the City Guards were around. They could get in trouble for talking about the queen in such a way. The City Guards would be especially vigilant this morning when emotions were running high, expecting fights to break out, or even lootings and runaways.

"I should get back," Dela said. "It's only another hour until The Choosing, and I don't want my mother to get worried."

"Of course."

Already people were gathering near the platform at the base of the castle's walls where the names would be called. The number of people called would be twenty or more, and everyone would want to hear each and every name, just in case either they or someone they loved—or even hated—was called upon. People jostled shoulders to get the best spots near the front, not wanting to miss anything.

Dela leaned in and gave her friend a quick hug. "Good luck."

"You, too," Layla said before turning and running off in the opposite direction, quickly engulfed by the crowds.

Clutching the warm pastries to her chest, Dela headed home.

Her father was standing outside the front door, frowning at her as she approached. "Where have you been? Your mother is worried sick."

"To get breakfast, Pops." She lifted the paper bag containing the treats. "And I'm not a child anymore. I turned into adulthood four years ago, when I was sixteen. I'm only still living here because of—"

Dela cut herself off, realizing she was about to say it was only because of them. She didn't want to say anything hurtful, not now. They were good parents, all in all. Her mother worried too much, and her father could be a little gruff, but considering the hand life had dealt them, she didn't have much to complain about. She knew other girls who'd been put out to work in the brothels as soon as they'd turned sixteen—or sometimes even younger when the parents lied about their ages—and the money earned was given back to the household. At least she'd been allowed to learn a trade that didn't involve her lying on her back or being on her knees.

Her mother appeared, dressed in a long version of Dela's tunic, which brushed the older woman's ankles. "There you are. I was worried."

"I know, Mama. I'm sorry. But I brought your favorites."

She pushed the paper bag into her mother's hands. Johanna opened the bag and burst into tears.

Alarmed, Dela asked, "Don't you like them anymore?"

She swiped away at her tears. "Yes, I do. I love them. I'm just so frightened that tomorrow you'll be gone."

"I'll be fine, Mama. Just eat now. We have to leave soon."

"You need to eat, too." Johanna reached into the bag and pulled out one of the pastries and handed it back to Dela. "It's important you stay strong, just in case …"

"Everything is going to be fine, Mama. Wait and see."

Dela took the pastry her mother offered her and brought it to her mouth, only to discover her appetite had vanished and a cold worm of worry had replaced it.

CHAPTER 2

WARSGRA

He lifted his axe and brought it down directly over the neck of the boar. The animal didn't even have time to squeal before it collapsed to the ground, and hot blood spurted from the cut. The dying animal kicked its legs a couple of times, jerking in its death throes.

Warsgra sent a prayer for the boar's spirit up to the mountain Gods as the final breath left the animal's body, and it fell still for good.

Not wanting to let anything go to waste, Warsgra dipped his hand to the wound of the dying beast and allowed his palm to fill with the hot fluid. It warmed his skin, and, before it got the chance to cool, he brought the blood to his mouth and drank deeply.

He gave a grunt of pleasure. That was good. The blood would fortify him, and he needed fresh meat for the journey ahead.

Warsgra straightened, and with one fist—the one not holding the axe—he pulled his long, wavy brown hair away from his face. Though he was standing at the base of the Great Dividing Range, the mountain range that ran almost all the way through the middle of Xantearos, he wore only shoulder protectors, a loincloth, and thick, animal skin boots. He'd grown up in this environment his whole life and didn't feel the cold.

The thought made him growl in irritation. He was going to have to travel with other folks soon. Their puny bodies and need for multiple layers made this trek even more of a chore. He'd have preferred to take only a few more of his own kind, the Norcs, or even go it alone, but this was how peace had remained among the other folk living on the Western coast, and he didn't want another war breaking out. While he might have the brute strength so lacking in the other races, he appreciated that they had their skills. The Elvish could be cunning, and some of them even had magical abilities, though they were no longer allowed to use them, and the Moerians were dangerous fighters, skilled on horseback and with a weapon of any kind.

No, it was better that he swallow his pride twice a year so they all worked together. The crops weren't enough on this side of the mountain range to keep everyone fed, and while he was happy hunting and eating meat for every meal, the women and children of his clan were not.

Even worse than traveling with the other races who lived on this side of the coast was meeting with the humans a little beyond the midway point of the Southern Pass. As much as he disliked the Elvish and Moerians, he despised the humans. They needed to send multiple amounts of their number just to make it halfway through the pass, and by the time they met with him and his clan, they were exhausted and terrified. They were a pitiful sight to behold, and he still didn't understand how they'd managed to keep hold of most of the Eastern coast all these years. Yes, their numbers were great, and their ability to build and design far surpassed his kind, but every time he came face to face with one, all he could think was how he'd be able to crush them with a single blow from his fist. He was grateful that his interaction with them only ever needed to be limited to exchanging goods. If he was forced to travel with them for any amount of time, he imagined he would struggle to hold back his natural instincts to crush them.

"You're prepared for tomorrow's journey?" asked his clan mate, Jultu Rockrider, as he strode toward where Warsgra stood over the now dead boar.

Jultu was as big as Warsgra, but his family was less important among their kind. Warsgra's family had been around in the early days of the Treaty, and Warsgra and his ancestors had fought hard to make sure they were the leaders of their clan. Other clans of Norcs lived across the foothills of the Great Dividing Range, but Warsgra's was by far the largest and most powerful. The area given to the Norcs during the Treaty was known as the Southern Trough, and Warsgra's clan's position at the entrance to the Southern Pass was the most highly sought. The mines the Norcs worked were rich with coal in this area, and, carved out of the mountain side on both sides of their camp, was evidence of their work. No other clan would be stupid enough to challenge Warsgra, however. He would crush them in an instant if they tried.

Warsgra straightened. "I am now. Are the bison ready for the morning?"

"Yes, and the carts are loaded with coal. We just have to hope the Elvish and Moerians arrive by sunrise."

"They will." He snorted. "Or they'll have to travel alone."

"You know that isn't how things work, Warsgra," he warned. "Don't break a treaty that's a hundred and fifty years old just because you have no patience."

Warsgra shrugged. "I have patience. Just not for their kind."

"There's a reason we all came together, remember. It wasn't so long ago that our kind was almost wiped out by the mountain Gods. Don't disrespect them by making light of their powers."

Warsgra knew of their powers. His great grandfather had almost been killed during one such journey, and the tales of how he'd survived had raised his family name to what it was today.

"It's not the Gods I make light of, it's the people I'm due to travel with." He sighed and lifted his hand in defense. "Okay, okay. Relax, Jultu. I won't do anything to jeopardize things. I'll smile sweetly and be nice." As though to demonstrate his ability, he pulled his full lips back and exposed a line of strong white teeth.

Jultu lifted a bushy eyebrow. "You look more like you're thinking of a big meal than being friendly."

He burst out laughing and smacked his naked thigh. "Aye, or a good young female to bed."

His clan mate joined the laughter. "That, too. When are you going to choose yourself a wife, Warsgra? People are talking, and everyone wants a good wedding. Plenty of time to get drunk and have sex."

The weddings of his kind took place over a week, and most people couldn't remember their own names by the end of the celebrations.

The smile fell from Warsgra's lips. "I have no wish to get married. Especially not if it's only to give the people an excuse to drink wine and fuck. The last thing I need is some woman thinking she has a hold over me, or even worse, little rugrats crawling around." He pounded his fist to his massive chest. "I'm keeping my freedom."

"You'll end up old and dead, and with no one to continue your name, if you're not careful, Warsgra."

"But people will sing songs of my strength and courage for generations to come."

"Even great heroes can be forgotten," his clan mate warned.

Warsgra snorted. "Then they weren't that great."

He set to work with his axe, gutting the boar to be spit-roasted, and then hunks of meat would be wrapped in cloth to take on the journey. Several other members of his clan would be coming along in the morning, helping to drive the carts loaded with coal which the bison would pull. Because of the location of their home, already at the base of the Great Dividing Range and only a matter of hours from the Southern Pass, they didn't have as far to travel as the Elvish or the Moerians. The Elvish lived farther south, in the Inverlands, where the temperatures were cooler again. And the Moerians preferred the warmer climes of the north, where the Vast Plains stretched, allowing them to run their horses and hunt the animals that ran alongside them. Their rivers held gold, which they brought in exchange for grains from the humans, and the Elvish brought with them diamonds, mined from the most Southern point of the Great Dividing Range. It seemed crazy to him that the humans would exchange things that could be eaten for things that simply looked pretty when hung around their scrawny little necks, but it seemed humans valued beauty above full stomachs.

He looked across his homeland. The houses were created from rock and animal skin, and fires burned outside most of them to keep away unwanted visitors during the night, and keep the inhabitants warm. Living under the shadow of the mountain range made the Southern Trough a hard land to live on, but it was their land, and any complaints instantly made them look weak. Weakness was not an attribute welcomed among the Norcs. Weakness got members of your family killed, and other Norcs didn't want weak members to breed yet more weak stock into their population.

This time tomorrow he would be leaving his homeland behind, something that filled him with mixed emotions, and Warsgra didn't do emotions well.

He just had to wait for the others to arrive.

CHAPTER 3

DELA

Clutching her mother's hand—for her mother's reassurance more than her own—they made their way back to the city square. Dela's father followed, even quieter than usual, and though he didn't say as much, Dela knew he was worried about the results of The Choosing, too.

The streets seemed ten times busier than they had been only an hour earlier. Everyone was moving in the same direction, and they were caught up in the flow, hurrying to stay afoot. Falling down with this many people around would most likely only get you trampled.

The narrow streets opened onto the square. Dela let out a breath, taking in the vast expanse of heads and bodies. She craned her neck, trying to spot Layla. Was her friend here yet? She wondered if she'd recognize any of the names called this time. It would be a terrifying but amazing thing to leave the city walls and head up through the Southern Pass to meet other races. Dela had never properly met someone of another race. She'd caught glimpses of them, and seen paintings, but that was all. Would they be horrifying? Would the Norcs be as brutish as they were rumored to be, the Elvish be as devious, and the Moerians as uncivilized? She'd heard the stories, just as anyone growing up in Anthoinia had, but to come face to face with them would be something else entirely.

Not that such a thing would happen to her. Her brother had already been called, and the chances of another member of her family going would be thousands to one.

Was that a dip of disappointment she felt?

Immediately, guilt flooded through her. Her brother had died doing such a trip, and she was thinking of it as an adventure, a way to escape her parents' home and this city, and see the world outside. She shook her head at herself. How selfish she was.

A pair of blue eyes locked with hers over the crowds, and Dela pulled herself from her thoughts and lifted her hand in a wave. Layla was standing a little way off, surrounded by her numerous brothers and sisters, so many Dela often got them mixed up or forgot their names.

From the direction of the platform, a horn suddenly sounded, and Dela jumped. Around her, the crowd fell quiet, only people coughing and distant dogs barking disrupting the now fraught silence.

It was time.

Layla threw her a thumbs up sign, and Dela gave her a tight smile in return.

The horn blew out a melody, and, from the castle above, King and Queen Crowmere began to descend, walking the vast stairway that led down to the city square below. The massive gates opened, and they stepped through. The king and queen were both in their thirties now and were yet to produce children—something people were starting to question in private, but would never dare to do so in public.

A murmur rose around the crowd, people commenting on how beautiful Queen Crowmere was, with her waist length, shiny dark hair, and how handsome the king, with his full beard and broad shoulders.

It was hardly surprising. Dela thought almost anyone would look amazing with that amount of finery on their bodies. The queen was dripping with jewels—huge gold necklaces around her neck—and her fingers must have been so heavy with all the jewels Dela was surprised she could even hold her hand up to offer them a wave. Many of those jewels would have been acquired during the Passover. It seemed strange to Dela how they gave away food, causing some of the city to suffer and starve, in order to get their hands on yet more precious gems when it seemed to her that they had quite enough. She understood the races on the other sides of their lands weren't as fortunate to be blessed with their climate and crops, and so this was the only thing they had to trade, but Dela didn't believe it was all done out of the goodness of their hearts.

King and Queen Crowmere wouldn't be leading The Choosing, but were always present during. The head of the City Guard —a man in his forties, with a massive black beard, called Philput Glod—had that responsibility. And, from the way his smile stretched from ear to ear, Dela thought he probably enjoyed the task, too.

"Welcome to The Choosing," he boomed over the crowd. "Twice a year, at the changing of the seasons, we gather here to learn who will be the next Chosen. Those Chosen will embark on a mission to not only provide those less fortunate than ourselves with grain to feed their families, but also to return with coal to keep our furnaces stoked, and with gold and jewels to ensure our city remains wealthy. This time is called the Passover, and is what keeps our glorious country of Xantearos at peace. Those Chosen are honored to be serving their city."

Glod pulled out a scroll, and, as he unraveled it, read out the names.

Her mother's hand tightened around Dela's as names were announced. With each one, there came a gasp of shock or a cry of surprise. It was a mixture of congratulations and commiserations, depending on the situation. For young men, as Ridley had been, this was supposed to be a time for them to prove themselves.

"Layla Buckley," Glod called out.

Dela's heart stopped, and she swung around to look in the direction she'd last seen her friend. No, not Layla. Layla stood with her hand to her mouth, her blue eyes wide and round with shock.

The names continued to be called out. Dela barely heard them, thinking instead about how her best friend would be leaving tomorrow for several weeks. She had to come back. She had to. Dela didn't think she could cope with losing her as well.

She tried to focus on the other names being called. She recognized a couple—an older man, Wayneguard Norton, and another male a little older than she was, who'd been at school with Ridley.

"Dela Stonebridge," the Guard called out.

Dela felt as though someone had punched her in the chest. Beside her, her mother let out a cry and fell into her arms. Numbly, Dela hugged her, but her mind was spinning. Had she really just heard that? Had he called out her name?

"It's okay, Mama." She patted Johanna's back. "I'll be okay. I'll have Layla with me."

"I can't do this again," her mother sobbed. "I just can't."

Her father stepped in. "She has to, Johanna. She has no choice. You know what happens to absconders."

Those who tried to run from their duties would be tracked down. They were apprehended and beheaded on the same platform the names were being announced from now. It was a way of making sure everyone knew what would happen to them if they absconded from their job.

Tears streamed down her mother's face, and Dela desperately wished there was something she could do to take them away. But this was out of her hands. Short of claiming she was pregnant—which she most certainly wasn't—or dropping dead, she'd be going with everyone else to leave for the Passover tomorrow.

"I need to speak with Layla," she managed, still in a daze. Her friend would understand how she was feeling. It was a small relief, but at least they'd be together. Of course, it also gave Dela someone else to worry about—another person she cared about being taken by The Choosing. There were dangers along the way, but sometimes people simply weren't healthy enough to make it there and back again. The journey to the foothills of the mountains was an easy enough trip, but once the group started to ascend into the Great Dividing Range, through the Southern Pass, things could go wrong very quickly. Dangers lay in all directions. If timings were done badly, and either the white cloud descended, or the west wind blew, they might lose everyone.

The other races on the Western coast did things differently. Where Anthoinia saw it a case of safety in numbers, the other folk sent their most fierce warriors.

But that was how things had always been done.

The Eastern coast of their lands was rich in agriculture, with a more temperate climate, which the humans had always reigned over. And the Western coast was rich in minerals—coal needed to keep the furnaces of the Eastern coast burning. To prevent either parts of the lands and its people from struggling, it made sense to exchange goods twice a year. Of course, the Western coast could grow a few crops, and the Eastern coast could cut down trees, but it wasn't enough to live sustainably. This way of doing things had been happening ever since the Treaty had been put into place, and nothing was going to change now. If they lost a few people during the journey, it was almost to be expected. The mountain passes were the only ways to reach either coast of Xantearos, other than navigating the entire coast, which was even more treacherous, and would take months, or else to go by sea. The sea held its own dangers, with rough storms and sea monsters that could drag a ship down with a single tentacle. And no one went to the Northernmost point of Xantearos. The Northernmost point was called Drusga, which translated as Valley of the Dragons, and was made up of volcanoes and hot pools, and was rumored to be the place where the dragons used to live. Of course, dragons hadn't been seen for hundreds of years, and no one was crazy enough to want to go to Drusga and find out if rumors of their demise were true.

No, the Southern Pass, though with its dangers, was without doubt the safest option.

Her mother released her hand, though Dela sensed her reluctance, and Dela pushed her way through the crowds to where Layla was surrounded by her many siblings, each hugging and kissing her. Her friend spotted her approaching and pushed her brothers and sisters out of the way to open her arms for her. Dela fell into them, and they held each other tight.

"Oh, by the Gods, Dela. I can't believe we've both been chosen."

"I know. I know." She unfolded herself from her friend's arms to look into her face. "At least we'll be together."

They locked eyes, and Layla nodded, tears shimmering in their blue depths. "Yes, at least we'll be together."

"So, what happens now?" Dela asked.

Layla glanced back at the platform, where the City Guard was rolling up his scroll, and the king and queen were being ushered back into the safety of their castle. "We have tonight, and then we leave at first light."

* * *

Dela woke early the following morning, before the sun had begun to rise. Her mother had cried into the early hours, while Dela had lain in bed, a strange mixture of fear and excitement swirling inside her.

She'd barely slept, and, when she had, her sleep had been filled with vivid but confusing dreams of soaring across a night sky, the world a dark and empty space beneath her.

She didn't want to feel the excitement. It felt like a betrayal to both her mother and Ridley. She shouldn't be excited doing something that had brought death to her family. Yet the idea of getting beyond the city walls and seeing something of their country set her pulse racing. What would it be like out there? They were always told that the walls had been built for their own safety, to keep out the wild creatures that roamed in the lands, but now she was being sent out into them.

Like most of the people who lived in Anthoinia, Dela didn't own much. She had the clothes she'd worn the previous day for The Choosing, and a second near identical outfit. Moving as quietly as possible, she set about gathering her few possessions and stuffing them into a bag which would strap across her shoulders. Meals would be provided along the way—after all, they'd be traveling with numerous carts filled with food. It wasn't as though they'd be able to starve the people tasked with delivering them. They'd be given a ration of water, but would also be expected to find water along the way, presumably when they set up camp for the night.

That same thrill of exhilaration shot through her again. She'd be sleeping under the stars, unprotected from whatever else lived in the kingdom. Her hand went to her dagger. She thought she'd be grateful to have the blade on her, and wondered if Layla had something similar. If she didn't, Dela would see if they could swing by the blacksmiths before they left and pick her up something to protect herself with.

All of the people called in The Choosing were due to meet back at the city square at daybreak. It was almost that time now, but the idea of waking her mother to say goodbye made her feel wretched. A part of her was tempted to just kiss her mother's cheek and sneak away before she woke, but though it would be easier on her, she didn't want her mother to be even more upset that they'd not had a proper goodbye.

Instead, she crouched at her bedside, in much the same way as she'd done the previous morning, and shook Johanna awake.

She woke with a start. "Is it time?"

"Yes, Mama. I have to go."

She moved to swing her legs out of bed, but Dela's hand on her arm stopped her. "You don't need to come, Mama. It will be easier if I do this alone."

Johanna stared into her face, her eyes shiny with tears, her jaw tight, her lips pressed together. Dela knew she was trying to hold it together for her sake, and she loved her mother even more for it.

"I'll come back, Mama. It will just be a matter of time."

She reached in and hugged her mother tight.

Her father had woken by this time, so she leaned in and kissed his hairy cheek.

"You can take care of yourself. I know you can." His gruff voice cracked, and she appreciated the small show of emotion from him. It must be hard. She knew her father loved her, and while her mother was allowed to cry her tears, men simply weren't allowed to show emotion in their society.

"I will. I'm tough, Pops. You know that."

"'Course I do. We'll see you when you return, okay?"

She nodded, tears of her own threatening, and a painful lump constricting her throat. Dela didn't want to lose it, knowing it would only make things harder. She remembered their goodbyes to Ridley the morning he'd left, how, even though they knew it was possible he might not return, they hadn't really believed he wouldn't. They'd even joked and jested with each other, telling him not to go getting himself eaten by any monsters. Ridley had been excited about going, and though there was an undercurrent of worry, they'd been proud of him, too. He was a man, taking on the world. He'd taken off the ring he always wore—the one with the shiny black stone with a thread of red running through it—and pressed it into her palm. "Take care of this for me, Sis," he said. "I want it back when I return." She'd kissed him and promised she would. But when only a small part of the convoy returned, their lives had been thrown into the black hole of knowing he was gone and he wasn't ever coming back.

This was different now. There was the very real possibility of the same thing happening again, and she didn't know how her parents would be able to cope if they were left completely alone. What was the point in continuing if you lost both of your children? The world would be empty and meaningless. At least in death, there was the possibility they would be together again, assuming Ridley didn't do something that condemned his soul to the underworld before he died.

Unable to speak, knowing that doing so would reduce her to tears, she secured the pack containing her few possession on her shoulder and turned to leave what had been her home for the past twenty years. Feeling her parents' eyes on her, she glanced over her shoulder, and then lifted her hand in a wave. Her lower lip trembled as her mother clutched her father and sobbed on his shoulder. She wanted to tell Johanna it would be all right, promise her that she'd return, but they all knew it was a promise she might not be able to keep.

As her footsteps took her through the narrow streets where she'd grown up, putting space between her and the house, a part of Dela's soul grew lighter. She wasn't happy to leave her parents — far from it—but she felt the responsibility of being the remaining child like a backpack weighing her down.

From the homes she passed, people peeped out.

They called out to her, "Good luck."

"May the Gods bless your journey."

"Winds speed to you!"

She wasn't someone who'd ever liked attention before, but their well-wishes made her stand taller, her shoulders back. The children whispered behind their hands, their eyes widening with awe.

Dela hadn't asked for this—none of the Chosen had—but she still felt special in that moment.

She stepped into the open area of the city square and glanced up at the castle towering over them. How were King and Queen Crowmere feeling that morning? Did they give any thought to the twenty souls being forced beyond the city walls? Or were they still sleeping peacefully, not a single troubled thought in their heads to wake them?

Across the other side of the square, Dela spotted Layla. She was talking to the man who'd been in Ridley's year at school. She recognized a couple of other people, too. An older man in his fifties with a good beard of silver and solid shoulders, who she believed was called Norton, and a couple of men around the ages of thirty years, too. She was relieved to see that she and Layla appeared to be the youngest of those Chosen this half-year. It was difficult for everyone involved when someone who had only recently passed their sixteenth year was Chosen. Though legally they were adults, it was hard for people not to still view them as a child, especially for the family involved. To be called up during The Choosing on the very first time you were eligible to enter was very unlucky indeed.

Layla spotted her and ran over. The two women clutched each other tightly, knowing exactly how the other one was feeling without having to say a word. They had each other, and that was something, at least.

"The carts are already outside the city walls," Layla said. "We'll be heading out shortly."

Dela surveyed the small crowd. "Is this everyone?"

She was asking more than she was saying—had anyone absconded? But Layla nodded. "Yes, I think so."

"Good."

The last thing she needed her parents to have to see was one of their own decapitated in the square because they'd tried to get out of their duties.

A couple of the men, including the older one, strolled over.

"Dela Stonebridge," he said, putting his hand out to her. "You think you're ready for this?"

She shook the offered hand, making sure her grip was as firm as his. "As ready as anyone else here," she said. Because she was young and female didn't automatically make her weak or incapable. "It's Borton, isn't it?" she asked, deliberately getting his name wrong.

He dropped her hand and cleared his throat. "Norton. Wayneguard Norton."

She exchanged a secret smile with Layla "Ah, yes, of course. My apologies."

"Hey, Dela," the younger man who'd known Ridley said. His name was Brer Stidrisk, if she remembered correctly. "How are you feeling about all of this? It can't be easy, what with Ridley …"

He trailed off, apparently unsure what to say.

"No, it isn't, Brer, but we'll get through it. Thank you."

He ducked his head, the moment of compassion apparently making him uncomfortable.

Philput Glod, the head of the City Guard appeared on the same platform he'd made the announcements from the previous day.

"Welcome, everyone!" he called across the small crowd. "You have the honor this half-year to meet the other races—the Norcs, Moerians, and Elvish—for the Passover. We are not expecting you to come across any trouble, but, to be prepared, if you do not have a weapon of your own, please help yourself to something you will be able to manage." He gestured to a small pile of swords and knives off to one side.

Subconsciously, Dela's hand went to the hilt of her dagger. It may not be large, but she knew how to handle it, and she hoped that would be enough to defend herself and others if need be.

"Food and water has been provided for the first few days," he continued. "After that time, you will be expected to find water sources along the way, and you may wish to hunt to provide yourselves with fresh meat or fish."

"You ever hunted anything?" Layla asked Dela out of the side of her mouth, keeping her voice down.

"Only mice when they come into the house," she replied with a smirk.

Glod's raised voice drowned them out. "You will be provided with bedding rolls, and canvas to sleep beneath, and you will be responsible for their safe return. Is that understood?"

"He's more worried about the bedding rolls' safe return than ours," Dela murmured to her friend, and Layla covered a snort of laughter with her hand.

"Finally," he called out, "we wish that the grace of the Gods be with you."

That signaled the end of his speech, and everyone got moving, gathering what they needed to take with them. Dela was happy with her dagger, but Layla approached the pile of weapons with caution. She wasn't used to being armed, and Dela could tell by the twisting of her lips that her friend didn't know where to start.

Layla reached down for a sword, but Dela's hand on her arm stopped her.

"Go for something smaller," she suggested. "The sword will be too heavy for you to wield, and it will weigh you down during the walk."

Layla gave her friend a grateful smile, and selected a dagger similar in size to Dela's instead. It wasn't made from the same steel as Dela's dagger, so was still heavier, but the weapon was better suited to Layla's hand.

Dela hoped neither of them would need to use the weapons.

Glod led the way, guiding them from the city square, through the roads of Anthoinia. A few people stood on the sides of the streets, clapping and patting their backs as they passed by, as though they were knights off to war.

The motley crew of the Chosen shuffled their way forward,

navigating the lanes toward where the Great Gates barred the city from the lands outside. Through the gates waited a convoy of carts containing the hundreds of sacks of grains which they'd be exchanging with the other races in return for minerals.

Dela's stomach began to churn. This was it.

Before them all, the Great Gates creaked open.

CHAPTER 4

ORERGON

His twin black braids flew out behind him as his horse's hooves thundered across the ground. They were late, the sun having risen two hours earlier, and he knew he wouldn't hear the last of it from that oaf of a creature, Warsgra.

The mountain peaks of the Great Dividing Range towered over them. At his side, two of his fellow Moerians rode. Unlike the Norcs, who needed to travel with huge bison pulling even bigger carts of coal, the mineral they traded with the humans only took up the space in the leather pouches on the horses' backs.

Despite the body heat he'd generated from the hours of riding, Orergon could already feel the difference in temperature here compared to his own homeland. Though the Southern Pass would be clear, the tops of the mountains were tipped with snow and ice.

The changing of the seasons happened twice each year—winter giving way to summer, and summer giving way to winter. Only then were the weather conditions suitable for traveling through the mountains. It was deemed too dangerous to try to get through the Southern Pass at any other times of the year, and the Northern Pass through the Great Dividing Range was deemed dangerous at all times of year.

As the pounding beat of their horses' hooves brought them ever closer, Orergon was able to make out the thin lines of smoke rising into the air from where the Norcs lived. Soon their stone homes would come into view. Why any creature would choose to live in the shadow of these mountains was beyond Orergon's comprehension. Yes, farther north had its dangers and challenges, but at least it wasn't covered in snow and ice for months of the year. Not only that, everyone knew the mountains held dangers of their own. If the mountain Gods looked down on them, they could wipe out entire populations with a single curse.

Even the air here was different, making it harder for him to catch in his lungs. This wasn't his first time to this region, and he doubted it would be his last, but he was already looking forward to getting this over with. If it wasn't for his tribe's need for grain, which grew less and less with each passing summer on the plains, he wouldn't be here at all. But what were a few worthless pieces of metal in return for feeding the women and children of his tribe? If the humans thought it was worth their while, then he could afford to take a few weeks out of his life to keep the peace between each of their kinds.

"Orergon!" One of his riders pulled their steed to flank his. "Over there."

His rider lifted his hand to point south, and Orergon followed his line of sight. A small group of figures moved in the distance, and in the bright morning sunlight he caught glimpses of silver white hair. The Elvish.

"At least we're not the only ones to be late," he said, sitting higher on his horse's back. Unlike how humans rode, Orergon didn't use a saddle. He didn't understand how anyone would want to use one. There was no better way to get a feel for a horse and improve balance than riding how nature had intended. He and all his people had been riding this way for as long as he could remember, and he thought it bizarre and laughable that a human would want to put a big lump of leather on top of what was a perfectly comfortable horse back.

Like them, the Elvish only needed to bring a small company with them. They didn't ride horses, but instead rode the backs of large, majestic deer. The leader of their group sat higher on a regal stag. Orergon loved his horses, and had no wish to trade, but he had to admit that they made a sight with their massive antlers. The Elvish were smaller in stature than the Moerians, so though the deer backs weren't as broad as the Moerian's horses, they were easily strong enough to ride. The Elvish home of Inverlands gave way to more snow and ice, with rocky ridges and crags, and perhaps the deer's more delicate footing was better suited to that environment.

Orergon counted their number. It looked as though their leader had brought four of his kind with him, twice as many as he'd brought, but far less than the humans. Each half-year, it surprised him how many of their own kind the humans sent on this journey, partly to exchange what to him appeared to be worthless metal. It wasn't as though the Moerians didn't wear decoration, but they took feathers from the hawk to give their feet flight, and hide from the buffalo to protect their skin from the sun. He couldn't see what good the small pieces of metal would do them. The kinds of people the humans sent over baffled him as well. When the Moerians had to take on long journeys, they sent their strongest men and women, but the humans sent a strange combination of men and women, old and young. He knew from ancient tales that the humans had fighting men called knights, and yet they didn't send their knights on these exchanges. Instead, they sent numerous of their weakest kind, and each exchange Orergon watched their weakest fall to exhaustion and hunger. Not that it made any difference to him. He'd work to protect the lives of his own kind. The others could do whatever they liked.

The small band of Elvish had diverted course slightly and were now heading in their direction. Orergon guessed they had decided they'd be better to approach the Norcs together. The head of the clan, Warsgra, could be a violent, oafish creature, and was sure to be in a bad mood due to their unintentional tardiness. Perhaps, like the humans, the leader of the Elvish had decided there was safety in numbers. Not that Orergon was afraid.

The two groups grew closer until they were near enough to greet one another.

The leader of the Elvish was tall for his kind, but still not as tall as Orergon, though neither was anywhere near Warsgra's towering six feet eight frame. He wore his white blond hair to his shoulders, the strands appearing as light and delicate as spider's webs. Through the strands peeped the pointed tips of his ears. His eyes were a light blue, appearing almost silvery when the sunlight caught them. He wore a kind of armory fashioned out of a metal that looked as lightweight at his hair.

The leader of the Elvish pulled his stag to a halt, and then, light-footed, jumped to the ground.

Orergon also dismounted, and he lifted his hand, exposing his palm, as a sign of greeting. "Prince Vehel Dawngleam. Good to finally make your acquaintance. Your brothers have always spoken highly of you."

Vehel ducked his head. "I'm honored to meet you, too, Orergon. I, too, have heard much about you. I thought we'd be better approaching the Norcs as a united front. Warsgra's reputation precedes him."

Orergon laughed. "Yes, he's not the most lighthearted of men."

The Elvish prince shrugged. "Though his own kind appear to think highly of him."

"They're all frightened he'll use that damned axe of his on their necks, that's why." He remembered the two men flanking him. They'd not dismounted from their horses, and Orergon knew it was because they were protecting his back. They had no reason to believe the Elvish would want to cause them any harm, but it was their role to protect their leader, no matter the circumstances.

"These are my tribesmen, Aswor," he nodded to the man on his left, "and Kolti."

Both men were similar to him in appearance. They had his deep skin tone, dark eyes, and black hair. Their hair wasn't as long as Orergon's, however. As leader of their tribe, he was the only one allowed to wear his hair past his shoulders. Should he ever lose his position of power, his hair would be hacked off at his nape to show everyone that he was no longer their leader.

Vehel nodded in his direction, and then introduced his own men. "And these are my brethren—Ehlark, Folwin, Athtar, and Ivran."

Each of the men also appeared similar in appearance to the leader of the Elvish, but, like his own men, none of them had dismounted.

If his knowledge of Elvish history was correct, Vehel was the youngest of three brothers, and was the son of the Elvish king and queen of their region. No one other than the Elvish recognized them as royalty, but he was royal among his people. That made Vehel an important person, though Orergon detected something in the other Elvish men's eyes. What was that? Boredom? As though they couldn't quite be bothered to be here. It seemed strange to him. Vehel was an important man, and yet something about the ones he traveled with made him think otherwise.

"Shall we proceed?" he said.

Vehel ducked his head. "Very well."

Orergon remounted his horse—a chestnut stallion called Corazon—and pulled Corazon around to face the mountains and the home of the Norcs ahead.

CHAPTER 5

VEHEL

As far as the other races went, Vehel could just about stomach the Moerians. The Norcs, however, were a different matter.

As they approached their home of the Southern Trough, Vehel tried not to show his dismay at the way the Norcs lived. This was their main place of residence, but he would be excused from thinking it was a camp that had been erected during a long journey. Any kind of luxury—other than women, meat, and wine—was considered a weakness for the Norcs. The Moerians lived basically, too, but they didn't display the uncouthness of the Norcs.

The Elvish, however, like their home comforts. Blankets of silks and furs, comfortable clothing, homes filled with beautiful things. Where they resided in the Inverlands, the climate was substantially cooler than the Vast Plains of the Moerians, and so they needed these items to stay warm. Of course, it was cold at the foothills of the mountain range as well, but the Norcs were certainly big enough to withstand the cold climes. They looked as though their mothers had been mated to a bull, and the Norcs were the result of that coupling. Big, hairy, with no manners Vehel could appreciate.

Still, he had to be nice for the moment. Their pescatarian diet was getting harder and harder to maintain, and they needed this exchange with the humans. He'd been alive for one hundred and fifty years, and, in that time, he'd witnessed the changes to the climate of their kingdom. On the Eastern coast where the humans reigned, they still had the sun and rain, but the weather on the Western coast was becoming more extreme. Both their lands down south, and the Moerian's hotter climes in the north, were getting less and less rainfall every year that passed, making it even harder to grow crops in both the hotter and colder lands. On the coast, they foraged shellfish, but those, too, were growing fewer in number. They also sent their kind out on ships to catch fish, but they were losing more and more people and boats to the sea monsters that lurked in the depths. They claimed more victims until people were too frightened to fish. It was far from being an ideal way to live, but at least this exchange with the humans twice a year bought them a little more time. Vehel didn't want to think of a time when he may need to move his people to different lands. Doing so would undoubtedly mean clashing with a different race, and they'd lived in peace for so long now, he didn't want to give anyone a reason to start a new war.

Vehel dug his heels into the side of his stag, and they picked up pace as they approached the Norcs' home.

They'd been noticed, people gathering from their homes to watch. The women were almost as big as the men, with thick thighs even larger than Vehel's, and shoulders to match. With the brute strength of this clan, Vehel didn't understand why they were content to live and roam in the foothills of the mountains, rather than try to cross and take far more habitable spots on the Eastern coast. Perhaps they simply weren't clever enough to consider such a thing, or maybe they were afraid of the humans with their weapons and buildings and walls. The Norcs probably wondered the same sort of thing about the Elvish, with their propensity toward magic, but the Elvish part of the Treaty meant them signing a promise not to do magic, and over the years folks had not only forgotten how, but such a thing was now frowned upon.

He couldn't imagine the Moerians living in a different environment than where they currently resided. They rode for days across the Vast Plains, hunting and surveying their lands. To take them out of there and force them to live elsewhere would be like taking the fish from the sea and expecting them to thrive in a pool.

As they got closer, the scent of meat roasting on a spit filtered through to his nose. The others could smell it, too, and his stomach growled. Even though he did not eat meat, he could appreciate the reason others did. No, they would make do with the dried fish and bread they'd brought for the journey.

Movement came from the Norcs, people muttering and breaking away to create a clear path. A huge man with long, wavy brown hair and shoulders twice the width of Vehel's broke through the crowd. A similar sized man followed him close behind.

Vehel forced a smile to tweak his cheeks, and he jumped from the back of his stag and handed the rope harness to one of his men.

Beside him, Orergon did the same, climbing from his horse's back to stand beside the animal.

"You're late," Warsgra growled as he came to a halt before the other two men.

"Apologies," Orergon said, lifting his hand, palm facing Warsgra in a greeting. "We had some unexpected delays."

Warsgra lifted his bushy eyebrows at Vehel. "You, too?"

"Yes. The lands are getting wild. The Gods don't like us passing through them so easily."

"Let's hope the Gods are more favorable on this leg of the journey," Warsgra said. "I know the mountain Gods always favor my kind, so perhaps they will look kindly on you if you're traveling with us."

Orergon's smile appeared frozen on his face. "We have our own Gods who I'm sure will watch over us. We have a gift for them, too."

Warsgra snorted. "Sure."

Vehel bit down on his anger. There was no need for Warsgra to be so dismissive of other cultures. It wasn't as though his own was the leader in anything, even if he liked to think it was.

Warsgra turned and strode away, heading deeper into the compound, and assuming the others would follow. "We will eat and allow you an hour to rest, and then start the journey through the Southern Pass. The weather looks fair, and it should only take us a couple of days to reach the point where we are due to meet the human convoy." He glanced back over his shoulder at them, sweeping aside his thick hair. "Assuming they're not running as late as both of you, of course."

Vehel scowled at his back, and then exchanged a glance with Orergon. Though they were opposite in looks, Vehel thought they both were most likely wearing identical expressions of frustration right now. He wasn't sure how he'd get through the next few days without wanting to send a lightning ball into the middle of the Norc's chest.

A large fire pit was burning in the middle of what appeared to be the compound's main square. Above the pit, a massive headless boar had been spiked and was now turning on a spit. The fat from the beast dripped into the flames, causing it to sizzle and smoke. Vehel wasn't interested in the meat, but he appreciated the warmth. The temperature would continue to drop, the deeper they headed into the mountains, and while he was used to a cooler climate, that of the great mountains could prove to be deadly on occasion. The weather could turn in a moment, and what was previously a fine day could easily turn bad.

But it wasn't always the turn in the weather that caused the deaths, but what was held within the weather that should be feared. Creatures existed in the Great Dividing Range that couldn't be killed by normal methods, and even brute strength and bravado like Warsgra was displaying wouldn't be enough to defeat them.

The Norc might believe the mountain Gods looked kindly upon his race, but sometimes the dangers came from the underworld, and those dangers had little to do with the Gods.

CHAPTER 6

DELA

They'd only been on the road for two days and one night, and not yet reached the most arduous part of their journey, and already they had lost people. The first to collapse had been an older woman Ellyn Rudge, who'd begun to complain about her hips within the first hour of the walk, until finally she'd given in and collapsed on the side of the road. There was no space on the carts filled with sacks of grain, and though they'd tried to convince the older woman to ride on top of the sacks, she'd cried that she was frightened she'd fall off, and refused.

They'd left her with some supplies and a blanket for warmth, and promised to bring her back on their return.

Dela still felt awful leaving her there, however. Who knew what kind of dangers might approach her in that time.

The next to fall on the wayside had been a middle-aged man, who'd tripped and done something bad to his left leg. They'd tried to fashion a walking stick for him, but his progress had been impossibly slow, and they couldn't slow down to match his pace. Again, they'd offered the ride on the bags of grain, but they couldn't keep doing that for everyone who was struggling. The weight the oxen were pulling was already huge, and they couldn't keep adding extra people to the top. They'd exhaust the beasts and never make it to their destination, and that would never do.

It seemed incredible to Dela how a place of such beauty could hold such dangers. Between here and the Great Dividing Range which cut through the middle of their lands, the ground was flat and offered them incredible views of the jagged, snow-topped mountains. The sky was a brilliant blue, with only a few clouds gathering near the peaks. The climate of their kingdom meant green grass sprouted in every direction, and clear blue streams ran by, glacial water that was clean enough to drink right from where it flowed. Ever since she was a small child, she'd been warned of the dangers outside the city walls, of the haunted forests whose trees pulled up their roots and moved when you weren't looking, and the ancient swamps that housed fearsome creatures in its murky depths, just waiting for an opportunity to pull an innocent rider down under the mud, but so far everything had been perfect. She almost didn't want to have to endure the busy, smelly streets of Anthoinia again, preferring the fresh air and open spaces.

She was grateful to have Layla with her, and she'd formed some friendships with a number of the other Chosen as well. They sang songs together to pass the time, or told jokes or funny stories to lighten the mood and take their minds off their blistered feet and aching muscles.

Her mind was never far from her brother as she trod the same path he'd taken three years earlier. She knew he'd been lost at some point in the Southern Pass, though she wasn't sure exactly where, which meant he'd definitely traveled the same road she was on now. She imagined her feet stepping in the exact same footprints he would have left, and the idea brought him closer in her heart.

"Whoa!"

The male voice came from the front of the procession. It had sounded as though it belonged to the older man, Wayneguard

Norton. Norton had elected himself as leader of the troop, and no one had put up much of a fight to stop him from doing so. It wasn't a job any of them wanted.

The carts all came to a halt, and the oxen snorted their displeasure at the change in momentum.

"What's going on?" Layla asked Dela.

Dela shook her head. "I have no idea."

The young man who'd been at school with Ridley, Brer, was also walking with them. Those of a similar age group had automatically banded together. "I think there's something up ahead. I guess we'll find out."

The last of the carts drew to a halt, the oxen scraping at the dirt road with their hooves. Dela left her spot near the back of the group and moved closer to the front to see what was holding things up.

Norton stood at the front, stroking his beard like it was a cat, a frown causing the lines on his forehead to deepen. Ahead, a river rushed across the road, but a curved stone bridge ran across it, allowing them access to the other side. She still couldn't see what the problem was.

"Why have we stopped? Is the bridge down?" She stood on tiptoes to try to see if she'd missed something.

"You don't know what that is," he replied, not looking at her.

"A bridge?" She felt like she was pointing out the obvious.

"It's a Devil's Bridge. The Devil helped to build it, so he takes one soul of every party trying to cross."

Dela wasn't even sure she believed in devils. Seemed to her, the Gods caused enough problems without them needing to worry about devils as well.

"It's just an old wives' tale. I'm sure it'll be fine."

"Are you going to be the first one to try it?" he asked. "All tales stem from something, however much the truth may have been bent in the telling. No good thing comes from crossing that bridge."

"Do we have any other options?" She viewed the river, which churned and foamed against its banks. It was too fast moving to try to get the oxen and carts through, and if the force of the water turned the carts over, they'd lose all the grain as well.

Their words were picked up and passed back through the convoy.

"What is it?" someone called from the back.

A second shout. "Why have we stopped?"

"Devil's bridge," a different person shouted back.

A female voice this time. "A what?"

"Cursed …" came the hushed whisper in return.

"This is crazy," Dela said out loud. It was just a bridge, and in the bright sunshine, it was hard to imagine there was anything bad going on with it.

Leaving the convoy, she trotted down to the side of the bridge. The ground grew sodden beneath her boots, and she turned side on, her arms stretched to keep her balance. She wanted to get a good look under the arch, where shadows swallowed the bright sunlight.

"Dela!" a male voice called out to her, but she ignored it. They could come down with her if they wanted. No one was stopping them, but so far she was still alone. Only inches from the tips of her toes, the rocky riverbank lay. Water rushed by, passing her to continue beneath the bridge and vanishing into the distance.

Dela leaned out, trying to get a better view. She didn't know what she thought she was going to see, but she knew she needed to check.

Though the underside of the bridge, particularly the part where the stone met the riverbank, was shrouded in shadows, there was nothing she could see that would make her think something would try to snatch them if they crossed.

"There's nothing here," she shouted up. "It just looks like a regular bridge."

"You can't see a curse," one of the older women called back.

Dela sighed and rolled her eyes. She turned and stomped her way back up to the road and jammed her hands onto her hips. "Do you have any better suggestions? It's not as though we can just turn around and go home."

"She's right," Norton said. "We have to go across. We don't have any choice."

Layla looked at her, chewing her lower lip anxiously. "It'll be okay, won't it, Dela? You definitely didn't see anything?"

Dela shrugged. "I didn't see anything, but my knowledge of such things is no better than anyone else's here."

Norton stepped forward, taking charge. "Okay. We have to go across."

One of the older women burst into tears.

He continued, "If you choose not to cross, we can leave you here, but you'll be alone and without shelter for many days to come. That's your choice, of course, but you can't blame anyone but yourself if something happens to you."

Worried mutters went about the group. A few moments of bravery, versus days and nights on end alone. Dela knew she was going to be crossing. Not only was there no way she'd want to be left behind, but she wasn't completely sure there was even anything to be afraid of. The sun warmed her shoulders, birds tweeted in the surrounding trees, and the water gurgled by. It was a beautiful day and felt as far from the devil as possible.

No one volunteered to stay behind.

"Right." Norton nodded. "I suggest we keep moving, then."

The drivers of the carts yelled, "Yah!" at the oxen to get them moving again. The carts wheels creaked, the weight crunching stones and dirt beneath them. The oxen snorted and stamped their hooves, but reluctantly started forward.

A hand slipped into Dela's, and she looked over to see Layla's pale face. "It'll be okay." Dela squeezed her friend's hand in reassurance.

Layla nodded, but her expression was tense, her lips a thin line.

Dela's chest tightened. She shouldn't feel responsible for her friend—they'd ended up in this situation in exactly the same way, and they were the same age—but she couldn't help it.

"Come on. Let's get this over with."

Norton had led the way, taking the first steps across the bridge, while the carts filled with the bags of grain began to follow. They were a good number, and it would take time to cross. Dela figured she'd rather go quickly than wait until the very end.

She gave Layla's hand a tug. "Come on."

They exchanged a smile then started forward. The bridge was wide enough to allow them to walk side by side with the grain carts, meaning they didn't have to wait. Others were doing the same, no one apparently wanting to be the last to cross.

The oxen grew more agitated than normal, needing some extra "Yahs!" and taps with the whip to get them across.

"They don't like it," Layla said nervously.

"It's just the rushing water below them. It's normal for them to be anxious about it."

She hoped she was right.

They stepped onto the bridge.

It was solid and well-built. Those who'd first mounted had already reached the opposite bank and were now over safely, but still Dela's heart raced, and her mouth grew dry. She didn't believe there was anything to be afraid of, but her body was telling her something different.

They needed to get across, though. They had no choice.

Step after step brought them farther over the bridge. The oxen kept moving, snorting hot air, and others followed. The usual chitchat and song had quieted from the group, the tension simmering between them like heat.

They were halfway across now.

"Almost there," she said.

A sudden scream rang out in the bright day, and Dela spun around to see who had made the sound. The oxen behind them spooked, their walk becoming a gallop, causing the man driving to yell in alarm.

It took Dela a moment to see who'd screamed.

A woman in her thirties, who Dela thought was called Huda, was on her knees, her hands over her face.

Dela's stomach contracted, suddenly loose and watery, and her heart became trapped birds' wings in her chest.

"Go," she told Layla, giving her a shove in the direction of the opposite bank. "Get across."

"What are you doing?" Layla cried in alarm.

"I don't know yet."

She ran back across to where the woman was on her knees. Others had backed away, clutching at each other in fear and alarm.

Dela dropped to the ground in front of the woman. "What's wrong? What's happened?" She pulled Huda's hands away from her face.

"I can't see! I'm blind."

Dela reared back and clamped her hand to her mouth. "Oh, by the Gods!"

The woman's eyes were filled with blood.

Huda blinked, and blood ran in twin rivulets down her cheeks. She opened her mouth to speak, but instead of words, more blood appeared in a bubble between her lips.

Dela scrambled back in horror. She wanted to help, but she didn't know what she was supposed to do. She had no medical training. Being the youngest child of two, she hadn't even been there at the birth of her sibling. Could the woman have been ill before they'd set out? Dela hadn't noticed her appearing to be sick, but this might just be a coincidence.

The woman's ears were bleeding now. Blood, so much blood.

Huda coughed and choked and made a strange gurgling sound

before falling face down on the bridge. Dela darted forward again, meaning to try to help in any way she could, but something made her stop. The bridge moved beneath Huda, the ground suddenly becoming wet, like sand on the coast. A few of the others had hesitantly started to approach to see if there was anything they could do to help, but Dela waved them away.

"Move back!" she cried. "Get away!"

The woman wriggled and squirmed. The blood seemed to mix with the brick of the bridge, which now didn't look like brick at all. Dela could barely believe what she was seeing. The more the woman tried to fight, the less solid the stone she was lying on became, until eventually she began to sink.

"We need something for her to hold onto," she cried.

But the woman barely seemed able to lift her own head, never mind drag herself to safety. She wasn't even screaming any longer, but instead continued with those horrific gurgles until those fell silent, too.

The liquid stone rose up, like two arms on either side of her, surrounding her as though in an embrace, and then pulled her down. She vanished into the rock, and the moment she disappeared from view, the rock became solid again. Other than the smears of blood she'd left behind, it was as though she'd never even been there.

Dela stared at the spot, breathing hard and trembling all over. Then she turned and ran across the bridge to the other side and down the side of the bank to get a look beneath the bridge in the same place the woman had vanished. Could she have come through the other side? But no, there was nothing. It looked exactly as it had when she'd checked the first time.

People were softly crying in shock. Spilled bags of grain from where the oxen had spooked lay on the road.

Nobody moved or spoke for a moment, a sense of disbelief over what they'd just witnessed falling over them all. Layla cried into her hands, and Dela went back to where she was standing to put her arm around her friend's shoulder. Her own eyes were dry, but her head was spinning. She felt as though she'd just walked into a nightmare.

She'd seen magic before, but they were parlor games—making something vanish and reappear, or changing a dove to a rabbit. Though she'd heard tales, she'd never seen anything like that.

"It's sorcery!" someone cried, breaking the silence.

Another person yelled, "Witchcraft!"

Norton grunted. "No, the devil claimed his soul payment."

They had no choice but to move on. There was nothing they could do for the woman now.

They would need to come back this way, and would have to come back over the bridge again. People set about calming the oxen and hauling the sacks of grain back onto the cart.

Dela peered into the distance, to where the jagged tips of the mountains rose into the innocuously bright blue sky. This was only the start.

There would be far worse ahead.

CHAPTER 7

WARSGRA

"We're moving out!"

Warsgra beckoned his strange mixture of fellow travelers with a wave of his arm and kicked the flanks of his massive mountain goat to get him moving. He set his sights on the journey ahead. They were only a matter of a few hours from the entrance to the Southern Pass, and right now Warsgra just wanted to get this whole thing over with.

Just having the other two races around irritated him. The Elvish leader, Vehel, refused to eat his boar, which was insulting enough.

The Moerian, Orergon, was slightly less annoying, but his inability to tolerate the cold riled Warsgra. Orergon and his companions always seemed to get the best spot beside the fire, which made him clench his teeth and ball his fists in annoyance. Then the dark-skinned man went through a ridiculous routine of kneeling and praying to the mountain Gods, as though that would make the blindest bit of difference. The Gods did whatever the hell the Gods wanted, and getting on your knees wasn't going to change anything.

His clansman, Jultu, clapped him on the back. "Only another

seven more nights or so, and we'll all go our separate ways." He'd clearly sensed his leader's irritation.

Warsgra grunted. "Only if things run smoothly, which you can never bet on. And even then, seven nights is seven nights too long."

They were a strange crew, that was for sure, with the Elvish on their deer, and the Moerians on horseback. The Norcs preferred to ride huge mountain goats, big enough to take their weight, surefooted enough to find their own way along the mountain passes, and tough enough to be used in battle. Perhaps the other races found their choice of ride strange, but a goat as large as his was far hardier than a horse, which, other than its hooves, had no form of defense. His goat, with its massive curled horns, could crush a man's ribs if it butted him, and Warsgra would always choose an animal with that kind of power behind it than a horse.

He had a saddle made up only of animal skin, and rope tied around the goat's horns gave him some control, though he trusted the animal's choice in route more than his own. It seemed to have a natural instinct for which rocks would move beneath foot when stepped on, and knew to avoid them.

Warsgra led the way, with Jultu at his side, riding an animal not quite as big as his own, but close. Behind them came a number of carts laden high with the coal his clan had mined from the sides of the mountains. Each cart was driven by another member of his clan, each with several large bison pulling it.

The Elvish came next, riding their deer, with the leader, Vehel, on his stag. The Moerians brought up the rear, their horses' hooves skidding occasionally against the rock and creeping ice.

Warsgra was comfortable heading deeper into the mountains. Despite the dangers, this place was home to him and his kind. Besides, there were dangers everywhere across these lands. Just because some were more inaccessible than others, didn't mean they should be feared any more. This wasn't the first time he'd completed this journey, and he was sure it wouldn't be the last.

"How many humans do you think will survive this time?" Jultu asked him, a note of humor in his tone. "Half of what set out, or less?"

"I've no idea, but every time we meet with them, I understand a wee bit more about why they settle the way they do. They're not travelers, that's for sure."

"They used to be, back before the war. They were all over these lands. It's only since the Treaty that they've remained in the one place."

Warsgra snorted. "Then the Treaty didn't do them any favors. I'd prefer to remain fewer in number and stronger in body than let anyone and everyone procreate and settle down, expecting to be fed and taken care of. At least with our kind, we know the weak aren't going to survive long, and so they won't go on to make weak babes of their own."

Jultu nodded in agreement. "Their strength is in numbers. A single human could be crushed in an instant, but it's the way they keep coming and coming that has worn other folk down. It's like a termite—barely noticeable alone, but a whole army could raze a place to the ground."

"Not if we squash them one by one."

Jultu chuckled.

Behind them, the carts rocked and rolled. The Southern Pass was the lowest point of the Great Dividing Range, and for the most part was relatively flat—well, as flat as a mountain range got. On either side, the steep, jagged cliffs of the mountains rose high, blocking out the sunlight. The summit of the mountaintops meant they gathered clouds around their peaks, which also did nothing to help the amount of light down here. They could handle a few clouds. These kinds brought nothing more than the occasional snowstorm. It was when the Long White Cloud came in that they had to watch themselves. Those things could swallow people like a wave, leaving only death and destruction in their wake. It had been several years since he'd last seen it sweep across the Great Dividing Range, however. There were plenty of things in this life that brute force worked against, but the tales of the things people saw when caught inside the cloud weren't one of them.

An uncharacteristic shudder worked its way down Warsgra's spine, and he hoped Jultu hadn't noticed. Showing he was spooked was never going to be a good thing.

The thunder of hooves approached, and he turned to see Orergon, together with one of his men, galloping up behind them. The dark-skinned man pulled his horse to a walk when he reached them.

"Problem?" Warsgra said.

Orergon shook his head, his twin braids shivering with the motion. "No, I just thought I would see what you think of the traveling conditions this time around."

"They're fine. Same as every half-year." A smirk touched his lips. "Why? Too cold for you already? It's only going to get colder."

The Moerian wore plenty of animal skins, with furs around his shoulders and topping his boots. It was a complete contrast to Warsgra's own outfit of loincloth, boots, and shoulder protectors. The other man didn't have the sort of muscle he did. He guessed it meant Orergon's bones grew cold more easily.

"I'm fine," the other man replied. "I figured if we have several days together, we might as well learn how to become traveling companions."

By some miracle of the Gods, Warsgra managed to hold back his retort. He'd rather be traveling this road alone than with this whole sorry menagerie of animals, and he wasn't even talking about the ones with four legs.

The Elvish appeared so weak, with their small bodies and pale skin. Yes, he knew they lived far longer than the Norcs, and the one riding somewhere behind him now was probably four times his age, but being old wasn't something that impressed Warsgra. He wasn't even sure how the Elvish had managed to secure their place in the Treaty. They must have used magic, because he didn't think it had been done through battle alone.

A number of hours after first entering the Southern Pass, they stopped for a break. There was no snow on the ground at this time of year, at least not at this altitude, so there were enough grass and shrubs for the goats, deer, and horses to graze on. The travelers divided themselves into small groups and got fires going, settling down to eat whatever rations they'd brought with them. Warsgra still had a decent chunk of the boar left over, which he shared with Jultu and his other men, all of them tearing into the meat with their teeth. He glanced over to see the Elvish chewing at their dried fish pieces and crunching into items of fruit and was unable to hold back a smirk. No wonder they didn't grow very large. It was hardly enough to sustain a child.

Vehel reached into the satchel at his hip and pulled out a smaller bag with a string top closing the opening. As he was sitting there, Warsgra watched him tip the contents out into his slender, pale hand.

Warsgra swallowed the last of his meat and pushed himself to standing. Trying to appear nonchalant, he wandered over to where the Elvish prince was sitting.

"What do the humans find so fascinating about those things?" he asked.

Vehel looked up at him, his silver white hair falling over one shoulder of his armor. "They're rare, and hard to find. Apparently, that makes something precious in their minds." He tipped his palm from side to side, allowing the small, clear rocks to roll together.

"I don't get it," Warsgra admitted.

Vehel raised fine white eyebrows. "No, neither do I, but we each have things we find precious, too—certain herbs, the metal we make our armor from, the twine of the Urbubor tree that is almost invisible underwater which makes it perfect for fishing."

"All practical things," Warsgra pointed out. "What possible use could they get from a few small rocks?"

"Perhaps it will remain a mystery." He jerked his chin toward the continuing passageway through the rock. "How much farther have we got to go before nightfall?"

He glanced over his shoulder in the direction the Elvish prince was indicating. "A few more hours."

"And the temperature will drop then?"

Warsgra frowned. "It's not the cold you should be afraid of."

Vehel held his eye with his ice-blue gaze. "I'm not afraid of anything."

A slow smile crept across Warsgra's lips. "Good to hear."

Perhaps he could grow to like this one after all.

CHAPTER 8

DELA

The mood among the group had changed greatly since they'd left the bridge.

Though Dela had always known this journey was going to be dangerous, it hadn't quite seemed real until she'd watched a woman bleed to death and then be sucked though the apparently solid stone of a bridge.

Now she saw danger in everything. In every sway of a tree branch, in every squawk of a bird, in every cough or sneeze of the people she was traveling with. She jumped at the slightest sound, and still hadn't managed to subside the shaking that had taken over her limbs the moment the woman had started bleeding from her eyes. Had something like that happened to her brother? The Chosen who had returned from the same trip he'd been on claimed they'd been attacked by an unseen force in the mountains, but maybe they'd been lying. Perhaps they'd been trying to spare Dela and her parents all the nightmares the truth would have caused.

The thought of Ridley dying in such a way twisted at Dela's guts. She couldn't help but picture him alone and terrified, and every part of her wished there was some way she could turn back the clock and change the outcome of him being part of the Chosen three years earlier. But such a thing was impossible.

Dela made a mental promise to herself. No matter what happened to her on this journey, if she made it home again, she wouldn't tell her parents the truth of the things she'd seen. It would be a small comfort, but at least she'd be able to give them the chance to sleep at night without being plagued by nightmares.

Within a couple of hours, night began creeping in.

They chose a clearing beside a small copse of trees, just off the side of the road. The trees offered them some shelter, while they were able to still see the road from east to west. They'd not come across any other travelers yet, but that didn't mean they weren't on the road. There were plenty of people who chose to live outside of the city walls, and those same people were known to be dangerous. Dela couldn't help feeling, however, that the most danger lay within the things they weren't able to see. They could fight off other people with swords and stones, but they couldn't fight things like dark magic.

They stopped and began to string canvas from the branches of trees to at least give them some shelter from the dangers that lurked out there. Fires were lit, water was gathered from a nearby stream, and rations were handed out to each person.

Dela found herself settled around a fire with Layla, Brer, Norton, and another man in his thirties called Gilford. Layla had barely eaten, but instead stared into the fire, chewing on the corner of her thumbnail. Norton sat with a knife and a piece of wood, whittling it down into something Dela didn't recognize yet. No one had mentioned directly what had happened. It seemed pointless, as they couldn't change anything, but Dela found she couldn't remain quiet. Thoughts and questions churned over and over in her head, and in the end she couldn't prevent them bursting from her tongue.

"What do we do if we come across another Devil's Bridge? Do we try to cross it?"

Norton's lips pressed together. "Let's pray to the Gods that we don't come across another one."

"But we will, on the way back," she insisted. "We'll have to cross the same one again."

"We have to make it back alive first. But then …" He gave a hiss of exasperation and threw the piece of wood he'd been carving to the ground. "I don't know! It's not as though I asked to be leading up this whole thing. I was Chosen just like the rest of you. I didn't volunteer. I don't know anything more than anyone else."

The older man got to his feet and paced away from them, his head shaking. It was strange, but Dela found some comfort in his words. She didn't like to be afraid, but it was good to know she wasn't the only one who felt that way. It didn't make her weak or a bad person, it just made her normal.

"We just have to keep going." She lifted her voice so Norton would hear. "Keep going and take care of each other the best we can. We don't have any other choice. People do come back from the Passover. Every six months, the Chosen return. We're not the first, and we won't be the last, but we have to remember this isn't a certain death sentence. People do come back." She did her best to ignore the twisting in her gut as she remembered one of the people who *hadn't* come back.

Norton's back was to them, but his shoulders slumped, and he turned around to face them. He ran his hand over his graying hair. "You're right. My apologies. I didn't mean to behave like a child."

She shrugged. "Apology accepted."

Norton came and took his place around the fire and picked up his whittling once more. Dela exchanged a glance with Layla, and her friend gave her a smile and a nod and started to eat the rations she'd been staring at for the past hour.

* * *

Mid-morning the following day, they approached the entrance to the Southern Pass. They walked alongside the carts still laden with the bags of grain. The oxen were starting to slow after several days of walking, but they still appeared strong and unhindered by the huge weights they pulled. The same couldn't be said of the people, and though they knew it would add more weight to the carts, they took turns hopping up on the bags of grain to give their feet a rest.

Dela was sporting a number of huge blisters, but she did her best to ignore them. She worried about Layla. The other girl appeared to have already lost weight, her face becoming gaunt. If Layla grew too weak to continue the journey, what would Dela do? Could she continue without her, and leave the others even more people short, or would she stop with her friend and do her best to take care of her? They were already down from twenty members of the Chosen to only fifteen, having lost people along the way. What if they were attacked and didn't have enough people to fight off the assailants? The possibility of being robbed of this grain was very real, and Dela was thankful for the knife at her hip. They'd all been offered different weapons with which to defend themselves and their produce before they'd left on this journey, but these weren't a group of warriors she traveled with. She thought herself capable of being able to defend herself, but that was about all.

The flat tundra leading to the Great Dividing Range gave way to sudden mountain slopes. Grassy fields were overtaken by outcroppings of rock. The temperature noticeably dropped. The atmosphere of the group became even more tense, if such a thing were possible. Approaching the mountains was like facing a giant.

The gap of the Southern Pass opened up like a yawning maw through the mountain range, threatening to swallow them. Despite the bright day, the sides of the mountains threw deep shadows across the pass, making it appear as though it was almost in darkness.

The fables told that when the Gods were creating the lands, they caused the mountain range to erupt right through the middle of the land, dividing west and east. But when they looked down, they realized the mountain range was too inhospitable and would mean the two sides of the lands would never meet, so one of the mountain Gods, Oreus, reached down with both hands and scooped two massive pathways through the mountains—one in the south and one in the north—giving them a way to meet. But at the same time, he put a curse on each of the passes, that only the best and bravest would be able to make the journey from one side of the country to the other.

Dela didn't believe for a second that they were either the best or the bravest, but they were here.

The hardest part of their journey was about to begin.

Layla was riding one of the grain carts, and Dela looked up at her and lifted her hand in a wave. They could do this. The distance they had to travel into the Southern Pass wasn't as far as for the folk entering from the western side, so they were due to meet about one third of the full distance across.

A thrill of excitement prickled through Dela. She'd never met any other races, not properly, anyway. She'd come across them on occasion in the market square when they'd entered the city walls to sell something of importance to humans, such as an ancient artifact they may have unburied, or when a higher class human had purchased a lower class race as a slave, but she'd never actually had a conversation with one of them. In many ways, they were like humans. They had two arms and legs, and a head, but there the similarities ended. Some were huge like giants, and others more diminutive in size. Their skin came in different shades, and she didn't understand their cultures. Some were versed in magic, while others ate only meat and lived like wild men. Would she even understand when they spoke? She knew they were supposed to have a universal language, but different dialects were bound to have developed with them all living in such different lands. Years ago, before the Treaty, they shared the same lands, and the city of Anthoinia didn't have its high walls. She couldn't imagine everyone living side by side, working together and living together.

Of course, things hadn't stayed that way. They wouldn't have needed the Treaty, otherwise, and their lands wouldn't have been divided up the way they had. And they wouldn't need to have The Choosing, or the Passover either.

But that was the price of peace.

CHAPTER 9

VEHEL

The first night in the Southern Pass went by without event. Vehel and the other Elvish set up camp. Each race stuck to their own kind, though they were forced to remain nearby due to both the narrowness of the Southern Pass and for their own safety. There were things that lived in the mountains that could end any of their lives in a single instant, and if the Gods decided they'd only survive one night in the mountain pass, then that would be the end of them. Vehel was used to setting up camp wherever they ended up, but the vast sides of the mountains towering on either side made everyone nervous. A single rock fall could crush their shelters and whoever slept beneath them.

The Elvish took two-hour stints keeping watch, rotating through the night, so while four of them slept, one was always on lookout. Vehel never reached a point of deep sleep throughout the entire night, a part of him primed for something to happen, ready to leap into action. Plus, he had all the different noises of the other men sleeping around him. He was used to the company of his group, but hearing the Moerians pray through the night, and the Norcs snore and grunt in their sleep, was enough to keep anyone awake.

The Elvish weren't used to being in a large group. Because of their long lifespans, and because each couple only ever had two to three offspring, their numbers always remained low. The Elvish's strength didn't come in their number or size. They had other abilities on their side when it came to war. Though they weren't big either in population or stature, they had magic on their side. Since the Treaty, however, the Elvish had been sworn not to use their magic. The other races saw it as too great a threat, and should they ever use magic, they would see their part of the Treaty revoked, leaving them open to their part of the kingdom, the Inverlands, being invaded. But that had been several hundred years ago now, and because the Elvish hadn't been using magic, the youngest generations—himself included—had not been taught the old ways.

It had been Vehel's grandparents who had fought in the Great War, and those same grandparents who'd signed the Treaty. His parents were the king and queen of the Elvish, and had been alive when the Treaty was being signed, though they'd only been young Elvish of thirty or forty years old back then. Vehel was one hundred and fifty-three years old now, but he was still the youngest of his brothers, Vehten and Vanthum. His father, the Elvish King, made no attempt to hide the fact he thought far less of Vehel than he did his brothers. They were both larger in stature, and though Vehel was still of a good size for his kind, his father saw this as a disappointment. No matter what he did, he was never as good as Vehten and Vanthum. They were better than he was with a sword, better at literature, and they were funnier and easier to be around. Both his brothers had previously been on this journey and returned with all lives still intact, but also with gifts for the king and queen, their parents. A winged Marmoset they had trapped, or a candy made from the Moonflower—the sweetest and rarest plant in Xantearos. It was their way of showing their parents that not only were they able to accomplish what had been asked of them, but also that they found it so easy they were able to add extra tasks to their missions.

Vehel did his best to make it appear as though he was capable of getting the diamonds to the humans and returning with the grain, yet that niggling feeling that he'd somehow end up failing wouldn't leave him be. Maybe a hundred and fifty years of his father telling him of his disappointment in him wasn't so easy to shake off.

If he did this, however, and brought home something even grander than the items his brothers had returned with, then the king would have to acknowledge that he was an equal to his brothers. Yes, he was third in line, and the chances of his ever ruling the Elvish kingdom were slim, but at least he'd garner some respect.

When morning finally arrived, Vehel felt sluggish from the lack of rest, but he forced himself to pull his weight, dismantling the makeshift camp and stamping down the remains of their fire. They fed and watered the deer before getting them ready to move on. He found himself watching the leaders of the two other races while he worked, envying the easy banter that passed between them. Both Orergon and Warsgra appeared so comfortable in the presence of their people, where Vehel watched every word he said and every action he made.

With the camp packed up, and the Norcs and Moerians also ready to continue, Vehel pulled himself up onto the back of his stag. Even the animal didn't belong to him, having been loaned to him by his father's stables. His Elvish kin—Ehlark, Folwin, Athtar, and Ivran—rode either side of him on their smaller deer. Though they rode with him, they were his father's men, and a part of him knew they would report back to their king on how they thought Vehel behaved, and whether or not he did their kingdom proud and represented them accordingly. If things went wrong, they'd be sure to report back to his father about that, too.

Traveling with the Norcs made for dirty work. Their huge

beasts pulling the carts left shit everywhere, and the coal filled carts caused a black dust to fill the air, choking his lungs and settling on his armor. The Norcs themselves were also filthy, throwing meat bones to the ground when they finished eating, pissing wherever they stood, yelling to each other in great, booming voices. Vehel could be a hard man when he needed to be, and would kill if the necessity arose, but he couldn't help but look down on how rough the Norcs, and in particular their leader Warsgra, were. He struggled to see the reasoning behind it. You could be a good, strong leader without resorting to spitting on the ground every few minutes.

The way the leader of the Norcs looked at him reminded him of his father, too. A kind of disdain, and a way of letting him know he was only putting up with him because he had to. He didn't need to prove anything to Warsgra. After the next few days, he hoped he'd never have to see the other man again.

The sound of their convoy traveling was immense. Horses' hooves clacked behind them, and the creak of the wheels of the coal carts and the snorts of the bison filled the air. Men called to one another, while others sang a ballad of old, and someone else coughed repeatedly.

"I normally prefer to make less noise," he said from the side of his mouth to Athtar, who rode beside him. "We must be alerting everyone in the area to our approach."

Like the rest of his kind, Athtar had white blond hair and pointed ears. The rest of Athtar's features were also pointy—his chin and nose in particular. Athtar was about fifty years older than Vehel, but was not born to royalty, and had worked for his father for many years.

"If someone tried to attack this convoy," Athtar replied, "they're a braver man than I. Taking on each of the races' strongest people? They might as well sign their own death warrants."

It wasn't the mortals who worried Vehel, however. The stories of the creatures that lurked in these mountains were told from generation to generation. Just because many of them hadn't been seen for centuries didn't mean they no longer existed. It wasn't as though the Elvish were able to cover every inch of Xantearos to find out. There were too many remote places inaccessible by their kind. Tales used to speak of dragons dominating the skies of Xantearos, but the great beasts hadn't been seen in hundreds of years, and it was believed the last was killed off during the Great War, or that the volcanic region of Drusga where they lived had erupted and drowned the last dragons in molten lava as they slept.

Vehel sat straighter on his stag. "Still, a little caution doesn't go unwarranted."

Athtar lifted his fine white eyebrows. "Would you like me to tell Warsgra to keep it down?"

Vehel gave a laugh. "I don't think the man would know how to be quiet if his life depended on it."

"No, probably not. He does seem to like the sound of his own voice."

They both looked to where the big man led the way, his thick curly hair reaching halfway down the middle of his naked back. He certainly didn't seem to feel the cold of the mountains either, and it was getting colder with every step taking them deeper into the pass.

They rounded a bend, and for a moment Vehel lost sight of Warsgra and his companions.

A sudden yell of shock met his ears, and the next moment, the bison pulling the carts drew to a halt, nostrils flared and ears flat back against their skulls. They stamped the ground with their hooves, and their snorts of breath created white plumes on the chilled air.

Another cry of fright set Vehel's heart racing. He exchanged a glance with Athtar, who nodded in response, and Vehel lifted his heels and kicked the flank of his stag to get him moving.

He rounded the corner to find Warsgra and his men flailing

and yelling as though a swarm of Bottlehead wasps was after them. Warsgra swung his axe, but Veher couldn't see what he was swiping at.

Then he caught sight of it, something black and furry, about the size of a large rat, but with six legs that protruded from its fuzzy body like spider's legs. It darted up Warsgra's thick thigh. Warsgra spun around and let out a roar. Vehel spotted a second of the creatures, clinging to Warsgra's long hair with its spindly little claws. From the expression on its face, it looked like it was laughing.

He'd never seen anything like this before. He stared around, and saw Warsgra's men were in similar positions. Little creatures clinging to their bodies. Some of the things started to climb the carts, spooking the bison further. They couldn't have the bison breaking free of their yokes, or have them tipping the carts, or making a break for it. They needed that coal. Even though it wasn't the mineral the Elvish exchanged during the Passover, it was imperative they each make it to the meeting and were able to complete what they pledged. Failure to do so might mean the breaking down of the Treaty, and no one wanted to go back to a time of war.

Even more of the creatures were clinging to the craggy rock walls of the Southern Pass. What were they? Little rodents of some kind, but that appeared to have a strange kind of wicked intelligence in their dark beady eyes.

Vehel felt a pulse of energy flood through him.

He'd experienced this energy before, but it still took him by surprise. He held it back, unable to give in.

But he couldn't sit there and do nothing.

He jumped from his stag, his feet hitting the ground of solid rock. Around him, his fellow Elvish did the same. The Moerians were right behind them, and he heard Orergon give a yell of surprise as he saw what was happening. One of their horses let out a whinny and reared up onto its hind legs.

Vehel drew his bow from where it was attached to his back and pulled an arrow from his quiver. He drew it back, aimed, and let the arrow fly. The arrow speared first one, and then two of the little creatures, so they looked like miniature hogs on a spit. He drew another arrow and repeated the motion.

All around, everyone was fighting. The Moerians let out war cries and charged with the spears they favored. The Norcs swung axes, chopping down on the beasts, splitting them in two. But no matter how many of the creatures they managed to kill, more appeared to be coming. They ran over the rock face, skittering toward them. If they weren't careful, they'd be overrun and there would be no way they'd be able to fight their way back from that. What did the things want? To kill them? Take their food? Or did they simply not like the convoy in their territory?

He pulled another arrow and let it fly, spinning on his toes just in time to bat away another one that had leapt at him from the pass wall.

Athtar was struggling. He had two attached to each leg and was unable to let loose an arrow with them in such close proximity.

That same feeling of energy burned up inside Vehel again. He wanted to push it back down, knowing it would be frowned upon. But he needed to help, and fighting the creatures with hand to hand combat wasn't working. He could feel his consciousness pulling away from the edges, centering to the fire inside himself. Turmoil wrenched him from side to side. It could work. It would help.

But, no, magic wasn't allowed. It was banned for the Elvish, and doing this could put everyone in jeopardy.

Vehel was delaying too long. As he looked around, he saw his traveling companions becoming overwhelmed, beaten to the ground by numerous little furry bodies, swarming over them like ants over the rotting corpse of a locust. The energy grew stronger inside him, and he suddenly realized he might no longer have the strength to hold it back, even if he wanted to. This was the reason he wasn't the fiercest fighter or the most enigmatic of his brothers. It was because he had something else inside him, and he'd known all this time that if he didn't keep a tight rein on it, he would show himself for what he really was.

He clenched his fists and jaw, and even though more of the creatures flung themselves at him, he didn't react. He focused purely on what was happening inside him now. The energy building until he knew he could contain it no longer.

With a cry that came from the bottom of his lungs, he released the power inside him. Automatically, his fingers sprang open, and with them his eyes, though he hadn't even realized he'd closed them.

The gloom of the Southern Pass was transformed. A blinding blue light burst from the palms of his hands. Those around him shielded their eyes with the backs of their arms, but, more importantly, the light sent the strange little creatures scattering. Where it touched them, their wiry black fur smoldered, and they let out high-pitched shrieks before bounding back up the side of the mountain face.

With the last of the things gone, the light vanished from Vehel's hands, and he dropped to one knee, his head down, gasping for breath. He was drained, as though he'd given it everything he had.

A hand on his shoulder made him lift his head. Warsgra looked down at him, his bushy eyebrows drawn together, his green eyes darkened with concern. "Are you all right?"

Vehel managed to nod, and Warsgra put out his hand and pulled him to his feet.

He sensed the piercing gaze of his own kind on him and couldn't meet their eye. He knew what they were thinking—that he shouldn't have done that. Magic was forbidden in order to keep the peace of the Treaty, and he had just used it.

The clop of hooves approached, and Orergon pulled his horse

up beside him. "Thank you, Vehel. I don't know what we would have done if you weren't here."

"I … I …" he started, unsure of how to finish.

Warsgra raised his voice, as though he wanted every man in the Southern Pass to hear. "What just happened here was necessary. We all know the use of magic is forbidden, but if this Elvish prince hadn't used his, we'd might all be dead by now. If not dead, then we'd have lost all our animals and be making the rest of the journey on foot. I hope I can trust each and every one of you to appreciate that, and keep your mouths shut. Be warned, if you do not know how to hold your tongues, I can help you along by removing it for you." He lifted his axe and brought the flat of the blade down on his palm.

"And believe me, I am not skilled with such delicate work. You may end up losing your entire head."

CHAPTER 10

ORERGON

Orergon believed every word of Warsgra's threat.
He looked back at his own tribesmen and lowered his head in a nod to them, to tell them he agreed with what Warsgra had just said. He wasn't going to pretend that traveling with an Elvish prince who had the ability to do magic didn't make him nervous, but he'd only used that magic to help them, not harm them. In fact, Vehel revealing to them that he had such an ability probably caused him more harm than it did them. And from the way his Elvish companions were now glaring at him, Orergon didn't think his own kind would be supporting him either.

But if Vehel hadn't done what he'd done, they might all be having their flesh chewed by a swarm of little six-legged rodents by now. They owed it to him to keep his secret.

The group was more subdued as they gathered themselves and continued on their way. They still had a couple of nights before they reached the meeting point, where they'd make the Passover for the humans, and for the first time Orergon wondered if they'd make it. This wasn't the first time he'd completed the trip, and there was always the possibility of danger, yet for some reason this time something felt different.

Was it simply because Vehel was here with them? One or the other of Vehel's brothers had accompanied them previously, and neither had given any sign that they held the ability to do magic inside them.

No, he didn't think the feeling of unease originated from Vehel being with them. It was bigger than that. The mountain felt different, as though its craggy faces held something portentous.

Orergon ran over the rituals he and his tribesmen had gone through before and during this journey, making sure they hadn't forgotten to give thanks to each of the Gods and asking for their blessings. Of course, Orergon knew the Gods didn't always listen. After all, hadn't they gone through every ritual known to their kind before his wedding day, and then on the day his son had been born? He'd prayed and made sacrifices, as had the rest of his tribe, wishing them well and praying to the Gods that his son would grow to be a strong, generous, noble man to take over his father's place as tribe leader.

His heart contracted at the memories. They'd done everything within their power to wish them good fortune, but none of it had mattered in the end. The Gods had done whatever they wanted anyway.

Digging his heels into the flanks of his horse, Corazon, he pressed forward to catch up to where Warsgra still led the group, mounted on his huge, white mountain goat. Orergon was no fan of the Norc leader, but he knew these mountains better than any of them.

He slowed to a trot beside him. "How are you feeling about this trip?"

Warsgra glanced over, frowning. "How do you mean?"

"Does it feel different from those before it?"

His frown deepened. "In what way?"

Orergon was starting to get frustrated at the way the big man kept answering with questions of his own.

"I'm not sure, exactly. Things just feel differently this time.

Where did those creatures come from? Why haven't we seen them before?"

Warsgra shrugged. "The mountains cover a vast area. There's no way we could ever know all the creatures that live here."

"Yes, the mountain range does, but not the Southern Pass. We've traveled this way, twice every year, for a long time now, and not come across them."

"What are you suggesting?" he grunted.

"I'm not sure." He thought hard. "That something happened to push them toward us, perhaps. Or that the Southern Pass itself doesn't want to be crossed this time."

"The Southern Pass doesn't have its own thoughts and ideas, Orergon. It's just rock, like the rest of the mountains."

"Very well, then perhaps the Gods don't want us to pass this time."

Warsgra gave a booming laugh. "I'm sure the Gods have better things to do than worry about the likes of us."

"I'm not so sure."

Not feeling as though he was getting anywhere with the Norc, Orergon allowed his horse to slow, pulling back to join his tribesmen once more. The Elvish prince, Vehel, continued to ride his stag, but Orergon noticed how he slumped slightly, as though his head had grown too heavy for his body. The other Elvish rode alongside him, and Orergon noted how they exchanged glances with each other, but never with Vehel.

Warsgra may have threatened to cut out the tongues of anyone who spoke of what Vehel had done to save them, but he wondered if that applied to the Elvish, too. Orergon had a strong feeling that if they were all blessed enough to return to their homelands once the Passover had been completed, Vehel would be reprimanded greatly for what he'd done. They just had to hope news of his use of magic wouldn't spread to the Eastern side of Xantearos. Orergon didn't even want to think about the repercussions if such a thing happened. Part of the agreement of the Treaty was that the

Elvish no longer continued to use magic, and the humans would view its use as breaking it, even though it had been done to save lives.

The rest of that day's traveling ended without further trouble. They set up camp, fires were lit, and meals were passed around.

The next day, if all went well, they would be meeting with the human convoy traveling from the Eastern coast. Then the Passover would be complete and they'd all be able to return home.

CHAPTER 11

DELA

Spending the night sleeping beneath the shadow of the towering cliff faces of the Southern Pass had been the most terrifying thing she'd done in her entire life. She'd thought sleeping on the roadside had been bad, worried they'd be attacked by wild animals, marauders, or worse. But somehow she found the walls of the Southern Pass to be even more menacing. Her gut told her this place was bad, and she wasn't able to let her guard down for a moment.

The result was that she got little sleep that night. The chill of the place didn't help either, and though she knew they were in the mountains now, she felt as though she was in a place the sun never touched. By the time she rose in the morning, the cold had settled in her bones, and she wondered if she'd ever feel warm again.

They worked together to break down camp, and she noted she wasn't the only one who'd been affected. Everyone looked exhausted and worked with bone-deep weariness.

"I keep thinking of home," Layla said as she rolled up the canvas they used as part of their shelter. "I never thought I'd miss my brothers and sisters, but now I'd give anything to be back with them, everyone fighting and laughing." She gave Dela a sympathetic smile. "I can't imagine how it's been for you over the last few years, knowing you'd never get to see Ridley again. It's only been a few days, and I already feel like I'm missing a part of myself by not being with them."

Dela lifted her hand to the ring she wore on a string of leather around her throat. The circumference was far too large for her to wear around her finger. She'd worn it around her neck ever since he'd given it to her as a reminder of him—not that she was ever going to forget him. Still, it made her feel closer to him to have something of his so near her heart.

Layla must have seen her reaction, as she winced. "Sorry, that was really thoughtless of me, wasn't it?"

Dela forced a smile. "No, you're allowed to miss home. It's not your fault Ridley didn't come back. I don't want people to think they're not able to talk about their own families because of mine."

Layla finished shoving the canvas into a bag, and then reached out and squeezed Dela's hand. "We're almost on our way home," she said. "We'll do the Passover today, and then we'll be able to turn around and go back to a hero's welcome."

Her thoughts went to the Passover, and her stomach churned at the thought of meeting the other races. What would they be like? Would they welcome them with warm greetings, or would they treat them like the enemy? Many years had passed since the Great War, but still there must be some residing resentment. After all, humans had taken the entire of the Eastern coast, while the other folk had been forced to divide the more inhospitable Western coast between themselves. Yes, the human population was larger, but Dela knew if it had been the other way around, and humans had been forced to take a smaller chunk of land that was harder to live on, they wouldn't have let things lie.

"Let's move on," Norton called as they stashed the final remains of their camp onto the carts. "Only a few more hours, and we'll be there."

Her heart fluttered with excitement, and the weight that had been pressing her down since entering the Southern Pass lifted. They were almost there, and then they'd all be able to go home.

The group began to walk again. Even the oxen had slowed now, their pace heavy, as though they struggled to lift their own feet. Their chests heaved, their breathing labored, even though they'd only just started back out after a night's rest. Perhaps they'd slept as badly as she had? Dela suddenly realized they'd say goodbye to the oxen when they did the Passover. It wouldn't only be the carts they'd give to the other folk. They'd need something to pull them with as well. She reached out and placed her palm against the shoulder of the animal closest to her. Its skin was warm beneath her palm, the hair covering it coarse and scratchy. But she was thankful for the small amount of heat bringing the feeling back to her fingertips. Her heart tightened at the thought of giving the animals away. It was stupid to get attached to working beasts, but she felt like they'd gone through a lot together.

The blisters on the backs of each foot had burst a couple of days ago, and now were forming crusts that kept rubbing off on the backs of her boots. The tips of her toes were also blistered, and every muscle in her body ached. She'd always assumed it would have been her feet and legs that would have suffered the worst, but it was her lower back that pained her most, and she walked with a stoop, her hand pressed on the base of her spine.

"You look like your mama when you walk like that," Layla commented, teasing her.

"And you look like your brother, Donald," she retorted. Donald had been born with one leg noticeably shorter than the other, and walked with a lurching limp. Layla reached out and smacked Dela playfully on the arm.

Dela was pleased her friend was with her, and that she'd made it the full journey. She couldn't imagine how much worse this all would have been if they'd not had each other.

"We'll be seeing the other folk soon," Layla said. "What do you think they'll be like?"

Dela shook her head. "I have no idea."

"I hear the Norcs are big and rough, and they tend not to wear many clothes. I wonder how much of their naked bodies we'll get to see."

"Layla!" Dela's mouth dropped in surprise at her friend's comment, and she looked around to see a twinkle in her blue eyes. She didn't know how she had the energy to be thinking about such things. Dela was so exhausted she could only think about her own bed.

"Oh, what? Don't be such a prude." She jabbed her in the side with her elbow. "It's not like you haven't thought about it."

She widened her eyes. "I haven't! Not like that, anyway. I mean, they're ... different."

"Dela, I've known you your entire life. I saw you vanish around the back of school with Pete Jameson when we were sixteen. Don't make out to me like you're some blushing virgin."

Okay, she wasn't, but losing Ridley had put an end to all thoughts of anything like that. She'd known then that she wouldn't be looking to marry and start up a family of her own any time soon. She needed to stay with her parents and make sure they were all right. Besides, it hadn't been much of a loss. She'd never been able to picture herself like Layla's mama, with multiple kids hanging off her legs. Maybe this was what she'd wanted all along, to be able to leave the city and explore what existed in the rest of the country. Was that why she hadn't been as frightened as she'd thought she'd be when her name had been called? Had a part of her not only been expecting this, but been looking forward to it?

Considering everything that had happened, the notion felt wrong on every level. But though she wanted to be home and tell her parents she was safe, a little part of her soul died at the thought. Would that be it for her, then? Once a person had been one of the Chosen, they weren't entered a second time. So she'd return to Anthoinia and go back to living with her parents, and that would be it for her life.

The hours passed as they plodded onward, heading deeper into the Southern Pass. With each footstep, Dela's excitement grew. In her mind, she pictured the meeting. She imagined shaking hands with these unusual people, of noting every feature to mind so she could go home and recount in detail how they had all been. Maybe they'd even ask questions of her, wanting to know what life was like back in Anthoinia. Surely she couldn't be the only one interested in how the other races lived?

"Shh." Norton lifted a hand, and they all slowed. The oxen and carts came to a halt behind them. "Do you hear that?"

Dela's ears strained, trying to pick up on what Norton was talking about. So far, other than the sounds their convoy made, the Southern Pass had been ominously quiet. There was the occasional small rock fall which rumbled down the sides of the mountains, or an eagle which gave a mournful shriek overhead, but that was all. Now, however, something had changed. At first she thought it might be the distant sound of thunder, or even a waterfall somewhere up ahead, but then she realized it was the sound of numerous feet—animal and man—and the rhythmical crunch of cart wheels on the rocky floor.

She looked to Norton. "It's them!"

He nodded in reply. "Let's hope so."

She knew what he meant—that they'd better hope it was the people they were supposed to meet rather than another group of travelers who might mean them harm. But no one traveled through the Southern Pass unless they absolutely had to, and during the Passover was pretty much the only time anyone needed to. The rest of the time, the two sides of their country remained divided.

Dela's stomach flipped in anticipation. They were finally going to come face to face with the other races.

"Let's keep moving," Norton said, beckoning everyone forward.

Dela pushed to the front, and Layla followed. A couple of the men, including Norton, were also up front. Perhaps they were as eager to meet the other folk as she was. She had no reason to fear them—they were all here for the same thing.

This part of the Southern Pass was long and straight, offering them a view into the distance. The acoustics of the place must have carried the sound between the cliff faces, as another few minutes passed before dots appeared in the distance and gradually began to grow larger.

It was them.

She exchanged a nervous smile with Layla, and they kept walking. Dela suddenly forgot all her aches and pains in light of this far more exciting development. A small part of her was disappointed, however, knowing that as soon as the produce was exchanged, they'd be turning around and heading home, and the adventure would be over.

As the distance between them shortened, Dela was able to make them out more clearly.

"Bunch of freaks," Brer—the guy who'd been at school with Ridley—muttered.

"Shut up," she snapped. "You don't know how good their hearing is."

He cocked an eyebrow. "Yeah, like a dog's."

She leaned out and punched him in the arm.

"Ow! What was that for?"

"These are important people. The other races send their best to the Passover, unlike us."

"They're not people, though, are they? Isn't that the point? Besides, I thought you of all of us would be a bit more wary of them."

His words made her straighten, and her stomach clenched. "What's that supposed to mean?"

"We don't know what happened to Ridley. Maybe he got on the wrong side of one of these guys."

Dela scowled at him, not wanting to even entertain the thought. "There are plenty of dangers on this journey, and anyway, they were attacked by something. The others lost sight of him, and that's all we know. I'm not going to start putting blame on others when no one really knows what happened."

Brer shrugged. "Suit yourself, but if it was my only brother, I think I'd have tried a little harder to find out what attacked him in the first place."

His words stung, and she twisted her face away, not wanting him to see her angry tears. She hadn't been able to do anything more to find out the truth. She'd been left as the only child of her mother and father, and she wasn't about to leave them alone to go off on some pointless quest. The Chosen who'd returned from the Passover that year had already told her everything they knew, and they were the ones who'd been there. How was she ever supposed to find out more than they already knew? She probably would have died trying and then would have left her parents with no children at all. She wanted to fight her corner with Brer and explain all the reasons she hadn't fought harder to find out exactly what had happened to Ridley, but she clamped her mouth shut. She told herself it was because this wasn't the time, but deep down, the niggling worm of doubt tried to raise its head. Maybe she didn't want to fight with him because she knew he was right.

Dela pushed Brer's words aside and focused on the road—and the people—up ahead.

Now they were closer, she was able to make out more detail. Leading the way was a man with massive shoulders and long, brown hair. His chest was bare, exposing massive pectoral muscles and thick ridges of abdominals. She wondered how he could stand the cold. He was riding what appeared to be a huge, hairy white goat, with horns that protruded in thick swirls from its forehead. Beside him rode a similar looking man, and behind them came the carts of black coal they were to exchange. So they were the Norcs, she thought. The ones everyone said were rough and uncivilized. Behind them, a male with white blond hair sat astride a magnificent stag. The Elvish. This one might even be considered royalty among his own kind, though of course the human royals didn't acknowledge them as such.

Bringing up the rear were a number of men on horseback. Their skin was the color of tanned hide, their hair long and black. The man leading their group wore his hair in twin braids which lay down the front of his leather covered chest. None of the dark skinned men had saddles for their horses, preferring to ride bareback. These were the Moerians.

Her heart pattered in exhilaration, and Dela picked up her pace, so eager to meet them that she inadvertently became the one leading their convoy.

CHAPTER 12

WARSGRA

"There they are," Warsgra grunted. "Sorry looking bunch, too."

Julta glanced over at him as they rode closer. "Cut them some slack, Warsgra. They've come a long way, and they're not built for these conditions."

He snorted. "Soft and fragile, that's what they are. They have no business coming this way at all. The mountains are our home."

"Let's just get this over and done with, and then we can bid them farewell."

They got closer, the human's small shapes becoming more defined. Most of them walked alongside the carts of grain pulled by oxen on yokes, much the same as the bison who pulled his carts of coal, only less built for these conditions.

They got closer still, and Warsgra frowned. If his eyes weren't deceiving him, the one who appeared to be leading the group was a young woman with hair that looked like golden flames. Unlike many of the shuffling, limping group, she held herself tall, her chin up, her shoulders back. He didn't see any fear in her eyes, only interest, and he couldn't tell if that pissed him off or not. He normally enjoyed seeing a flicker of fear in a stranger's eyes, especially when they saw the size of both him and his axe. An older male human walked close behind her. A lover? No, too old. A father, perhaps? Not that it mattered to Warsgra. Humans didn't interest him; it was the contents of the carts that got his attention. His clan didn't want for much and their needs were few, but the grain would allow them to make bread for the next six months, and would keep small bellies full, and the women content. Whenever he returned with the carts filled with grain, his people cheered and ran alongside them, knowing they'd be fed for another six months.

He was close enough now to see the young woman in detail. In contrast to her hair, which looked as though it were made of the gold the Moerians carried, her eyes were a soft brown. Her nose was small and delicate, her lips full, her cheekbones high. A slender neck vanished beneath a smock-like top which hid her shape, and she wore thick leather pants and heavy boots. He liked the practicality of the way she dressed, reminding him of Norc women. There was no room for finery when survival was at stake.

The humans stopped where they were, and he pulled his goat to a halt. Knowing he had nothing to fear from these humans, he jumped from the animal's back and handed the rope-reins over to Jultu.

"Greetings," he said, stepping forward. "I hope the journey wasn't too arduous."

He could feel the young woman staring at him, and he was tempted to stare back. Normally, the humans were frightened of him, his size and strange dress, and the way he was twice their size. He was used to them stuttering and being unable to meet his eye, not gazing at him unflinchingly the way this woman was doing.

"See something you like?" he said instead, smirking as her cheeks colored and she glanced away. His stomach dipped in disappointment, and he found himself regretting that he'd said anything. He had been rather enjoying being the focus of her clear gaze.

That was fine. He didn't need the interest of some young girl with limbs so spindly she looked like he could snap her across his knee. They had a job to do.

"We'll divide the grain between our three races," he said. A third for the Norcs, a third for the Moerians, and a third for the Elvish.

Behind him, both Orergon and Vehel had dismounted. These humans didn't look like much of a threat, but he still sensed both Orergon's and Vehel's men grow more alert as their leaders approached the humans.

Vehel reached into the satchel at his waist and removed the small pouch which contained his contribution to the Passover— the diamonds.

He held them out to the young woman, who took them and handed them behind her to the man at her shoulder.

"Don't you wish to inspect them?" Vehel asked her.

She shrugged her narrow shoulders. "Inspect them for what? I don't know what I'm looking for."

The man behind her appeared to, however, as he tipped the pouch, emptying the tiny clear gems into his palm.

The woman, however, didn't even glance back. Instead, she looked between them each—him, Vehel, and Orergon—as though she was studying them. Warsgra held himself straighter, even though he already stood a foot above the others, and pushed back his shoulders. He wasn't sure he liked sharing the woman's intense gaze with the other two.

"And you?" she said, nodding at Orergon. "Do you have your exchange ready?"

Orergon lifted his hand in the greeting of their kind, exposing his palm to her. "Of course." He nodded back to one of his men, who stepped forward. The gold was heavy, and had been carried on satchels slung across the horse's back. There was substantially more of it than of the diamonds—something Warsgra couldn't fathom, why one should be more precious than another—and he handed it over to the woman.

She dropped slightly under its weight. "Heavier than I was expecting," she said, before turning around and handing it to the man behind her.

He'd already put the diamonds back in the pouch.

What prevented them from just taking the precious materials and not returning home? It wasn't as though they were interested in feeding their families with them, like he was. Were they so frightened of the king and queen who ruled over them that they'd never even consider taking the goods for themselves? Or perhaps the goods simply had no value to them. Unless you knew someone who would buy them, they were worthless, and he was sure most of these people had never left their homeland before.

This part of the Southern Pass was wide enough for them to allow two carts to pass each other, which was why the timings were done as they were, so they'd meet up in the widest point. The bison pulling his carts of coal would continue forward, and be taken by the humans, while he would take the oxen. The oxen weren't much good to him on the mountainside where his clan lived, but they would make good enough roasting meat.

"Let's move them on," he called.

The humans would need to take control of the bison, and his clansmen would take over driving his portion of the oxen. He assumed both the Moerians and the Elvish released their oxen into the wild once they'd arrived home. It wasn't as though the Elvish ate meat, and the Moerians had plenty of space to accommodate them. The animals probably went on to have good lives roaming the Vast Plains, assuming they weren't eaten by the local wildlife, of course.

The exchange started, with the humans who'd been driving the grain carts jumping down. Some gave the animals they'd been driving a pat on the flank or a scratch behind the ear, and Warsgra did his best not to roll his eyes at the display of affection. These were beasts for work or food, not to be treated like some kind of pet.

His men also climbed down from the coal carts.

But then he caught sight of the young woman who'd been leading their group. Instead of paying attention to the exchange and making sure her people were going where they needed to be, she was standing with her hands jammed against her hips, staring into the distance at something behind them.

"What is that?" she said, so softly it was as though she was speaking to herself.

Warsgra glanced over his shoulder to follow her line of sight, and his stomach curdled.

Where the tall cliff faces of the Southern Pass met the sky, there was now only a streak of white. It was so thick, he couldn't see where the mountain cliffs ended, or the peaks of the range beyond. He'd seen this before, but from a great distance. He'd never seen it so close, and even as he stared, it grew closer, as though it was being blown down the Southern Pass toward them, though he could feel no wind on his face.

"Move!" he bellowed. "Everyone, move, now!"

Confusion rippled among the motley crew of beings, but no one stirred. They didn't know what direction they were supposed to be going in, or what they were even running from.

The young woman turned to him, her eyes wide. "What is it?" she said, and this time he knew the question was directed at him.

"It's the Long White Cloud."

Understanding dawned on her face, and with it came horror.

"We need to go back," she cried, turning to run toward her people. "Turn the carts around. We have to get out of here."

He wanted to tell her not to worry about the carts, that they'd be faster on foot, but he saw how weak and fragile her people were, how many of them had been riding the grain carts when they'd arrived. His own people were either riding by goat, or driving the coal carts.

He wouldn't normally have offered to help humans, but something about her and her desperation, made him offer.

"Leave the grain carts. Get your people up on the coal carts. You don't have time to turn them around."

She looked up at him, her brown eyes wide in her pale face, and then nodded. She took off again, her hair flying behind her as she ran from person to person, directing and helping them where she could.

Both Orergon and Vehel had remounted their animals, and they drew up alongside them.

"If we continue this way," Orergon said, "we'll be entering the Eastern side of Xantearos, and we'll be breaking the Treaty."

Warsgra tightened his jaw. "If we don't go this way, we're all going to die."

Orergon pressed his lips together and nodded. Then he turned to Vehel. "Can you do anything to stop it?"

They all knew what he meant. They were talking about the way the Elvish prince had rid them of the little furry creatures that had attacked them the previous day.

But Vehel's light blue eyes widened, and he shook his head. "It doesn't work like that. I have no idea. I've never faced this before."

"None of us have," Warsgra said. "Not like this."

He looked back again. The cloud was already noticeably closer, barreling down toward them. The things that lurked inside the cloud were the sort of things parents told to their children at night to make them behave themselves. The living didn't get swallowed by the cloud only to come out alive and unscathed. If it reached them, the death toll would be unfathomable, and he didn't even want to give a thought as to the ways in which they would die.

They'd managed to get the humans onto the coal carts. A few

still ran around aimlessly, and he spotted the young woman and a couple of others among them.

"Get the girl," he said to Orergon as she ran by.

Orergon reached down and caught her by the arm, hauling her up and onto the back of his horse. But instead of thanking him for helping, she struggled to get down again.

"What are you doing?" Orergon asked, exasperated.

"My friend is over there. She needs me with her."

Warsgra glanced over to where a skinny woman of about the same age as the redhead ran from cart to cart, moving over supplies. He jabbed his heels into the side of his goat and galloped up to her.

"Leave that, silly girl. You won't need blankets if you're dead."

Then, just as Orergon had done, he reached down and hauled her up and swung her onto his goat to sit behind him. He glanced over to Orergon and the woman, and was relieved to see she'd stopped fighting to get down.

"Let's move!" he roared, and, with no other choice, they left the oxen still tethered to the grain carts, snorting in panic, as the Long White Cloud approached.

CHAPTER 13

DELA

Dela felt dizzy with fear as she clung around the waist of the Moerian leader. They galloped down the Southern Pass, back in the direction they'd just come. With no saddle on the horse, Dela dug her knees into the animal's wide belly and held on tighter to the man in front, terrified she was going to fall and be trampled under the hooves of all the beasts running alongside them, or rolled under the wheels of one of the coal carts.

But that wasn't her biggest fear. No, her biggest fear was the white plumes of clouds that now blocked her view of the entire Southern Pass behind her. The cloud was so thick, it was impossible to see through. It filled space between the walls of the Southern Pass, rising high into the sky, as tall as the mountains themselves. And the cloud was gaining on them, moving far faster than any of them could. They'd never make it to the exit of the pass, where they stood a chance of finding shelter. It had taken them two days to get here from the entrance. Yes, they were traveling far faster now, but even so, their survival felt hopeless.

She tried to keep sight of where all her people were, but they'd all mixed in together now and were impossible to spot. She caught glimpses of them, of Layla riding behind the Norc man, of Norton riding one of the coal carts, of Brer on the back of one of the Moerian horses. Goat, horse, stag, carts. Human, Elvish, Moerian, and Norcs. They were a strange ensemble of beings, but right now they were united in one thing, and that was putting distance between them and the Long White Cloud. If it swallowed them, they most likely wouldn't make it out alive.

Behind them came the terrified shrieks of fear of the oxen they'd abandoned. Her heart shattered at the thought of their terror and panic. They wouldn't be able to turn around on their own, not with the carts still attached to their yokes, and there hadn't been enough time to move between them and unhook them. Besides, having numerous untethered oxen running through the Southern Pass would only have hindered their own escape. Dela knew all of this, but it didn't stop her from feeling terrible about it. She never liked to think of anything in pain, human or beast.

They were never going to make it. The animals they were riding would collapse of exhaustion long before they reached the entrance to the pass. Those still pulling the coal carts were already lagging way behind, and they had a long way to go. Every time she looked back over her shoulder, the wall of white cloud appeared to be getting closer. It was almost as though it was chasing them, but such a thing was insane. It didn't have a thought process to be able to do that. It was just a cloud, something made up of water particles suspended in the air.

But Dela knew the stories. She knew how this thing swallowed men up whole, and never spat them out again—not alive, anyway. She'd always liked to believe they were only fairytales, but, now she was seeing it for herself, she could understand where those stories had come from.

Her arms wrapped tighter around the man directly in front of her. Because of the pace they were riding at, she had no choice but to lean into him, pressing her face and body up against his back. He was strong and lean, and even though there was no saddle, he felt as secure on the horse as though he were a part of it.

Risking lifting her face from his shoulder, she looked around, trying to spot Layla. The last time she'd seen her friend, Layla was being whisked onto the back of the mountain goat by the huge Norc leader. He lifted her as easily as he might have swung up a small child.

At first Dela couldn't see her, but then she spotted her not too far behind. She'd been blocked out by the massive bulk of the Norc's torso, but Dela had recognized him, and then spotted Layla's dark hair flying out behind him. She wished there was a way they could communicate, so they could reassure each other that everything would be all right, but such a thing was impossible.

A massive crack sounded from behind them, and with it came a shriek of fear and pain. Dela's heart lurched and she twisted around to see what had happened, certain the cloud had caught them and claimed its first victims. But instead she saw that one of the wheels of the carts had come loose, and in doing so had tipped to one side, throwing everyone off.

She spotted Brer among the people now picking themselves up off the ground.

Dela bashed the Moerian on the shoulder with her fist. "Stop! We have to go back!"

But he didn't even slow.

"Did you understand what I said?" she cried in his ear. "They need us!"

"If we go back, we die." His voice was deep and heavily accented, and she barely caught it above the thundering of the horse's hooves and snorted breaths.

He wasn't going to stop; she had no doubt about that. Men like him didn't get to be leaders by making stupid decisions, but she wasn't a leader. Far from it.

Dela braced herself, and then released her hold on the Moerian and jumped from the back of the horse.

She hit the ground hard, smacking her shoulder and hip, but managing to lift her arm to protect the side of her head. She rolled a couple of times and tucked herself into a ball, aware of the hooves thundering past her head. Someone yelled, but she didn't know who the shout was directed toward.

When she felt as though the main group had passed, she unfurled and got unsteadily to her feet. The people who'd been on the cart were still helping each other up, and she broke into a limping trot to go back and see what she could do.

Brer caught sight of her and waved her away. "What are you doing? Go! Run!"

"I couldn't just leave you all."

The bison were long gone, chasing after the others, dragging their broken yoke along behind them, drawing grooves in the dirt.

Dela went to help the others up. She glanced back again to see the cloud even closer. She froze, mesmerized by it. Did she see things move within its folds? Black shadows only barely hidden …

A hand on her arm yanked her away.

"By the Gods, Dela," Brer said. "What are you doing?"

She blinked. "What?"

"You're just standing there, staring. We need to go!"

She realized she had been, too. The approaching clouds, or at least what she'd thought she'd seen in them, had rendered her useless. If Brer had not yanked on her arm, she could easily have stood there until they swallowed her.

The thought made her shudder, and she started to run, taking after the others. It was frantic confusion, with people of different races and animals everywhere, all trying to get away. She lost sight of Layla, and then Brer. She wondered what had happened to Norton, too. There were too many people and animals around to spot anyone. Everyone was moving too fast, just a glimpse of a dark head, or the flash of a boot.

Hooves pounded the ground, but they weren't running away from her, but toward her. She looked up to see the white-haired Elvish leader—a prince, hadn't they said?—pull his huge stag up next to her. He leaned over, offering his hand.

"Take it." He looked down at her, his blue eyes intense.

She'd be stupid not to take the offer of help. She'd done what she could, which hadn't felt like much at all, but why let herself die?

With a nod, she reached up and took his hand. He was only a little larger than she was, but from the way he pulled her up, she could feel the strength in his lithe muscles. Even with all the chaos going on, he was an incredible sight. His armor appeared to be the lightest of steels, and she suddenly remembered her dagger. Of course, Elvish steel. That's what the armor must be made from. That, combined with his white hair and pale blue eyes, he was truly beautiful.

The breadth of the stag's back wasn't as great as a horse's, and she hoped she'd be able to stay on. There was a saddle of sorts, but it wasn't like the kind of saddle she'd seen used back in Anthoinia.

"Hold on tight," he told her.

This wasn't the time to feel shy or awkward about putting her arms around an Elvish prince—even though she did. He whirled the animal around, and then they were moving again, a gallop which meant they passed all those on foot. She felt wretched every time they flew past someone, but what could she do? The animal would be crushed to the ground if everyone tried to climb on. Anyway, who was she to tell an Elvish prince what to do? He'd come back for her, though she didn't know why. Perhaps it was because she'd been at the head of the convoy when they'd first met, and she'd been the one to take the goods in exchange. Maybe they all thought she was someone important, and that was why they'd tried to help her. It was different than how she thought they'd be. Rumor had always been that the other races held a kind of disdain over the human folk, but so far they hadn't treated her that way. They'd probably never get the chance to find out she was a nobody, anyway. The cloud was still gaining, and she couldn't see any possible way they'd be able to outrun it. Already, the horses and other animals were starting to tire and slow, and they weren't even a halfway out yet.

"Can we fight it?" She spoke loudly into the Elvish prince's ear so he'd be able to hear her above the racket of hooves and feet running.

He looked over his shoulder at her. "Fight the cloud?"

"Yes, or at least whatever is in it."

He shook his head. "I've never met anyone who has."

"Maybe no one ever tried," she shouted back.

"More likely no one ever survived to be able to tell us about it."

Dela bit her lower lip and glanced back again. The fallen cart with the bison had been swallowed now, vanished within its thick, white billows. What was happening to them in there? Was it utter madness?

"We're never going to outrun it like this," she cried. "There must be some other option."

"This is all we can do," he called back. "I'm sorry."

She held on tighter as he pushed the stag faster still.

CHAPTER 14

VEHEL

Vehel had glanced back and spotted the young woman with the red-blonde hair trying to help others of her kind to their feet. He waivered for a moment, knowing his Elvish companions wouldn't think highly of his actions, but then he'd pushed aside his worries and pulled the stag around and gone back for her. Chances were they wouldn't survive long enough for Ehlark, Folwin, and the others to report back to his parents and brothers, anyway.

He didn't know what it was, but something drew him to the human woman. She commanded his attention from the first moment he'd laid eyes on her when she'd been standing at the front of the human convoy. He'd expected her to be exhausted and broken—as most of the others she traveled with appeared to be—but instead she'd taken charge, making eye contact with each of them, even Warsgra. She didn't appear intimidated in the slightest.

And then he'd watched her throw herself from the back of Orergon's horse, and he'd wondered if she was brave or just crazy.

Either way, he couldn't let her struggle, and so he'd turned his stag around and gone back for her, and now she was sitting right behind him, her arms wrapped around his waist, shouting instructions into his ear. He wasn't used to people doing that either, especially not humans. Of course, she didn't know who he was, but he figured in this situation, they would probably all die the same way.

Death was an excellent way of bringing everyone to the same level.

Vehel didn't want to think about everyone dying here in the Southern Pass, but he was starting to accept its inevitability. The human woman was right when she said they wouldn't be able to outrun the cloud. Their only chance was if the cloud stopped encroaching and began to withdraw, but at the pace it was currently rushing at them, he doubted it. He'd witnessed avalanches in the mountains of his home in the Inverlands, and the Long White Cloud reminded him of this, how the snow bundled toward them, picking up pace as it gathered momentum down the mountainside. The only difference here was that the cloud was utterly silent, whereas an avalanche sounded as though the entire of Xantearos was coming to an end.

His men hadn't made any attempt to follow him when he'd turned back for the girl, but he saw Orergon had done the same thing. It was only because he was closer to the back of the group that Vehel had reached her first.

So, he wasn't the only one who thought there was something special about her.

Orergon maneuvered his horse to bring it alongside Vehel's stag. He didn't address the woman, or mention what she'd done.

"Can you do what you did last time?" Orergon called out to him. "Can you use your abilities to stop it?"

The woman perked up at what he was saying, and he felt the weight pressing against his back increase as she leaned into him. "What? What abilities?"

They both ignored her.

"It's not that simple," he called back. "I don't have control over it."

"But it's something," Orergon insisted. "Surely we have to try. We can't keep going much longer."

He was right; people were already falling back. Up ahead, one of the horse's front legs gave out beneath them, pitching the rider forward, over the animal's head and to the ground. Those who were on foot were a long way behind them now, and the cloud was almost upon them. He didn't want to hear their screams when they were swallowed up.

To his surprise, a small fist hit him on the shoulder. "Hey, what ability?"

He glanced around at her, unsure of how to react. He was an Elvish prince, and no one had ever thumped him on the shoulder before—well, his brothers had plenty of times, but certainly no one of a lower standing, and definitely not a human girl.

But Orergon didn't give him a chance to respond. "He can do magic. We were attacked by creatures farther down the pass, and Vehel was able to get rid of them."

"Vehel? That's your name?"

He nodded and called back over his shoulder, "What are you known by?"

"Dela Stonebridge," she shouted in his ear.

"Well, Dela Stonebridge, you should know that magic is forbidden."

She didn't give up, continuing to shout over the sound of the pounding hooves and the heavy breaths. "But if you can do something, shouldn't you try?"

"I agree with the human girl," Orergon called over to him. "You need to try. We're going to lose people soon."

"There are humans here, Orergon. Say there is the slightest chance I save them, what then? They go back to Anthoinia and tell their king and queen that the Elvish prince used magic? That would be enough to start another Great War. The humans would have a reason to try to take back our lands for themselves, and what would happen to my people then? Yes, I might save the handful of lives here now, but it could ultimately cause the deaths of thousands of others."

"I won't let them," the woman—Dela—yelled from behind them. "We'll force everyone to keep it a secret."

"That won't work. It's different among the inhabitants of the Western coast—we all have the same thing to lose—but the humans won't feel as though they'll lose anything. They'll tell their families, and then their families will tell their friends, and before we know it, the whole of Anthoinia will know. The City Guard will take it to the king and queen, and that will be the start of a new war."

"So you're just going to let us all die!" she cried.

"I don't even know if I can do anything. I don't exactly have control over it. There's a chance nothing will even happen."

Her arms around his waist tightened. "But you have to try!"

The urgency in her voice settled deep in his soul. How had this all become his responsibility? The idea that he could save all these lives was insane.

"Where's Warsgra?" he asked Orergon, still riding alongside them.

"Up ahead."

"He'll need to know what we're doing."

Orergon kicked his heels into his already exhausted horse and galloped away to find the Norc. Around him, the air of desperation and futility grew thicker. Those on foot cried that they couldn't go on, and some of the animals pulling the carts stopped walking and refused to move, no matter how much they were coaxed. He didn't want to be the one to decide if these people lived or died, or be the one to possibly start another war, but what kind of position was this to be in? If he wasn't able to do anything —which he doubted he could, anyway—at least they'd all die with him trying. Dying while attempting something heroic and giving people hope was surely better than dying surrounded in nothing but fear and futility.

Orergon reappeared with Warsgra at his side, still mounted on his huge white goat. Like him, Warsga had a human woman sitting behind him. They came to a halt, and the two women reached out to each other, their fingertips meeting across the space between them. From the look in their eyes, Vehel could tell they meant something to each other. He'd have thought them to be sisters if they hadn't been so opposite in looks.

"Orergon says you're going to try the thing you did with those creatures that attacked us the other day," Warsgra said.

Vehel nodded. "I can't promise I'm even able to do anything, or that it will have an effect, but I've agreed to try."

"If you don't, we're all going to die," he stated.

"I'm aware of that."

The last time it had happened, he hadn't even thought about it. The feeling had simply filled him, and he'd released the energy toward the creatures. He wasn't even sure he'd be able to do it again.

He climbed from his stag and turned toward the approaching cloud.

Chaos faced him.

People cried, dragging themselves away, while others were swallowed by the cloud, screaming. Most of the animals they'd been riding were faster than the folk on two legs, but a couple of carts had tipped in the chaos, trapping the bison beneath. They struggled beneath the wood and piles of coal, the whites of their eyes showing in fear, nostrils flared. The cart was too heavy for the animals to crawl from beneath, and the white cloud quickly engulfed them.

Vehel closed his eyes against the bedlam and dug inside himself for the thing he'd spent most of his life repressing. He'd known since he was a young boy that he was able to do things most of the other Elvish had long forgotten how to do. Nursemaids caught him lifting his toys into the air with only his thoughts, or conjuring one item of food into another. He'd even brought a pet bird back to life after he'd found it lifeless in the bottom of its cage one morning. He'd only been six years old, and hadn't really understood why what he found so natural to do was so badly frowned upon. Before, he'd only received smacked hands in response to his magic, but that morning they'd beaten him badly. From that day forward, he'd done everything he could to ensure he kept his abilities hidden, even though he could feel them growing stronger. More than a hundred years had passed since he'd been a child, however, and keeping something repressed for so long meant it no longer felt natural to him.

The human woman, Dela, slid from his stag and came to stand beside him.

"I don't know what you've got planned," she said, glancing over at him, "but you really need to hurry."

He gritted his teeth. "I'm aware."

Others had picked up that there was something going on, and they began to stop fighting and running. People came to stand behind him or beside him, not so much his Elvish kin, who'd already tried to distance themselves as much as possible from him, but the other Moerians and the Norcs, too. Even the humans were sided with him.

Vehel closed his eyes. He reached deep inside himself, to where that nugget of buzzing power lived. He needed to release it, and even as he thought about it, the energy grew larger, swarming through his body and to his extremities. Yes, he still had it, and he'd be able to use it.

Question was whether it would make any difference.

"Hurry!" the woman cried. "It's getting closer."

He opened his eyes and threw the energy toward the cloud. Just like the previous day, blue light shot from his arms and hands, illuminating the normally gloomy Southern Pass.

It met with the wall of white, but didn't stop it approaching.

Instead, the light only served to reveal the things lurking in the cloud. Dark, demon-like creatures, some walking on all fours, others with horns protruding from the tops of their heads. Their hands were tipped in razor sharp claws, and, as he watched in horror, one of the Norcs was swallowed by the cloud. The big man swung his axe, but it didn't seem to injure the hellish creature. Instead, it let out a shriek, loud enough to make Vehel want to cover his ears with his hands, and swiped one clawed hand toward the man's throat. He dropped his axe and clutched a hand to the wound, but even through the translucent cloud, Vehel was able to see the spurt of blood that signaled his artery opening.

"By the Gods!" Dela's cry came from beside him.

He'd tried, and he'd failed.

There was nothing more he could do.

CHAPTER 15

DELA

They were all going to die.

The certainty settled in her heart, and her first thoughts went to her parents. They'd be left alone, and just like with Ridley, they'd probably never know for sure what had happened to their last remaining child.

"Dela!"

The cry of panic came from Layla. She was still on the back of the mountain goat, with her arms around the waist of the big Norc leader, but Dela knew she wouldn't want to die with her arms around a stranger.

"Layla!"

She reached for her friend, and Layla slid from the back of the goat and into her arms. "I'm frightened!" she cried.

"Me, too." Dela drew her dagger from her belt. "But we'll go down fighting, okay?"

Her lips pressed together and she shook her head. "I don't want to go down at all."

"Just stay behind me." She stepped in front of Layla, putting herself between her friend and the cloud.

The different races had begun to gather around their leaders now, ready to defend and protect. The only one who was left alone was the Elvish prince who continued to spill blue light from his fingertips. The look of fierce concentration on his face was both terrifying and mesmerizing at the same time. Did none of his fellow Elvish come near him because they were afraid? Or did they simply not approve of him trying to help?

She noticed how the other races stepped closer, however, offering a protection of their own. Where his own people seemed to have abandoned him, both the leaders of the Moerians and the Norcs had moved in. She'd not been expecting such a thing, assuming the races hated each other, in much the same way humans had always been taught to hate and fear what was different from them. This show of solidarity spoke to her, however, and she found herself staying close to him, too.

A big Norc, similar to their leader, was at his leader's side. "Stay back, Warsgra!"

But Warsgra stepped forward to stand beside him. "I'll fight these demons alongside you, not behind you." He brandished his axe.

The cloud was terrifyingly near now.

The Moerians' horses sensed the danger and whinnied and rose up on their hind legs, forcing the Moerians from their backs. Perhaps not wanting their animals to meet the same fate they were about to, the dark-skinned men with the shiny black hair allowed the animals to run, the weight of the men on their backs no longer slowing them down.

Together, they stood shoulder to shoulder, a strange infantry lined up in battle. Through the Elvish prince's magic, they were able to see what they were about to fight. Dela wasn't sure if that was a good thing or not. Her heart pounded, and her hand trembled around the hilt of her dagger, which she brandished. The Moerians all held spears, and the Norcs gripped their huge axes in two hands.

The cloud crept closer and closer. The demons inside

appeared unable to escape, needing for them to be inside the cloud rather than them reaching out to get them. Some people started to lose their nerve, staggering back and crawling away from the line of defense they'd created, but Dela and the leaders of the other races stood their ground. Perhaps it was madness, and she should be running, but this thing would get them eventually. She'd rather face it standing tall with a weapon in her hand than crawling on all fours and begging for her life.

The demons were close now, lunging for them as though they were divided only by a sheet of glass. She saw the wicked spikes of teeth in their gaping maws, and the evil flash of red in their eyes. They had nothing other than pain and death on their minds; that much Dela was certain of. The sound of their piercing screams was enough to turn her heart to ice, and combined with the screams of the people they'd already gotten hold of, made her want to jab something sharp into her ears, so she'd never have to hear anything again. Through the cloud, she could already see the rocky ground of the Southern Pass smeared with the blood of those already killed.

The Long White Cloud was so close now, trickling nearer, inch by inch. Dela stood with her right foot forward, her left back, brandishing the knife and ready for attack the moment the cloud swallowed her.

Instinctively, she held her breath, bracing herself, and had to stop herself closing her eyes against its enveloping mass. One of the demons had already set its sights on her, and it drew back its lipless mouth, revealing row after row of sharp teeth, and let out a hiss.

The cloud reached her, crawling over her body, and the demon lunged.

Without warning, Vehel's light changed. Instead of directing toward the cloud in a beam, it now circled them, enveloping them in a ball. The demon that had been lunging toward her hit the light and bounced off, its screams of rage filling Dela's ears.

She gasped in surprise, having fully prepared herself to be wrestling a demon right now. What had happened? Was the light somehow protecting them? She glanced to either side to find the light surrounding her in a sphere. But it was only large enough to encase a handful of people, and, purely due to their proximity to the Elvish prince and the fact he didn't have any of his own people with him, it was only Vehel, herself, the Moerian leader, and the Norc leader who were caught inside the ball.

Instinctively, she reached out for Layla, but though her friend was still behind her, she was no longer with her. The circle of light that had surrounded her had also divided her from her friend, leaving Layla on the outside, exposed and vulnerable.

"Layla, no!"

She tried to grab her, her friend reaching back, but the light had some kind of charge when she tried to reach through it that felt like a hundred Bottlehead wasp stings all at the same time. She pulled back her hand and let out a scream of pain and frustration.

"Stop it!" she cried to the Elvish prince. "Make it stop!"

But he no longer appeared to have any control over it. His eyes were wide open and glowing the same color as the light that now surrounded them, protecting them. His whole body vibrated with the power, and she thought it might kill him.

All around them was carnage. People screamed, and either fought or ran. Either way, it didn't seem to matter as they met their end, whichever choice they made.

The Norcs swung their axes wildly, hacking at the demons attacking, and the Moerians let out shrill cries and lunged with their spears.

She saw the Norc who'd been by his leader's side this whole time battling hard with one of the demons, but even a man of his fierce strength and size was losing. Layla had run, and Dela caught sight of Brer and Norton also fighting back. She wanted to help, but she was trapped inside this damned orb.

The big Norc leader, Warsgra, gave a yell of anger and lifted his axe high above his head. "Let us out, Vehel! Bring it to an end!"

The Moerian with the twin braids tried to grab the Elvish prince but was thrown backward by his power.

Her mouth dropped open in fascinated horror as Warsgra gave a war cry and swung the weapon down with all his might.

The world exploded around them, like all the air had been sucked from the space they'd inhabited, and then flung them out again.

Dela flew through the air and hit the ground, the side of her head smacking on rock.

And everything went black.

* * *

Stillness was all around her.

The mayhem and terrified screams of being trapped inside the Long White Cloud had vanished.

Was it over?

Layla!

Her eyes snapped open at the thought of her friend.

Where the hell was she?

Dela frowned and then groaned as she pushed herself to sitting. Every muscle in her body hurt, and she winced, trying to stretch out her aching limbs. But she wasn't badly injured—nothing bleeding or cut off, except for maybe a bump to the head.

Blinking her eyes open to bright sunlight, she looked around. Confusion flooded her. She was lying on a flat rock that appeared to be on the edge of a cliff. An expanse of countryside stretched out before her, but she was no longer in the Southern Pass, or even in the mountains. And not only that, she wasn't alone.

Sitting on the edge of the rock, looking out over the surrounding area, was the Elvish prince. Vehel. He had his back to her, and she wasn't sure if he knew she was awake or even there.

That wasn't all. To the other side, lying face down, so his broad naked back was exposed to the sunlight, was the Norc, Warsgra.

She looked on the other side of her, already certain of what she'd find. Yes, there he was—the Moerian, though she was unsure what he was known by. Like Warsgra, he was also unconscious. She preferred to think that, rather than dead, but the unnerving way he was utterly still made her think he was more than just asleep.

Her chest tightened at the thought of her last memory, of how they'd been attacked by those things in the Long White Cloud. What had happened? Had she been knocked unconscious, and they'd somehow escaped and brought her here—wherever *here* was? But it didn't look anything like the mountains they'd left behind. Everything about the place felt different. A hot sun beat down on her shoulders and the top of her head. Even the air tasted different in her mouth. It wasn't possible for them to have traveled so long and far, and for her to remain unconscious the whole time.

Was this even real? Was she dreaming?

Dela spoke. "What happened?" Her voice was coarse, and the Elvish prince jumped at the sound.

He turned back to look over his shoulder at her. "My magic happened."

That wasn't much of an explanation. "I remember the light … the circle …"

He nodded at the unconscious Norc. "Warsgra did something to it when he struck it with his axe. I don't know what. One minute we were there, and now we're here."

Dela's confusion deepened. What was he saying? "Here?"

"From the little I've seen, and the temperature, I believe we're somewhere in the Northern region of Xantearos. I'm hoping when Orergon wakes, he'll recognize something and be able to tell us more."

"Orergon? Is that the Moerian leader's name?"

"Yes."

"And you're Vehel?"

"That's right. And you're Dela."

She nodded. Her mind raced at a million miles a minute. "I don't understand. We can't have traveled to the north already. It would take weeks."

"I think Warsgra somehow put a cut in reality, fractured a hole that we were sucked through."

"This is crazy," she whispered, her hand at her mouth. "What about all the people we left behind? What happened to them?"

He shook his head. "My best guess is that they're all dead."

Tears flooded her eyes. "Oh, no. Not Layla!"

She couldn't bear to think that she'd lost everyone—Norton, Brer, all the others, but especially Layla. She'd done everything she could to protect her friend, but by standing in front of Layla, instead of beside her, she'd nudged her out of the circle of protection. When they'd somehow been pushed through a layer in reality, Dela had left Layla in the Southern Pass.

Her heart tore in two at her loss, and she placed her face in her hands and let out a wail of heartbreak. She didn't care that this stranger—a prince, no less—was watching her grieve. If only she'd done things differently, if only she'd known. She'd have pushed Layla into the circle of light before taking her place there herself. Had Layla, in her final moments, witnessed the group vanish? Were her final thoughts that her friend had abandoned her in her greatest moment of need? The idea was as though someone had stuck a knife in her guts and twisted it with everything they had. She remembered this pain; it was the same she'd experienced when she found out Ridley had died. Helpless, futile, inescapable pain, combined with the unnerving anxiety that something even worse was about to happen at any moment.

She thought of Layla's family back in Anthoinia, and how devastated they'd be when they heard the news, and her own family, too, who would assume she'd died with Layla.

"What by the Gods happened?" a gruff voice sounded behind her.

She wiped away her tears and turned to see the hulking Norc on his knees, his hair falling around his face and shoulders, frowning around at everyone.

Sudden anger burst through her, and she lunged at him, her small fists striking him in the chest. He hadn't been expecting it, and even though she was half his size, her fury and momentum sent him sprawling backward, so he landed on his back, with her on top. She punched at his chest, and then went for his face, but he caught her wrists in his hands, holding her firm.

"This is your fault!" she cried, struggling against him. "It was your axe that did this! We'd all still be back there if it hadn't been for you."

"Whoa, girl. Stop your fighting."

She struggled even harder, but it was as though he'd clamped her wrists in stone.

He continued. "I don't even know what you're talking about."

"You hit Vehel's light with your axe, and it brought us here!"

He looked around, but sat up, still holding her wrists, so she fell into his lap, straddling him. She was painfully aware of how close to his bare chest she was, and how his muscular, hairy thighs were right beneath hers. Considering the Norcs lived in such cool climates, why didn't they wear more clothes? Warsgra, however, seemed to have completely forgotten he had hold of her, never mind that she was now straddling his lap.

"I didn't do anything."

Vehel had gotten to his feet and approached them now, nodding. "You did. I don't know how, but when you hit my magic, it split something. Didn't you feel it, too, as though all the air was being sucked out from inside the ball I created, and we were pulled with it?"

Recognition lit in the Norc's green eyes, and he nodded slowly. "Yes, I remember that part. And then ... nothing ..."

"We were all the same," Vehel continued. "I woke first, and saw the three of you still unconscious."

Dela tried to pull her hands from Warsgra again. He frowned at her, as though only just remembering she was there.

"Are you going to keep hitting me, wee girl?" he asked.

Sullenly, Dela pressed her lips together, glanced away, and shook her head. He released her, and she scrambled back to her feet, glad to put some space between them.

She looked over at the Moerian, Orergon. "Shouldn't someone check if he's all right?"

"Aye." Warsgra got to his feet and walked over. He shoved Orergon in the back with his boot. "You all right down there?"

That wasn't quite what Dela had meant. "Don't do that! You'll hurt him."

Warsgra snorted. "He's tough. He can handle a boot to the back."

"Not when he's unconscious."

Dela crossed over to him and dropped to her knees beside the unconscious man. His twin braids had fallen over his face, and she gently lifted one and moved it back so she could see him more clearly. Thick, jet black eyelashes rested on his cheek, and his lips were parted slightly as he slept. His nose was aquiline and strong, and where she'd moved the braid revealed high cheekbones.

His eyes shot open, fixing on hers. The surprise made her dart back, and he did exactly the same thing, so one moment they were staring into each other's eyes, and the next they were flinging themselves away from each other.

Orergon looked around in confusion. "What … how …?"

Vehel stepped forward and explained the situation again, or at least as much as he knew of it. "I hoped you might recognize something of where we've ended up," he finished.

Orergon got to his feet. He stood taller than Vehel, but not as tall as Warsgra. The clothes he wore were mostly leather, a contrast to Vehel's expensive silver armor, or Warsgra's general lack of clothing. He jammed his hands on his hips and looked around at their surroundings, a slight frown furrowing his brow.

"This isn't the Southern Pass," he said eventually. "Or the Vast Plains, either."

"We're aware of that," Vehel said, "but do you know where it is?"

The Moerian lifted his face to the air and sniffed. "North, definitely, and from the temperature, I think we're even farther north than the Vast Plains."

Dela shook her head in amazement. "That's just not possible."

"It is. It must be. Because we're here, aren't we? One moment we were in the Southern Pass, and now we're here. We all saw what happened with Vehel's magic and Warsgra's axe. Maybe we can't explain it, but we were all there when it happened. There's no point in trying to think otherwise."

"Maybe we can use the magic to get back again," Dela blurted. "Vehel, you can create the ball of light again, and Warsgra, you can hit it with the axe. It might take us back to where we came from."

"Do we really want to go back into the Southern Pass?" Warsgra lifted his bushy eyebrows in disbelief. "We'd most likely be dead right now if we were still there."

"We could be helping!" Dela snapped.

He snorted. "Helping feed the demons."

Dela lashed out, smacking the bulky muscle of his bicep. "Stop that. Those were our friends we left behind."

"And I suggest you stop hitting me."

She scowled. Making out that Layla and the others had become meals for the demons deserved a thump. It wasn't as though she could hurt him.

"They weren't friends of mine," Vehel said. "And I expect my father will throw a party for the whole of our kingdom when he learns I'm most likely dead."

His words shocked her. "You can't mean that."

He lifted his chin higher, as though owning his words. "Those other Elvish who accompanied me were only there to report back on how I'd conducted myself during the Passover. My father always believed I wasn't capable of leading such an important mission, and I guess I've proven him to be correct."

Her mouth dropped. "The white cloud descending wasn't your fault, and we'd probably all be dead right now if you hadn't used your magic."

He shook his head and glanced away. "If anyone has survived …" Then he corrected himself. "If any of your fellow humans have survived and manage to get back to Anthoinia, they'll recount what happened. They'll tell your king and queen that I used magic to save myself and the other leaders, and most likely say I kidnapped you. That's plenty enough for your king and queen to announce the Treaty broken and give them reason to put an army together to invade the Inverlands, and most likely the rest of the Western coast, too. They've been waiting for an opportunity like this. It wouldn't surprise me if they somehow set the whole thing up."

She could barely believe what she was hearing. "If anyone escaped, they'll tell the truth. They'll say you were trying to save us!"

He arched his fine white eyebrows. "You truly believe that? More fool, you."

Indignation for her own kind rose inside her. "We agreed to the Treaty, just as the rest of you did. There's no reason for humans to want to see it broken."

"Only access to all of the things they exchange food for every six months. It's their way of keeping us in control, making sure our populations don't grow as large as theirs. By controlling access to the ability to grow our own crops, we've never been able to have the sort of populations you have."

She thought to Layla's family, with its six children, and all the other large families in Anthoinia. Hers was an exception.

Something else occurred to her. "Elvish don't have large families anyway."

"We can't, because we live for so long. Imagine if human families all lived to be hundreds of years old and reproduced just as they do now. The population would be overwhelmed. But the same isn't true of the Moerians and the Norcs. They live a human lifespan, but they don't have big families either."

"Is this true?" She looked to Warsgra and Orergon.

Orergon shrugged. "We can't have children we're unable to feed."

"Plenty of families in Anthoinia have more children than they can feed," she pointed out.

"That's the human sense of entitlement. You all do whatever you want without even thinking about it."

Dela opened her mouth to protest, but there was no point. Nothing she said was ever going to make any difference. They'd had hundreds of years to grow their prejudices. Maybe they even had a point. Humans had taken half of Xantearos as their own, and divided the remainder up between the other races. They'd even taken the half that was fertile and easy to grow on, unlike the colder climes of the Inverlands and the scorched Vast Plains. None of the Western coast got much rain, unlike the Eastern coast, so they'd always known they'd struggle to grow a good harvest there, and so had control over food sources. The Treaty could have divided the lands from north to south rather than east to west, but they hadn't, using the Great Dividing Range as the reason.

She gave her head a shake. "Arguing about the Treaty isn't going to get us anywhere. We need to figure out how we're going to get home."

In a sudden surge of panic, she put her hand to her neck, terrified the string of leather she wore might have been pulled loose in the kerfuffle. But her brother's ring was still there, safely tucked beneath her tunic. Then she reached down to where her dagger was normally wedged into her belt, but the space was empty.

"By the Gods!" she swore.

Of course, it had been in her hand when they'd been dragged through to this other place. She'd been prepared to use it on the demon that had been looking at her with murder in its red eyes right before Warsgra had hit the orb with his axe.

"What's wrong?" Orergon asked her.

"I lost my dagger."

Vehel's bow and quiver of arrows had been strapped across his back when it had happened, and they were still there now.

Dela looked around, hoping she might spot the dagger somewhere nearby. A glint of silver in the sunlight caught her eye.

"Wait, what's that?"

She hurried over, and bent to the item. It was the metal tip of a spear. Dirt had been blown over the weapon, partially hiding it, and she used her hand to uncover the handle, and then picked it up.

"That belongs to me." Orergon walked over to claim it.

"So the rest of our weapons might be here somewhere as well." She looked to Warsgra, who nodded, and started to kick his way through the sand and dirt, hunting for his axe. They had bigger things to worry about, but at least if they were all armed, they might feel a little safer.

Orergon and Vehel helped as well, even though they already had their weapons. The soil was a dusty red and flew up into the air, coating their skin as they searched.

"Ah-ha!" Vehel exclaimed, lifting Dela's dagger.

A smile cracked across her face. It might only be a small thing, but, like her brother's ring, it felt like a beacon of hope, and she was happy to have something of home on her person.

"Thank you," she told the Elvish prince, taking the dagger from him. She squeezed the hilt tightly, before placing it back in her rope belt, and then tying the belt a little tighter to make sure she wasn't going to lose it again.

He ducked his head to her. "Welcome."

"There she is!" Warsgra growled. He pulled his massive axe out from the dirt and lifted the weapon above his head. The bright sunlight glinted off the shiny steel, then he brought the axe head to his lips and kissed it.

It was a small comfort, but at least now they were all armed. Of course, being armed hadn't helped them in the Southern Pass, but Dela hoped they'd left the Long White Cloud and the demons within it far behind them.

What lay ahead, however, she couldn't even bring herself to imagine.

CHAPTER 16

ORERGON

Orergon wasn't sure how he was going to explain to the others how far their journey was going to take them. The female human didn't look anywhere near physically strong enough to make such a journey, though he'd been impressed with the fire in her eyes and the way she'd hit Warsgra. It took some guts to stand up to someone of his size and temperament. Warsgra was going to suffer with the temperatures up here, and Vehel had the largest distance of them all to travel. Orergon wasn't even sure Vehel would be welcomed back in the Inverlands when he got there. From the things the Elvish prince had said, it sounded as though his own family were against him, though Orergon wasn't sure why. Was it because they'd been aware of Vehel's ability to do magic, and so had shunned him?

"We're going to need to find horses," he said. "There's no possibility of us doing this on foot. Even on four legs, it's still going to be challenging."

Warsgra nodded. "We need to find food and water, too." He turned to Vehel. "Any possibility of conjuring something up for us?"

Vehel shook his head. "It doesn't work that way. As you've

already seen, the magic has more control of me than I have of it. Maybe if I'd been allowed to train and practice since childhood, as I should have been able to, things would be different, but the humans put an end to that."

The woman threw her hands up in the air. "If you're going to blame me for every single thing my ancestors did for the next however many weeks it takes us to get home, then I'm just going to do this on my own." She stormed off, shaking her head, her long golden-red hair in a ponytail shimmering down her back.

"Where do you think you're going?" Warsgra called after her.

"I have no idea, but this whole 'humans are responsible for ruining everything' talk is going to get old very fast."

"But humans *are* resp—" Vehel started, but she spun back around and cut him off with a swipe of her hand.

"Maybe, but I was still more than a hundred years away from even being born, and while I appreciate that it all happened practically within your lifetime, for me it's a very distant event."

She turned away again and stomped off, picking her way down the stony hillside. Orergon stood with the other two males and watched her back as she put more and more distance between herself and them. He looked to one side at Warsgra, who shrugged his broad shoulders, and then to Vehel, whose lips twisted.

"Very well," Vehel said with a sigh. "I'll stop mentioning the human thing, even though it's the truth."

Orergon gestured to her retreating back. "She's going to get herself killed if you don't."

"And we care because …?" Warsgra growled.

"Because we were the ones to get her into this," Orergon replied. "Because like it or not, we've ended up in this situation together. Because if we don't figure out a way to work together, we'll all most likely end up dead. We've got hundreds of miles between us and the Vast Plains, and it won't be an easy journey. If we're going to make it back to our people, we need to work together."

"And you think she has strengths we can use?" Warsgra nodded toward Dela's retreating back. "The Norc females have more strength in their little fingers than she has in her entire body."

Orergon jerked his chin toward her. "She's brave. You saw her in the Southern Pass. She took charge when it was time to do the Passover. She wasn't intimidated by any of us. And then when we were about to be swallowed by the cloud, she stood at our shoulders, ready to fight. Yes, she might be small, but she's fierce, and she looked like she knew how to use that dagger."

He'd known a woman with the same kind of fierceness before. Because of her small stature, she'd been underestimated, but she'd proven herself to be a strong and brave warrior. But all the bravery in the world hadn't made her strong enough to fight the things that had killed her.

The thought of death made him think of those he'd lost in the Southern Pass as well, Aswor and Kolti. They'd been good men, and their families would grieve terribly when they heard the news of their passing. Their souls would be running with the wild horses on the Vast Plains now, assuming the demons weren't able to drag them down to the underworld with them. It wasn't something he wanted to consider, or even that he would mention to their families. He'd give them hope, and tell them they'd died bravely in battle, so when the family members rode across the plains with the wind in their hair, they'd be able to feel their loved ones' spirits running along beside them.

Orergon dragged his thoughts back to the present. The woman had already managed to put some distance between herself and them.

What other choice did they have but to follow her?

He exchanged a glance with the other two, who both wore the same, resigned expression he was sure was on his own face, and then shrugged and took after her. The sun beat down on their heads and shoulders. He was used to the heat and being out in direct sunlight, but both Warsgra, and especially Vehel, with his pale skin, hair, and eyes, would suffer if they were out in it too long. Up here, high on the rock ledge, there was no shelter, and they had no choice but to move. They'd be better traveling any long distances at night, and resting somewhere near food and running water during the day. Once they'd made it farther south, the temperatures would cool again, but that would still be weeks from now, and they would struggle before that happened.

His long strides meant he caught up with Dela quickly. Warsgra and Vehel were close behind. She didn't even break her stride or glance in his direction, and though physically this young woman was the weakest of all of them, he had the strange feeling that she was the one leading them.

"So," boomed Warsgra, "anyone actually know where we're going?"

"South," replied Dela from over her shoulder.

"And do we know what lies between here and south? Do we have villages we can head to so we can ask for their help? I'm a proud man, and not someone who asks for help easily, but I'd say our current situation probably needs it."

"This far north isn't owned by any of our kinds," said Vehel. "The inhabitants may not take too kindly on a group such as ours descending on them."

Orergon nodded in agreement. "And it's not as though we have anything valuable to trade in exchange for food or horses." He looked around. "Do we?"

"We have our weapons." Warsgra's fist tightened around the handle of his axe. "But we'd be fools to give them up."

"He's right," Vehel agreed. "We need our weapons more than anything."

"There won't be much need for weapons if we've died from heat stroke or starvation," Orergon pointed out.

Warsgra frowned. "There must be something else we can trade first."

Vehel placed his palm on the chest of his armor, right above his heart. "I can trade my armor. I may need it, but it will be worth it if we're able to get a couple of horses in return."

"Anything else? Jewelry?" He directed his question at Dela. "Don't you have something around your neck?"

She whipped around, her hand at her throat, her brown eyes bright with anger. "No! You're not having that. I don't care if I have to starve to death, or if I have to walk until I rub holes in the bottoms of my feet. Nothing will make me part from this."

"A simple no would have sufficed," Warsgra muttered.

She glared at him. "No. No, no, no."

He returned her stare. "I think we all understand you."

"Good."

She turned back around and kept walking.

"How many hours do you think we have left before it gets dark?" Vehel asked. "We should probably try to find somewhere to shelter before then?"

Warsgra gestured around them. "Shelter? Shelter under what?"

Orergon realized the Norc was right. The short distance they'd already walked had brought them to a lower altitude, but it still seemed there were mainly grassy flats and stony outcroppings. A few hills like the one they just navigated down, which he assumed would also hold similar flat stones jutting out of the sides. They could try to fit under one of the flat rocks for shade, but that didn't solve the problem of them not having any food or water. Food, they could manage without for a few days, but they wouldn't last long without a water source.

Keeping the sun over their right shoulders to ensure they were staying on the same path, they kept going. Warsgra muttered under his breath the whole way, while Vehel appeared lost in thought. Orergon noticed Dela had lost a little ground from her earlier lead, and he hoped she wasn't struggling too much. He didn't know much about her kind, but he knew she wasn't made to cover huge distances with the sun burning down on her, which was what was happening now.

Orergon increased his stride and caught up with her. "I wish I had some water to offer you."

He was expecting a sharp remark in return, but instead she sighed. "I wish you did, too. I don't think I've ever been so thirsty."

"We'll reach a river soon, I'm sure of it."

She glanced to one side, looking into his face. "You are? What makes you so sure?"

"We're at lower ground now, and besides, I've seen something."

Immediately, her back straightened and her head twisted from side to side, hoping to spot what he'd seen. "What? Where?"

He lifted his hand and pointed into the distance where a few specs of black dotted the otherwise unbroken blue of the sky. "Do you see those birds?"

She shot him a confused look but nodded. "Yes."

"They're grain feeders, meaning they don't get any kind of moisture from their foods, so they never stray too far from a water source. If they're over there, then we can be sure water will be close by, too."

Vehel had overheard them. "Is that true?"

Orergon nodded. "Of course." He couldn't imagine why the Elvish prince would think he'd tell her an untruth.

"So, that's good news," Vehel said.

Orergon hoped he *was* right. He knew the lands—it was what he'd grown up with, after all—but this was farther north than he'd ever been, and the truth was that he didn't know exactly what they were going to come up against. None of them did.

"Let's just keep going in that direction. Follow the birds. They'll lead us to water."

"That's good," Warsgra growled, "'Cause I'm about an hour away from drinkin' my own piss."

Dela glanced over at him, her nose wrinkled. "You wouldn't actually do that, would you?"

"If it meant life over death? Aye, of course, I would."

She shuddered.

"It won't come to that." Orergon shot Warsgra a glare. There was no need to make a bad situation even worse. He didn't know why he wanted to protect the human woman, but he found he did. Was it just because she reminded him of someone he'd lost? He wondered about the ring around her neck, too. She'd had such a vehement reaction when they'd asked about using it for barter. It clearly meant a lot to her. Did it belong to someone at home? A lover or a husband? Had they given it to her as a keepsake for her to remember them by while she was away? Was that same person now grieving at home, believing her dead? It was none of his business, yet he found his thoughts turning the possibility over and over.

Above their heads, the sun thankfully began to lose some of its strength, and the light took on a softer glow. Each of them had slowed their pace, but though the cooler temperatures made traveling easier, night would also bring its fears.

Shapes in the distance began to take on form. "What's that?"

He narrowed his eyes, trying to bring them into focus. "Trees."

Warsgra increased his pace, stomping on ahead of them. "Trees might mean water." His long legs took him ahead within a few strides.

He exchanged a glance with Dela.

"Is that right?" she asked.

He nodded. "I hope so."

She looked back at Vehel. "Any time that magic of yours feels like it's coming back, just say so. Something to get us there faster would be appreciated right now."

The corners of Vehel's lips twitched. His cheeks had grown pink under his pale complexion, and beads of sweat had formed at the hairline of his brow. He still wore a layer of armor, and even though it was made from Elvish steel and was the lightest metal known to their lands, it must have been stiflingly hot under there.

"Believe me, if I had any way of conjuring such a thing, I would have done so several hours ago."

She sighed. "Shame. Guess we'll have to keep on walking, then, though I hope I don't have to take another single step once this is all over."

"I can carry you."

The offer from the Elvish prince made both Orergon and Dela lift their eyebrows in surprise.

"I'm stronger than I look," Vehel added hastily. "All Elvish are."

Was Orergon right in thinking the pink to his cheeks had suddenly deepened?

CHAPTER 17

DELA

Dela's mouth dropped at Vehel's offer. She hadn't been expecting that.

"Umm, no, I'm okay, thanks."

"Of course."

He kept walking, picking up his pace as though to try to catch up with Warsgra. Carry her? Was that some kind of Elvish custom she wasn't aware of? Admittedly, she didn't know much about their kind—only what history and gossip had taught her. She knew they lived to be far older than humans, some of them as much as three hundred years old. She wondered how old Vehel was. He looked to be in his mid-twenties in human years, but in Elvish years, was he considered young or older?

She was using the thoughts of him to distract her from the way her tongue felt fat and fuzzy against the roof of her mouth, and her teeth kept sticking to her lips. Her spit was so thick, she struggled to swallow, and even her eyes were scratchy every time she blinked. Sweat had dried at her hairline and across her eyebrows, so when she ran her fingers across her skin, salt came away on her hands.

But as they walked, the silhouette they'd seen on the horizon began to take shape. Two hills appeared on either side, so they looked to be walking into a valley. Beneath their feet, the ground began to turn greener, and they had to navigate small clumps of bushes. It wasn't much yet, but she stayed focused on that copse of trees, and, as they covered more ground, the copse grew larger. It wasn't only one or two trees, but several, and the trees looked as though they stretched onward, too. The trees didn't just offer the chance of water being nearby; they would also give them some much needed shade.

At least her discomfort from her thirst helped to take her mind off losing Layla and the sort of turmoil her parents would be in now. They wouldn't know yet, she guessed. In fact, it might be a week or more before they learned what had happened. It all depended on whether anyone had survived and made it back to Anthoinia to tell their tale. If no one survived, the City Guard would have to send a search party out to find them, and put together whatever they learned to create a story of their own. Of course, she doubted they'd ever figure out what happened to her, unless she made it home herself.

Dela gave herself a mental shake. Not unless she made it home. She *would* make it home. She had to. She needed to be there for her parents, and tell Layla's family exactly what had happened. It had been one of the things she'd struggled with so badly after losing Ridley—the not knowing. If she'd known exactly what had happened to him, would it have saved her the sleepless night after night of turning over the possibilities in her mind? Or would it just have given her something different to obsess about, and the knowledge of exactly how he'd died would have kept her awake instead?

Warsgra was well ahead of them now. He stopped and froze for a moment, and she wondered what he'd seen, but then he turned back to them and yelled, "I can hear running water!"

Dela looked to Orergon, who'd been walking by her side the whole way, his handsome face serious, and she saw the first hint of a smile touch his dark eyes.

"You were right," she said.

"Yes," he replied, as though he'd always known he would be.

The promise of water made her pick up her pace. Every muscle in her body ached, and a headache had formed right behind her eyes, but she knew rehydrating would make her feel a million times better. It wouldn't change anything about their situation, but at least she'd be able to think clearly again.

They hurried forward. Warsgra had waited for them, and Vehel reached him first, and then waited for them to catch up. He hadn't mentioned the carrying incident again. He seemed like a gentleman, as did Orergon—though Orergon was more attuned to nature—completely unlike Warsgra.

They stood still, and her ears strained. "I can't hear anything."

"I can," said Vehel. "I heard it while I was some way away."

Orergon nodded. "I can hear it, too, but I've learned how to pick up on such sounds."

"Human hearing is never going to be as good as any of ours," Warsgra joined in. "You've forgotten how to use your natural abilities."

By the Gods! What was wrong with this man? It was as though he took any and every opportunity to have a dig at anyone around him, including her. She hated that, despite his brutishness, he was actually extremely handsome. Full lips, a strong nose, bright green eyes, and a strong jaw covered in a scruff of beard. His long hair fell around his broad shoulders, and sometimes she found herself staring too long at the size of his bicep. It wasn't far from being the size of her head.

Dela tried not to be disappointed at her useless hearing—it wasn't her fault she was made the way she was. The most important thing was that they were near water. Her parched mouth and throat wanted to scream out for it, but she didn't think she even had the energy.

"Use your great hearing and take us to the water, then."

"This way."

They passed one tree, and then another, then a couple clumped together. The ground started to dip and grow softer. She smelled it on the air, a dampness where there had only been heat before. Hope lifted her heart. It was such a simple, basic thing to hope for, but that was what her life had been reduced to for the moment. If she didn't find those simple things in order to survive, she'd never make it back to her parents.

The men had already started in the direction of the water, and she hurried after them. The ground became dappled in shade from the trees, and she was grateful for the break in the endless sunshine. But then she realized it wasn't only the trees that created the shade. The sun had reached the point on the horizon where it still offered light, but was no longer completely visible.

Night was upon them.

"There!"

It wasn't much, a babbling brook a mere couple of feet wide, but it was the most beautiful thing she'd ever seen. A cry of delight burst from her throat and she stumbled forward, landing on all fours on the bank. She didn't even care that the water seeped through to her knees. She leaned forward, so her face was only inches from the water, and cupped her hands. She dipped into the cool liquid and scooped the water up to her mouth and drank deeply. It was the sweetest thing she'd ever tasted, and she gulped it down, before retrieving another handful, and another, and another.

A hand on her shoulder made her pause. "Take it slowly," a voice said from behind. "Or you'll make yourself sick."

She turned to see Orergon behind her, frowning at her in concern. She wanted to tell him to mind his own business, but then her stomach did a strange, loud gurgle, and she put her hand over her mouth. When was the last time she'd eaten or drunk anything? It had been the morning they'd set out on the final leg of the trip down the Southern Pass, and that felt like a lifetime ago now. With her thirst quenched, her thoughts went to food. Maybe they'd be able to find something here. Fruit in the trees, or perhaps Orergon would be able to put his spear to good use and hunt them a couple of those birds they'd seen.

She glanced over at the others. Warsgra had planted his hands and knees in the mud on the side of the bank and drank from the brook by lowering his head to the water. Vehel crouched, scooping water with his hand, in much the same way she'd done.

"You haven't drunk anything yet," she pointed out to Orergon.

"I was waiting for everyone else to finish. We couldn't all take our guard away while we were drinking. It would make us too vulnerable, and we have no idea who or what might also have taken up refuge here."

He'd been watching out for them all, she realized. What kind of mental strength did it take to be dying of thirst, and yet hold yourself back? He didn't really know any of them, and didn't owe them a single thing, but still he put their safety before his own needs and protected them while they took care of theirs.

"Drink," she told him, pulling her dagger out from its place in her belt. "I'll watch out now."

He nodded his understanding, and she got to her feet and took a couple of steps away from the water, giving Orergon room to crouch at the water's edge. She straightened and looked around, staying alert for any sign of movement that might indicate something larger than a bird.

Sudden splashing came from the water, and she spun, brandishing her dagger. Her heart thumped, not knowing what she was going to find. She'd expected something to have lunged out of the water to try to pull Orergon in, but instead she witnessed Warsgra stomping around in the shallows, his head bent over the water.

She frowned at him in confusion. "What, by the Gods …"

But he lunged down, sinking his hand beneath the surface, and the next moment he pulled up a good sized fish in his fist, its scales glinting purple, blue, and green under the late day's sun. He whipped around with surprising grace considering his size, and smacked the fish's head on a boulder, before throwing it, barely flapping, onto the shore at Dela's feet. Her stomach growled in hunger even as the fish flailed in its final death throes.

Warsgra's head darted from side to side, his green eyes bright, his hair damp at the ends and in scraggles around his shoulders. Even Vehel had stopped what he was doing to look up and watch the mesmerizing show of the Norc fishing. It was like watching a bear in its natural territory—fearsome but beautiful. He darted down a second time and snatched up another fish, repeating the process of knocking it almost unconscious and then throwing it to the bank.

Dela whooped her joy and jumped up and down, clapping her hands. Only an hour earlier, all had felt hopeless—they'd been dehydrated, without shelter and starving, but now they'd sated their thirst, had the shelter of the trees, and they'd be eating well tonight. It didn't change how she was swimming in grief at the loss of Layla, and she didn't think anything would ever ease the ache in her heart, but at least the physical side of her pain was taken care of.

The thought of what was still to come towered over her, overwhelming her, but she knew she couldn't give in to it. If she did, she'd give up, and she had to make it back to her parents. She couldn't let them go to their death beds believing they'd lost both of their children.

Warsgra caught a third fish, and then ploughed his way back out of the river, the water sloshing around his muscled thighs.

"We don't have a fire," she said. "Can we make one?"

"We don't need a fire to eat. Fresh fish is good, and its flesh has plenty of water in it. It's good to eat like this." Warsgra picked up a flinty piece of rock and got to work on one of the fish, scraping the scales from its body, and then opening its belly with the sharp side of the rock. He scooped out the inside, and then picked up a dark, shiny, fleshy part.

"Ah, the liver. Best bit." He threw it into his mouth, chewed and swallowed.

Dela wrinkled her nose, but her stomach did gurgle. She'd eat the raw fish if she had to, but the idea of it roasting on an open fire was far more appealing. She looked around, spotting fallen twigs and leaves from the trees on the ground.

"I'm sure we can get a fire going."

She set about collecting what she could find, picking twigs up from the ground. The temperature meant everything was dried out, and she was even able to scrape brittle moss from the side of a rock to use as a bundle of fibers for the kindling. The men watched her for a moment, and then set about helping, snapping the larger branches down to a better size, before setting them up in a teepee shape.

She didn't have a flint and steel to create a spark, and so would need to use friction, which was a long and tiring way of setting a fire.

Dela put her hands on her hips and sighed, suddenly exhausted and not sure she had it in her to create a flame. "Surely one of you must have a flint and steel on your person?"

Vehel stepped forward. "Allow me."

He glanced over his shoulder, as though to make sure no one else was around who might be watching them, though she had no idea who he thought that might be. They hadn't seen another single soul since they'd been brought here from the Southern Pass. Then he held his hand over the little bundle she'd created. His eyes slipped shut, his hand trembled slightly, and then a small flame burst in the center of the kindling. The flame quickly ignited the rest of the wood, and within a minute it was crackling and burning bright.

"I thought you weren't able to do magic on demand?" she said to the Elvish prince, grinning up at him.

He shrugged. "Transporting four people through the ether is a little different than a parlor trick. And no, I'm not supposed to use magic, but I figure the worst of the damage has been done."

Orergon brought over one of the fish Warsgra had cleaned. He'd speared it through the body with a larger stick.

"Wash away those entrails. We don't want to attract larger animals."

"All the more to eat," Warsgra grinned.

Orergon smoothed down his braids. "Not if they eat us first."

The Norc laughed, deep and full-bellied.

Orergon looked to Vehel. "Do you really believe your use of magic in the Southern Pass might cause a second war?"

He nodded. "If the news gets back to the king and queen, yes, I believe they would use it as proof that the Elvish broke the Treaty, giving them reason to invade the Inverlands."

"That's only if news gets back," Warsgra said as he leaned in to turn the fish over the fire. "If everyone died back there, there won't be any news to get out."

Dela looked around at each of their faces. "So, we're hoping everyone died?" The thought caused a tightening in her chest, making her feel as though she couldn't breathe.

The Norc shrugged but didn't look at her, preferring to concentrate on turning the fish as he spoke. "Those few lives lost in the Southern Pass will be far less than what will be lost if a second great war is started among our people. You know how many died the last time? Each of our races lost over half of our people. Thousands of lives lost." He finally glanced over at her. "You want that to happen again?"

She shook her head, frowning. "No, of course not." But at the same time, she couldn't hope for everyone to have died. Doing so would mean wishing her best friend and all her traveling companions dead, too. "You must have had people you were with who you loved and trusted. You can't possibly wish them dead."

She watched the look in each of their eyes change and knew they, too, were thinking of the companions they'd lost.

"Of course," said Orergon eventually. "We all have people we've lost, but hoping for survivors when it might cause an even greater issue won't help anything."

"It won't matter, anyway," Warsgra said. "I doubt anyone survived those things in the Long White Cloud. We all saw them. They weren't letting anything get away."

They fell into silence as the truth of his words sank in, and yet still Dela couldn't help hoping. Maybe it would mean the start of a second Great War, but she also hoped that if Layla had survived, she wouldn't say anything about the use of magic. But it was an empty hope, and if her friend had survived, others would have, too, and stories would be told, just as they'd always been told, and people would learn what had happened, and that was bound to get back to Anthoinia.

The scent of fish cooking filled the air, and Dela's mouth flooded with saliva. It was all she could do to stop herself dribbling when she spoke. When the skin was crispy and the flesh grew white, Warsgra took the fish from the fire and divided it up onto leaves to share between them.

They ate heartily, wolfing down the meal. Fish grease made their lips shiny, and Dela didn't even care that she might have pieces of fish or scales sticking to her face. It was possibly the best thing she'd ever eaten, and she found herself grinning around at Warsgra, Orergon, and Vehel. They might be in one hell of a situation, but at least their bellies were full now.

They didn't need the heat from the fire. The temperature here was already balmy, and Dela wished she was able to strip off some of her clothes. She wore only a vest under her tunic, and wasn't sure how comfortable she felt undressing to her underwear in front of the others. Her hands and face were fishy, so she got to her feet and went back to the riverbank. She leaned over the water and rinsed off her hands and face, and then sat back again. She worked her feet out of her heavy boots, and then bathed her aching feet in the water's silky coolness. Her blisters had blisters, and the skin around her heels and soles had hardened and thickened. They weren't pretty feet, but she didn't need pretty right now. That would serve no purpose. No, she needed practical, and if callused feet would mean she'd be able to walk for weeks to come, then she'd embrace them.

The daylight was waning, throwing shadows across the water.

The others all washed off, and remains of the meal were thrown into the water to keep any larger predators away.

It was an unspoken agreement that this was where they'd be spending the night. They were all exhausted and needed to rest. Even though it would be cooler at night to travel, they wouldn't be able to go much farther that day.

It felt strange to Dela to sleep so exposed, only the night sky above them. But she lay back on the ground, her arms pillowed beneath her head to try to give her some sort of comfort. The men had all found their own places around the fire, and the talk had died off as sleep tried to claim them.

Within minutes, her arms were already stiff and aching, and she shuffled around, trying to get comfortable.

Movement beside her made her jump, and she turned to find Warsgra looming over her, his massive shape even more threatening in the moonlight.

"Here," he said, gruffly, holding something out to her.

She frowned, but reached out and took it. It looked like a dead fox or something similar in the dim light, but then she realized it was one of the shoulder protectors he wore.

"For your head," he said, before turning around and going back to the spot he'd picked out as his own bed.

A small smile touched her lips. "Thank you," she hissed over at him, but he'd already turned his back on her and didn't reply.

Dela placed the item beneath her head and shoulders and gave a thankful sigh. The shoulder protector smelled of earth, and animal, and something masculine, too. It gave her comfort in a world where there was very little comfort to be had, and she was finally able to close her eyes and sleep.

CHAPTER 18

WARSGRA

That night was one of the longest of his life.
Despite what he'd said to Dela about hoping everyone had died, each time he closed his eyes he was back in the Southern Pass, watching his men fight and die, while he'd been able to do nothing.

He'd watched Jultu fight like the warrior he was until he could fight no longer, swinging his axe at those demonic creatures, even though it never seemed to harm them. He'd swirled on his heels and cut low, and then high when a second creature was coming at him, screaming. Warsgra had wanted to get out and help, but the light around him prevented him from doing so. He'd seen the human woman struggle with the same thing, desperate to get out to save her friend and her fellow travelers. He'd admired her for that—she hadn't cowered away, frightened, but had stood, brandishing her dagger and ready to take on whatever was coming for her.

The last thing he'd expected when he'd brought down his axe, hoping to chop his way out of the Elvish prince's ball of light, was for them all to end up here. Wherever here was. He did feel partly responsible, and Warsgra didn't like feeling responsible for anything, especially when these people weren't even his clan. Okay, Vehel was as much responsible for this mess as he was, perhaps even more so, but the other two—Dela and Orergon— hadn't done anything to cause or deserve this.

There was something about the girl, too, that was niggling at him. He couldn't figure out why, but she reminded him of someone. Something about the shape of her face and the color of her hair kept taunting a memory out of him. Every time he looked at her, it felt like déjà vu, but for the life of him he couldn't figure out where he'd seen her before. It wasn't as though he made a habit out of hanging around with humans.

Warsgra dozed occasionally, but kept waking with a start, thinking he'd heard something over the rush of the river beside them, but each time it was nothing.

He was relieved when the sky finally lightened and then the sun created a thin line on the horizon. Just as he imagined the others did, he wanted to get back to his people. Who would try to lead his clan with both him and Jultu gone? There were a couple of younger Norcs who might put themselves forward for the job, but none who were good enough. They'd be too reckless and selfish to think about what the whole clan would need to survive. The possibility of a great war starting with neither him nor Jultu there to lead his people into battle also played on his mind. If the humans forced the Norcs to fight for what was already theirs, he wanted a great warrior leading them, not some young male who thought more with his balls than with his head.

The others were all still sleeping, so Warsgra pushed himself up to standing and went back to the river. It looked beautiful in the early morning light, gurgling and peaceful. He needed to see if he could catch some more fish for breakfast, and also figure out if there was something they could use to carry water. Though they could continue to walk alongside the river, at some point it would divert course or vanish underground, and they'd be thankful for any water they'd be able to take with them.

He lowered his face to the river and drank deeply. He kept his axe by his side, ready to fight should anything try to attack.

Movement came from nearby, and he spun around, lifting the axe and jumping to his feet.

"Only me," the human woman said. "I wanted to give you this back."

She held out the shoulder protector.

"Keep it," he replied. "You might need it."

Her brown eyes lit up. "Are you sure?"

"I'm sure."

"Well," she tucked it into the side of her belt, "thank you. I did sleep a whole lot better with it as my pillow."

Her face had been resting on the fur the whole night. It would have smelled like her hair. Maybe he should have asked for it back after all.

Warsgra frowned and shook the random thought from his head. This was a human woman. Sure, he could appreciate the fullness of her mouth and how pink her tongue was every time it snuck out to lick her lower lip, but the rest of her was too fragile. Okay, maybe her arms were shapely, and her legs looked long beneath those leather pants of hers, but she was nothing like the Norc females. They were solidly built, and you didn't need to worry about crushing a hip bone when you pounded into them. Hell, they fucked back as hard as they were able to take. This human woman however, looked like she'd need to be treated with a velvet glove. By the Gods, he wasn't even sure he'd fit inside her.

"What?" she said, jamming her hands on her narrow hips, and he realized he'd been staring as all of this had gone through his head.

"Nothing," he growled. "Just thinking how weak you look compared to Norc females."

Her eyebrows lifted, and a high flush of anger bloomed in her cheeks. "I'm stronger than I appear."

"Sure," he said dismissively, trying to hide what he'd really been thinking. The stirring in his pants told him his body hadn't quite given up on the idea either.

"I'm getting more fish." He dropped his axe to the ground and strode into the river, knowing the cool water would help him take his mind off things.

He felt her watching him but did his best to ignore her. He didn't need that kind of distraction. He needed to make it back to his people, and thinking about this woman that way wasn't going to make this journey any easier.

The others had started to stir now, too, Orergon getting to his feet and stretching out his long, lean back, while Vehel put back on the armor he'd removed before bedding down for the night. Warsgra ignored them both and stared back down into the water, peering through the rapids and waiting for the dark shadow of a fish to slip by. He remained motionless, not wanting to frighten the fish away.

But a sound came to his ears, one he didn't recognize. At first he thought it was the buzzing in his ears he sometimes got after being in battle, caused by the amount of noise hundreds of fighting Norcs would make, but then the sound grew louder.

Warsgra took his eye off the fish and straightened. He looked toward the shore, where Dela was drinking from the water's edge, and then toward the trees, where Orergon and Vehel remained. They'd all heard it, too—he could tell by the way they'd stiffened, slight frowns of confusion marking their brows where their minds were going through the same process as his.

The buzzing grew to an almost deafening sound, and confusion morphed to fear.

"Move!" he yelled to the others. "Hide."

A huge winged insect, with a yellow and black striped body which ended in a massive curved sting at the end of its tail, burst across the bushes on the opposite side of the river. It was the size of one of his mountain goats, and the buzzing it made was deafening. Its spindly legs hung from the underside of its body, and even though they looked fragile, Warsgra knew they'd have immense power in them. The creature hovered for a second, its bulbous eyes moving one way and then the other. Then it seemed to fix its sights on something.

"Dela!" Warsgra yelled. "Run!"

Her brown eyes widened as she saw the thing coming for her.

Back where they'd slept, Vehel had drawn his bow and arrow, and Orergon picked up his spear. Warsgra had left his axe on the bank, needing both hands to catch fish, and he deeply regretted that right now. With a yell, he ran, his legs driving through the water so it sprayed up in his face.

Dela saw the thing coming and turned to run, but it was so fast, it was already on her. Its legs wrapped around her back, and Vehel paused, unable to let the arrow fly as he'd be as likely to hit Dela as the creature.

Dela screamed and fought back, but it wasn't enough, and the flying beast lifted her into the air.

CHAPTER 19

DELA

The scream barreled out of her lungs as her feet lost contact with the ground, and she was suddenly suspended in the air. The massive insect legs that had caught her were like iron bars clamped around her torso, squeezing her tight. She wasn't sure she would even be able to breathe, and it felt as though each time she exhaled, the legs squeezed a little tighter, so she was unable to take the next breath in.

Beneath her, the ground moved in a blur. Where in the Gods' names was this thing taking her? To feed her to all its giant grub babies, she realized with horror. She didn't want to die as maggot food.

She barely heard the yells of the others above the insanely loud buzzing. The creature flew forward, banking in one direction, and then the next, whipping Dela's head from side to side. She struggled in the thing's grip, but the way it had grabbed her meant her arms were clamped by her sides. She couldn't even kick the creature as gravity forced her legs to hang down.

They followed the line of the river, zigzagging back and forth. Motion sickness and being unable to breathe deeply left her dizzy and faint. She didn't want to pass out. Though being unconscious might be a welcome parting from her current situation, the thought of not knowing what this creature was doing with her was even worse. She didn't want to wake up to find herself being chewed on by maggots, or having eggs laid into her skin. She'd do everything in her power to keep herself awake so she could fight back.

To her right towered a high, muddy riverbank, with several large holes dug into the side. As they drew closer, she saw a second of the insects emerge from one of the holes and fly off, the buzzing doubling in volume for a moment before it faded away. They were still flying at a breath-stealing speed, and as they flew toward the bank, Dela tightened every muscle and squeezed her eyes shut, preparing herself for impact, certain she would end up slammed against the muddy bank hard enough to break every bone in her body. Instead, sudden darkness surrounded her, and the buzzing stopped. Her ears were still ringing from the racket.

Cold, wet, muddy walls surrounded her. The insect held her close to its fuzzy underbelly as it crawled forward, taking her deeper into the riverbank.

Despite her fear and panic, Dela tried to formulate a plan. She hoped the creature would just store her here and leave again. In which case, she'd be able to simply crawl back out of the hole and run to safety. If the creature didn't leave, she had her dagger wedged in her belt. She didn't want to get into a fight with the thing, and worried that if she managed to kill it, its massive body would fill the hole, and she wouldn't be able to get past, and then she'd stand the chance of being stuck down here until she died a slow and painful death. No, she'd probably run out of air before that happened, and suffocate.

Panic threatened to overwhelm her and she bit down on it, knowing she'd lose the ability to think clearly and that it might be the death of her. Still, she felt as though she was trapped in a nightmare, and she desperately wanted to wake up.

Finally, the insect stopped. Its grip on her released a fraction, and she was able to suck in a breath of stale, mud-tainted air. But she remained as motionless as possible, not wanting to do anything to remind the creature that she was there. *Please go, please go, please go*, she prayed over and over. The insect continued to shuffle back and forth, but again its legs released around her, dropping her fully onto the muddy tunnel floor, so she landed on her hands and knees. Cool dampness sank into the knees of her pants, reminding her of the previous day when she'd first knelt at the riverside to take a drink. How she wished she was back with Orergon, Vehel, and Warsgra right now. What would they be doing? Would they try to find her, or would they assume she was dead and not waste any more time on her? She prayed they wouldn't give up. They barely knew her, and she was a human, who they all despised, but she hoped they'd seen something about her that would make them want to at least attempt to save her.

She couldn't rely on others saving her, however. No one helped someone who refused to help themselves.

As the insect gave her more room, she was able to slide her hand down toward her belt, where the hilt of her weapon rested.

She wanted the thing to leave, figuring that would be a far better option than her attacking it first. Getting into a fight with the insect was not how she wanted things to go, but she needed to be prepared for the possibility. She was still curled up beneath its body, but her hand slipped lower, her fingertips brushing the hilt of her dagger. Her fingers tightened around it, but then the insect moved. It had managed to turn itself around in the confined space, and Dela froze, her heart pounding as it moved over top of her. It was leaving! Thank the Gods!

She had to hold back a sob of relief as the insect passed back over her, its legs no longer surrounding her torso, only its tail above her now. She held her breath in the darkness, huddling tight into herself, trying to make her body as small as possible so it didn't notice her.

There was a sudden swiping through the air above her, and

something sharp punctured the back of her neck. Dela gave a cry of shock, unable to stay quiet any longer. The thing had stung her! Her fingers tightened around the hilt of her dagger, and she went to pull it out and stab the creature in the belly, but instead of pulling out the knife, her fingers barely moved.

A fresh spurt of fear blasted through her.

The giant insect continued the way it was going, leaving her alone in the wet, dark tunnel. It left the entrance, taking off into the air, the movement of its massive wings vibrating down the burrow. Through the gap it had left, she could make out a pinprick of light that signaled the entrance. All she had to do was get to it, just crawl down the tunnel far enough to drop out the end. She didn't even care that she'd most likely fall directly into the water beneath and possibly be carried away on the rapids. Anything would be better than dying in a black hole with the possibility of being fly-food. But when she tried to reach out to drag herself forward, her arm wouldn't even move. She kicked out a foot, but though the movement happened in her head, her body remained motionless.

A thin whine of fear escaped her throat, and her breathing came quick and fast. The sting on the back of her neck didn't even throb anymore, and the aching that had become a part of her since leaving Anthoinia what felt like a lifetime ago had also vanished.

She was paralyzed.

CHAPTER 20

VEHEL

Vehel had watched in horror as the giant fly picked up Dela and whisked her away.

None of them had been expecting it, and he sensed the shock of the other two as well, as what had happened finally sank in.

Then they all burst into movement, Warsgra reaching the bank and snatching up his axe, while Orergon began to run in the same direction the fly had gone.

He hadn't been able to let his arrow fly, knowing it might hit Dela. One of his arrows would kill her, and he couldn't risk it, but now he was wondering if being killed by one of his arrows would have been a kinder death.

"Come on," Warsgra bellowed as he took after Orergon. "It followed the river."

Vehel broke into a run, chasing the other two. That creature had moved at an insane speed, there was no way they were going to be able to catch up with it if it had traveled any kind of distance. He felt sick at the loss of Dela, how they'd all just stood there as she'd been snatched. The creature must have figured that she was the smallest of each of them and would make a good meal. A shudder ran down his back at the thought. No, that wouldn't be the end of her. It couldn't be. Somehow he knew they needed her if they were going to make it home. The three of them together would never make it. They'd end up killing each other without her to focus on.

His feet thumped across the soft ground, his breath growing heavy in his lungs. The other two were taller, their strides longer, and already they were ahead. He wished he hadn't put the armor back on after he'd removed it to sleep. Though the armor was lightweight steel, it was still steel, and was sure to be holding him back.

The brook grew wider, and then wider again, boulders protruding from the water, creating areas of still calmness, interspersed by flowing rapids. It was far from a brook now, and most definitely a river, which only seemed to grow wider and deeper the farther they ran.

"Keep your eyes open for the creature," Warsgra yelled from over his shoulder. "Or maybe a nest or something it might live in. That thing will have taken Dela back to its home."

Vehel didn't know what he was supposed to be looking for. One thing about coming from way down south was that the temperature was so much cooler, they didn't get giant bugs like that. Admittedly, they had some of their own issues with sea monsters living in their shores, but he'd never seen anything like that thing.

They followed the river around, looking out for any sign of where the creature may have taken Dela. Warsgra appeared frantic, his hand locked in his hair as he spun one way and then the next, trying to get an idea of where she'd gone. Orergon seemed more composed, his back straight and shoulders back, alert. Orergon was a hunter and perhaps was looking for signs Vehel hadn't even thought of.

No, Vehel's strength was in his magic, but his lack of training and control had let both himself and Dela down. If only he'd been trained, as he should have been, he'd have been able to conjure a spell to force the insect to release Dela.

"The Gods damn them!" he cried in frustration. "Where is she?"

They were all running out of steam now, slowing their pace, though he sensed none of them wanted to. But the weeks on the road had taken it out of all of them, not to mention the events of the last couple of days.

"We can't give up," Warsgra growled.

"We're not," Orergon replied. "But we need to slow or we might miss something."

They regrouped and continued along the riverbank at a slower trot. Vehel missed the grand stag he used to ride. The majestic beast would have carried him without complaint. He hoped the beast had made it out of the Southern Pass alive.

"What are those?" Orergon pointed at the opposite bank.

The riverbank was tall and topped with trees and bushes, but several large holes had been dug into the muddy wall.

They came to a halt, staring at the riverbank. No creature Vehel had ever seen dug such things, but this place was nothing like his beautiful homeland of the Inverlands, with its mountainous peaks and glacial waterfalls. He longed for the peace of his home, but then remembered what might be waiting there for him if he did manage to get back. Would he ever see his homeland again, and would he be welcomed if he did?

As they stood, watching, one of the huge black and yellow striped bugs crawled out of one of the holes and took flight. The moment its wings began to beat, the crazily loud buzzing filled the air once more, and Vehel had to resist placing his hands over his ears.

"Was that the same one?" Warsgra asked, looking to each of them.

Orergon shook his head. "I have no idea."

"How many burrows are there?" Vehel said, half thinking out loud.

They counted. Seven different holes in total.

"She could be in any one of those," he mused.

Orergon chewed on his lower lip. "The bug might still be in there with her, too."

Warsgra cupped his hands to his mouth. "Dela? Dela, can you hear me Shout out if you can."

"She might be hurt or unconscious," Orergon said. "She might not be able to shout."

Warsgra scowled. "Then we're going to have to go down each of those holes to try to find her."

Vehel frowned at him. "You're never going to fit down one of those. You'd barely get your shoulders in."

Warsgra fixed him in his intense green gaze. "Then I guess you'll be going down instead."

Vehel's stomach curdled, but Warsgra was right. Even Orergon would struggle to fit, and they couldn't risk him getting stuck.

"Take my spear." Orergon handed him the weapon. "If you meet one of those things in the hole, stab it."

"I suppose I should be thanking you," he muttered.

He unhooked his bow and quiver of arrows and placed them on the ground. They'd be no good in the confines of the burrow. Then he reached to the sides of his armor and took off the breastplate. Yes, it would have protected him, but the armor also made it harder for him to move. He had to focus on finding Dela and getting her out of there. The thought of her throwing her slender arms around his neck and hugging him in gratitude filled his mind. That was what he needed to focus on, not being stuck in a hole with the giant striped insects with stingers on their tails.

Vehel took hold of Orergon's spear and started to wade across the water. "Which one shall I try first?" he called back.

"The one the bug just came out of. At least you know that one is empty of its inhabitant."

Veliel gritted his teeth. He prayed Dela would be in the first one he tried, but he figured the chances were slim to none. No, they were seven to one. Assuming this was even where the insect had brought her.

He reached the other bank and slid the spear into the hole, pulling himself up and sliding inside. The walls were dank and coated in a wet, sticky mud that clung to his skin and clothes. He picked up the spear again and kept going.

"Dela," he hissed, hoping that if she heard him she'd be able to give him some clue she was there. "Can you hear me?"

But there was nothing, and he kept going, forced to remain on all fours, and keeping his head down. What would his father and brothers think if they saw him now—an Elvish prince crawling through the mud for the sake of a human woman? They would mock him until the end of his days, but it wasn't as though that would be any different than what he was used to.

The crown of his head collided with a wall, and he realized he'd come to the end. This burrow was empty. There was barely room to turn around, so he went backward instead, praying to the Gods that he wouldn't meet the owner of this hole as it arrived home.

He dropped out of the end, into the water and the bright sunshine, which he was grateful for. His coloring didn't normally appreciate the sun, but after being cooped up in that tunnel, he was thankful for it. He couldn't imagine how Dela was feeling if she was inside one of these things. He'd only been in one for minutes, but she'd be approaching an hour now.

That thought pushed him toward the next one. He was aware of the other two still standing on the bank, expectantly watching him.

"She's not there," he called over his shoulder. "I'm trying the next one."

He didn't wait for their response, but instead hauled himself into the adjacent hole. He wanted to call out to Dela, but he didn't know if this tunnel was vacant or not, and didn't want to alert any giant bugs to his presence. His body filled the space, blocking off most of the light behind him. He gripped Orergon's spear tight in his fist, hoping he wouldn't have to use it. While he was skilled with his bow and arrow, a spear was a different weapon altogether.

He lay flat, his belly in the mud, to be able to crawl down the tunnel by pulling himself forward with his forearms. The position allowed more light to flood in behind him, and let him see if he was approaching anything. Could he see something down there? His heart picked up pace? Was it another creature?

But no, he caught a glimpse of golden red hair in the small amount of light filtering from behind him.

"Dela!" he hissed. "Come this way. I'm getting you out."

But she didn't move. A stab of fear went through him. Was she already dead?

He moved quicker, pulling hand over arm to reach her, no longer caring how he was dragging himself through the mud. Damn whatever his family thought. In that moment, he didn't care.

Vehel reached her. She was on all fours, her forehead pressed against the bottom of the tunnel, her hair splayed across the mud. She was breathing, he was sure of it. Unconscious, then? He reached out and covered her hand with his own.

"Dela, we must move. The creature might be back at any moment."

But she didn't budge. Only the rapid speed of her breathing gave him any idea that she had heard him.

"Come on. We have to leave."

He grabbed her hand and pulled her forward. She slid toward him but made no attempt to try to move herself.

"What's wrong with you? We have to go."

He reached out and pushed her hair away from her face, trying to see her better to get an idea of what was happening. Her eyes were open, and they focused on him. He knew she saw him, but in the poor light he only saw terror and acute understanding of what was happening to her.

Realization dawned. "Did that thing do something to you? Can you not move?"

Her eyelids flickered up and down, but that was the only response he got. He remembered the huge stinger on the end of the creature's tail. That must be what the sting was for. It paralyzed its food and then stored it here in the cool damp until it was ready to be devoured.

He'd have to move her by brute strength.

Vehel started to drag her, the movement awkward in the confined space. The mud rucked up at her shoulders and chest, making it even harder for him to pull her. He had to scramble backward as well, at the same time as dragging her, and they weren't making quick progress.

A growingly familiar sound filtered to his ears.

Buzzing.

His heart stopped in his chest, his mouth running dry with fear. The insect was returning to claim its meal.

Shouts came from outside, muffled to him, still inside the burrow, though he was able to make out what was being said.

Orergon's voice. "Hurry, Vehel. It's coming back."

"Get out of there," Warsgra's deep tenor shouted.

Panic burst through him. He couldn't go much faster. The only way he'd get out of the tunnel any quicker was by leaving Dela behind, and that wasn't going to happen. He wouldn't let her think for even a second that he'd abandoned her when she was suffering like this. He didn't know why he cared about some human woman, but she seemed special. His life hadn't amounted to anything of great importance in his one hundred and fifty years, but *this* felt important.

He wasn't going to let her down.

CHAPTER 21

ORERGON

Orergon stood at Warsgra's side as the buzzing increased in volume.

By the Gods, why had he given his spear to Vehel? He had the feeling he was going to need it in the very imminent future.

"If it's coming back, we can't let it go in that tunnel," Warsgra said. "It'll trap Vehel."

Orergon nodded. "Yes, I know."

"So we're going to have to fight it."

They exchanged a glance, a silent agreement that they'd fight to the death if they had to.

He looked down to the ground, where Vehel had left his pile of armor and his bow and quiver of arrows. Orergon wasn't bad with a bow, but it wasn't his weapon of choice. Still, it didn't seem like he had the luxury of being picky right now.

"There!" Warsgra exclaimed, pointing to the other side of the river. He hadn't needed to point. There was no missing the huge black and yellow striped insect which appeared over the top of a small clump of bushes, and then dropped down to face the holes dug into the side of the muddy river bank.

They waited, every muscle tensed, watching. If the creature

didn't go near the tunnel Vehel was in, they could leave it be, but if it looked like it was going to block Vehel's escape, they'd be forced to take the creature on.

"Why hasn't Vehel come out yet?" Orergon asked Warsgra. "Do you think he found her?"

"Either that or he's stuck. Those are the only reasons I can think of."

"He's going to need our help."

Both he and Warsgra were too large for the insect to pick up and carry away, as it had done with Dela, but that didn't mean it couldn't cause them some serious harm with that huge stinger on the end of its tail.

The insect buzzed around the riverbank as though trying to figure out which was its hole. Orergon held his breath, hoping the thing would settle at a different hole than the one Vehel was inside. It buzzed around, like a honey bee at a border of flowers, but then stopped in front of the one they'd been hoping it wouldn't.

Orergon didn't hesitate. He lifted the bow and drew back, letting the arrow fly. It hit its mark, spearing into the insect's back. The buzzing grew higher in its fury, and the creature spun around, the arrow still protruding from its rear end. They'd taken the thing's attention from the hole, but redirected it to themselves.

Warsgra took a step forward, brandishing his axe in both hands.

"Hurry, Vehel!" Orergon shouted. "Get out, now!"

He wished he could go in and help, but his shoulders were too wide, and he was sure to get stuck. Besides, the insect was coming for them now, and he figured they were about to get busy.

The giant insect flew at them. Warsgra swung his axe, but the creature darted away. Not for long, though, as it bore down upon them again. Orergon pulled a second arrow and drew back the bow. He let the arrow fly, but missed the target this time, and it landed in the water.

Movement came at the hole Vehel had disappeared into. Feet appeared in the gap, quickly followed by legs.

The buzzing increased in volume, and Orergon looked up to find a second of the creatures appearing from over the bushes.

"I think it's called in some backup!" he shouted to Warsgra.

Warsgra followed his line of sight. "It may have released some kind of chemical when it was hit with the arrow, a way of calling in its friends when it's under attack."

"You mean we could have a big problem."

He nodded. "Exactly."

They could take on one of the creatures, maybe even two or three at a push, but many more and they'd be overwhelmed. They'd counted seven holes in total. True, not every tunnel might be currently occupied, but there might even be two or more insects to one hole. They had no idea how these creatures lived.

"Incoming!" Warsgra yelled and swung his axe at the second insect. The bug saw him coming and veered off at the last moment, but Warsgra managed to cleave off a part of one of its wings. It was able to stay airborne, but was no longer as agile, and it veered from side to side, unable to control its direction.

On the other side of the water, the remainder of Vehel's body slithered from the hole, as though the bank had just given birth to a mud-covered Elvish prince. Orergon watched from the corner of his eye, praying he'd pulled Dela out with him, but then the first creature attacked again, and he was forced to concentrate on that. It came right at him, its body curved so the sting was beneath it, and aiming directly at Orergon. Orergon pulled back the arrow. It was getting too close now, and he wouldn't have the space he needed to fire. Before he could let the arrow fly, Warsgra's axe came down in a swoosh, right before him, chopping off the insect's stinger. The thing let out a screech of rage—a sound he hadn't thought it capable of—and dropped to the ground in front of them. Warsgra lifted his axe again and brought it down on the creature's head, separating it from its body.

Orergon shuddered.

"We need to get out of here before more arrive," Warsgra said.

They looked over to where Vehel was now pulling an equally mud-covered Dela from the riverbank. She didn't look like she was moving, and Orergon had the horrifying thought that they'd been too late.

He plunged into the river to help Vehel. "Is she all right? What happened?"

"I think one of those things stung her. She's conscious, but she doesn't seem to be able to move or speak."

Vehel cradled her in his arms. His silver white hair was now stained pink from the red clay in the mud, and his face and clothes were streaked with dirt. But there was fierce determination in his light blue eyes, and though Orergon reached out to take Dela from him, he only held her tighter to his chest.

Her hair had fallen over her face, and Orergon swept it away. Vehel was right. She was awake—he could see the understanding in her brown eyes—and somehow that was worse than if she'd been unconscious.

"It's all right," he told her as they plunged through the water to get to the opposite bank, away from the insects. "You're going to be all right. We'll make you well again."

Warsgra had taken on the second bug, swiping at it with his axe when it bumbled by, unable to control which way it was going. The creature fell into the water and was swept away by a particularly rough part of the rapids.

"We need to get out of here before any more of its friends show up," he said, pushing his long hair away from his face.

They all nodded in agreement.

Their clothes were soaked from the waist down, but they'd dry out quickly enough.

"We need to put some space between us and the riverbank," Orergon said. "Use the trees as shelter."

"We don't want to lose sight of the river, though," Warsgra pointed out. "It's a life source to us, no matter the dangers."

He was right. They needed the river for water, and it was an easy source of food. Plus, they were more likely to stay on the right path if they followed the direction of the water.

"Agreed."

They moved away from the river, though kept it to their right. The trunks of the trees offered them shelter, while they still caught glimpses of the rushing water through them. Concerned more of the insects would detect members of their swarm had been killed and come after them, they kept up a brisk pace, not even stopping to rest.

After awhile, Vehel began to tire, and he handed Dela over to Warsgra. She looked tiny in the big Norc's arms, and he held her easily, as though she was no weight at all. She still hadn't shown any signs of the paralysis wearing off, and he started to worry that it might be permanent. What would they do then? They couldn't just abandon her, but they couldn't carry her for a thousand miles either. No, Orergon didn't want to think on that. They'd figure out a way to make her well again. They had to.

He thought of something. "Can you use your magic, Vehel? Is there a spell or something that might take the poison away?"

Vehel shook his head. "I keep telling you, I'm untrained in magic. It's banned, remember. How am I supposed to know how to do something like that?"

"Instinct?" he suggested. "You knew what to do in the Southern Pass."

"I didn't, not really. I went with a feeling, and look where that got us. What if I tried something and it was wrong? It might kill her."

"Death might be more merciful than being trapped inside her own body," Warsgra muttered.

"Don't speak of such things," Orergon snapped. "She can hear you, remember."

"And maybe it would give her some comfort to know we wouldn't let her suffer."

Orergon glared at him. Was the Norc really suggesting such a thing? How could he? But Warsgra didn't return the glare. He didn't even notice that Orergon was shooting him daggers. No, he was gazing down into Dela's face. The expression on the Norc's face softened, the emotion strange on such a tough male.

"Come on, Dela. You can fight this. I know you can. You're tough. You're not going to let a bug get the better of you."

Warsgra did care, Orergon realized. He might act like he was hard as stone, but there was a heart lying somewhere beneath that massive chest of his.

All they could do was keep going, though Orergon knew they'd have to stop soon. None of them had eaten that morning, due to what had happened with Dela, and they were running on empty. He said so to the others, and they agreed.

"We'll stop here for an hour and find something to eat and drink."

"It'll mean going back to the river," Vehel warned.

"I think we have to. It's our only source of water, and our main source of food."

Warsgra nodded in agreement. "I'll get some more fish, if someone else keeps watch. I think we're miles away from those things by now, but if one of them is coming up behind me, I'd like to know about it."

"Of course," Orergon said. "Vehel, can you get a fire started and watch over Dela, and I'll watch Warsgra's back?"

Warsgra gently placed Dela beneath a tree. It was unnerving to see her like this, with her eyes open and watching, but her body completely motionless. It must be terrifying for her as well, to not be able to move. Warsgra was right when he said death would be kinder than living like this, but it was far too soon to be making such a call. They'd fight for her for as long as they could.

Orergon had his spear back again now, so he followed Warsgra to the waterside to watch his back as he fished. For a society who lived mostly on meat, the Norc was an excellent fisherman. Orergon was a hunter, too, but the Vast Plains weren't a place where rivers were plentiful, and the ocean was many miles away from his homeland. The Elvish fished, but with nets in the sea, so they were lucky to have Warsgra with them—something Orergon never believed he would think. As they'd been walking, Orergon had checked the trees and bushes they'd passed for fruit. He spotted several bushes heavy with produce, but he didn't recognize any of it. The thought of picking something poisonous and getting everyone sick held him back. They would wait until they came across something one of them could at least identify. They weren't starving yet, and there was no point taking the risk unnecessarily.

With Warsgra in the water, Orergon braced himself, keeping his eyes open and his hearing sharp. He wouldn't let them be attacked again without being ready for it. This journey would take them many weeks, and he was sure that had just been the start of many challenges they would face. The insect had come out of nowhere, and they had let their guard down.

He wouldn't make that mistake twice.

CHAPTER 22

DELA

This was worse than being trapped in the underworld. Dela lay frozen inside her own body, staring out at the world but unable to interact. Was this it for her now? Was this how her life was going to be from now on? She'd wanted to cry when Warsgra had talked about death being kinder, had wanted to grab his arm and tell him he was absolutely right, but she couldn't even get a tear to fall from her eye.

Now she lay beneath a tree and watched Vehel work as he set about building a fire. As he'd done the previous day, he held his hand over the bundle of twigs and sticks, and his eyes slipped shut. Seconds later, the twigs burst into flame. It had been quicker that time. The practice was working.

She wished he would try something on her to make her better. She understood that he was worried he'd do something wrong and make her worse, but really, what could be worse than this? If he'd only ask her what it was she wanted, she was sure she'd be able to convey in some way that it was worth the risk.

With the fire going, Vehel came and sat beside her. His pale skin was still streaked with mud, though it had dried now. She must look a mess herself—not that it mattered. How she looked was the very least of her worries.

What he'd done for her had been incredibly brave. She couldn't imagine the sort of courage it took to climb into that hole after her. In fact, they'd all come for her. She'd glimpsed Orergon and Warsgra fighting the insects while Vehel had carried her out of the tunnel. They'd fought bravely, and they hadn't needed to do that. They could have just chalked her down to being lost, but instead they'd come after her and put their own lives at risk. They hadn't exactly hidden their dislike of humans in general, but their actions so far had made her think differently. Maybe she'd been a little prejudiced of them, too, before she'd had the chance to get to know them properly. She still didn't know them, not really, but she'd felt like she was getting to know them. Everything would change now if she stayed like this, however. The idea of them being forced to look after her while she was helpless filled her with dread, and she didn't want them to put their lives at risk either. She was going to be a hindrance for them and would slow them down.

At what point would they be forced to leave her behind?

Despair dragged down on her heart. No, she couldn't allow herself to think this way, or she would give up on herself. This paralysis was most likely only temporary and would wear off eventually. She had to keep believing that.

Warsgra and Orergon returned with freshly caught fish and some water, which they carried in the breast plate of the armor Vehel was no longer wearing.

"She won't be able to eat when she's like this," Warsgra said.

"What about water? Do you think she can drink, or are we likely to choke her?"

Dela wished she could answer, but she wasn't sure either. Her body's basic functions still appeared to be working—she could blink and move her eyes around. Experimenting, she swallowed some of her spit. Yes, she could swallow, so she could probably swallow food as well, if it was mashed up enough for her. Another thought occurred, and inwardly she groaned. What about needing the bathroom? Was one of the men going to have to take her and help her clean up afterward? No, she couldn't have that. She'd rather die first.

Warsgra got to work, cleaning and skewering the fish he'd caught, before resting the ends of the skewers on two rocks on opposite sides of the fire Orergon had got going.

Orergon and Vehel crouched on either side of Dela. Gently, Orergon supported her head, while Vehel tipped the pool of water, still held in his breastplate, up to her mouth. The water dribbled down both sides of her chin, dampening her tunic beneath, but some ran over her tongue and down the back of her throat, and mercifully her reflexes kicked in and she was able to swallow.

The scent of the fish cooking caused hunger to churn inside her, but she didn't think they would risk her choking on fish bones. She wasn't going to die of hunger any time soon. Better to wait until things got desperate. If Vehel wasn't going to try to use magic to make her better, then all she could hope for was that the fly's venom would eventually start to wear off.

They propped her back up again, and then the men took their places around the fire. When the fish was cooked, she could only look on, helpless, as they tore away at the flesh with their teeth, eating with a satisfaction she didn't think she was going to get any time soon.

"What do you think is happening down south now?" asked Vehel between mouthfuls of fish. "Do you think anyone is aware of what happened in the Southern Pass yet?"

Orergon shrugged. "It depends if there were any survivors, and if there were, how long it would take them to get back to Anthoinia."

"The journey from the city to the Southern Pass normally

takes the humans days, doesn't it?" Warsgra said, picking a fish bone from his teeth and flicking it to the ground.

Vehel nodded. "Yes, but that's when there's a big group of them, and they have carts filled with sacks of grain to maneuver. A solitary person could move faster."

"Especially if they were to come across one of our animals to ride," Orergon jumped in. "Humans know how to ride. Most of our animals fled, but if they were able to get on a horse and do the journey that way, they'd be far quicker."

Warsgra snorted. "Fear also is an excellent way of getting someone to move faster. Seeing what we did back there would sure be a good kick up the arse."

The men finished eating and got to their feet. They washed off the remains of the fish in the river, stamped down the fire, and got on the move again.

Warsgra bent to scoop her into his arms, and she wished she was able to put her arms around his broad neck to hold on. It wasn't as though she thought he would drop her, simply that doing so would have felt more natural. Her arms hung to the sides, and her head lolled. She hated being like this. Unable to move her head, she had no choice but to stare up at the leaves and branches of the trees above, and the blue sky peeping in between.

Warsgra's long, steady strides lulled her into a trance-like sleep, and before she'd even realized it had happened, she was no longer inside herself.

* * *

Dela soared through the clouds, weightless and heady with euphoria. There was no better feeling than this—the ability to fly. She burst through a cloud, the tiny particles evaporating instantly from the heat from her skin. It was like magic. One moment the cloud was there, and the next it had vanished. She turned her head to look at the empty space and held back the urge to whoop with joy. These were the best kinds of days, when the sky was blue and dotted with clouds. Some days she'd have to battle, putting her head down and barreling through thick clouds, or wind threatening to blow her off course, or rain pummeling her back, driving her toward the ground.

As she swooped down, the wind blasting against her face, the countryside below passed in a blur.

Was this how she was supposed to be now? Instead of being trapped inside her own body, she'd take on this different form and fly. Because she'd had this dream so many times before, and somehow she knew it was a dream, and yet it wasn't. Had some part of the universe known this would be her future and so had been building her up to a different way of life, a different consciousness?

She didn't know if she should be relieved or terrified. Relieved at the prospect of not being bound to her human body, but also heartbroken that she would never get her old life back again. It wasn't the old life she'd miss so much, but the potential for what might have lain ahead. Since she'd been picked as one of the Chosen, a new excitement had lit inside her. Though it had caused mixed emotions, a part of her had known that was a new start for her, and that life would become so much bigger than what had existed for her within the city walls of Anthoinia.

Only now it had grown far smaller—not trapped within walls this time, but within the confines of her own body.

No, that wasn't the reality. This was.

She closed her eyes against the wind rushing against her face and flew…

CHAPTER 23

WARSGRA

The human woman felt weightless in his arms, though he'd been carrying her for miles.

He glanced down at her sleeping face. Her full lips were slightly parted, and her dark blonde lashes lay on her creamy cheeks. Her red-gold hair hung down the side of his arm, her head cradled in the spot where the inside of his bicep met his elbow. He'd never thought it possible to find a human woman beautiful, but there was no denying that she was. Not only that, she'd shown a spark to her spirit, which he admired, and he found he missed her conversation—as spiky as it had been—as they walked. They'd only been a small group for a little over a day—four beings who should have nothing in common—and yet the loss of Dela's presence felt wrong to the very core of his soul, as though something had shifted in the universe that was never supposed to move.

No, he chastened himself, they hadn't lost her. She was right here, in his arms. He felt sure the venom wouldn't last forever. They'd get her back eventually. They just had to be patient.

Orergon held out his arms for her. "I'll take her for a while."

Warsgra shook his head and drew her closer. His shoulders

ached a little from being in the same position for so long, but she didn't feel heavy to him. It wasn't that he didn't trust Orergon to take care of her, but for the moment he was content to just walk with her.

They continued a little way, mainly in silence. The males had less to say to each other without Dela to spark conversation.

Orergon frowned, tilting his head to one side. "Can you hear that?"

Warsgra paused, his ears straining. He heard something and his stomach dropped. "It's not those giant flies again?"

The Moerian shook his head. "No, I don't think so."

Vehel had been quiet during the journey, but now he spoke up. "Sounds like a waterfall to me. We have a lot of them in the Inverlands."

Warsgra nodded. "I think you're right."

They'd been following the river up until this point. The waterway had widened in places, before narrowing off to the point where they thought they might even lose it underground, only to find it swelling again. The giant insects who'd snatched Dela hadn't made a second appearance.

As they continued, the trees began to thin out, and suddenly they found themselves standing on a precipice, looking out over a valley. The roar of the waterfall grew louder from where the river dropped off over the cliffside and into a pool below.

"Look!" Warsgra pointed out over the valley.

A small gathering of thatched roof cottages lay below them. A tendril of smoke wound into the sky from one of the chimneys, though Orergon assumed the fire was for cooking rather than heat. Though their journey had brought them farther south, it wasn't enough to have affected the temperature yet.

"What kind of folk live up this way?" Vehel asked, stepping forward to Warsgra's side.

Orergon shook his head. "They don't. No one owns this part of the lands. Even we Moerians don't come this far north."

Warsgra pulled Dela closer to his chest. "Might they be able to help her?"

Orergon glanced at the young woman's face. "Who knows? They might decide they'd rather cause harm than help."

"But we won't know without trying," Vehel said. "Those homes look innocent enough. The folk who live inside might be equally innocuous."

Warsgra grunted. "Or they use that as a trap to lure people in. Who lives this far out if they're good and kind to lost travelers? Surely they're more likely to be those who can't live nicely with others."

Orergon lifted an eyebrow. "Like you, you mean?"

"I live just fine with my own kind. It's everyone else who makes me mad."

Vehel nudged Orergon in the side, and pointed to something on the other side of the houses. "Have you seen those?"

Beyond the cluster of cottages were a number of fields where a small herd of ponies grazed.

"We need those ponies," Orergon said.

Warsgra wrinkled his nose. "My feet will be dragging on the ground if I tried to ride one of those things."

"That'll still be better than walking the next thousand miles."

He grunted again. "We need to think about the girl. I'll walk if I have to, but first we need to try to make her well again."

Orergon nodded. "Then we have to take the risk." He turned to the Elvish prince. "Are you still happy to trade your armor for whatever they can offer?"

Vehel nodded. "Yes, as long as they offer what we need."

Warsgra sucked in a breath. "Let's do this, then."

He started down the rocky cliff face which bordered the waterfall. After spending his whole life up in the mountains, such terrain didn't concern him. Normally, he'd be riding his mountain goat, whose footing was almost supernaturally sure, but he had learned plenty in his twenty-eight years and could get down this cliff easily enough, even with Dela in his arms.

Behind him, Orergon struggled to follow the same path, missing footsteps and sending flurries of rock down after them. Warsgra heard his yells of annoyance as he skidded, or a rock moved from under him. He figured if Orergon fell badly enough, he'd be there to break his fall. Vehel was doing better, having also come from a mountainous region. He also wasn't as tall, so his center of gravity was lower than the tall, lanky Moerian, making it easier for him to balance.

They picked their way slowly down to the bottom, staying away from where the spray of the waterfall hit the rocks, knowing it would make them slippery. So far, other than the chimney smoke and the ponies, there hadn't been any sign of life. Warsgra would have been surprised if at least one of the inhabitants hadn't noticed them climbing down the cliff toward their homes. Quietness always made him more nervous than a head on threat. A warning he could deal with, but he didn't like the thought of people sneaking up on them.

"Why's it so quiet?" Orergon echoed his thoughts as, one by one, their feet hit the ground. The waterfall emptied into a large pool, which then appeared to go underground. They'd finally run out of river to follow.

"I was thinking the same thing."

Vehel jumped the final few feet, the armor he'd put back on clinking as he did so. "Maybe they're on an excursion?"

Warsgra lifted an eyebrow. "Without their ponies?"

He hesitated and then handed Dela over to Orergon. He cupped his hand to the side of his mouth.

"Hello?" he bellowed. "Is anyone there? Our friend needs help."

He ignored the way the others winced at his volume. He'd rather march into this place, showing no fear, than scurry around like a bunch of frightened mice. Besides, he was too big to go unnoticed.

Warsgra strode toward the homes. Now that he was closer, he was able to see just how small they were. The height of the front door was barely up to his chest, and the windows were a fraction of the size they'd normally be. He was starting to get the impression that they wouldn't need to worry about these people too much. It made sense as to why they had ponies in their paddocks rather than full sized horses.

"Hello?" he called again. "We're not here to cause trouble. We're lost and we want to get help for our friend. She was stung by—"

His face suddenly collided with something, and he bounced back with the recoil.

"What, by the Gods!"

He felt as though he'd walked right into a wall, but there was nothing to be seen. He rubbed at his smarting nose, his eyes watering, and a streak of blood came away on his hand. Thank the Gods he'd passed Dela over to Orergon, or she would have taken the worst of the blow. But worst of the blow from what?

"What happened?" Vehel asked, coming at a jog to stop beside him.

"I'm not sure. I hit something…"

Tentatively, he reached out a hand. Sure enough, his fingertips met with a hard object, like glass or ice, and utterly invisible. "There's something here, protecting the homes."

Vehel frowned at him, but lifted his own hand and copied Warsgra's movement. "So there is. Extraordinary."

"Can you break it down?" he asked. "Use your own magic?"

"I don't know. I could try—"

Movement from one of the house cut off his words, and a small person—about the size of a ten year old human child—appeared. "You'll do no such thing," the person exclaimed.

At first, it was hard to tell if they were male or female. They had long, wavy red hair, and pointed ears like Vehel. But that was where the similarities ended. When the little person opened his or her mouth, they revealed a row of vicious looking pointy teeth. From the squareness of the jaw, and the lack of any breasts, Warsgra assumed this one was male.

"Fae," Vehel spoke from beside him. "You people are Fae."

The male Fae's head tilted to one side as it regarded him. "So, so? What is it to you?" His voice was high-pitched, and he spoke quickly, in a slightly jittery tone. "You're Elvish, aren't you?"

"Yes, I am. I just … I thought the Fae no longer existed."

"Oh, we exist, we exist. You southerners all seem to think anything that still resides in the north is extinct." His head tilted the other way, and his eyes—which appeared too large for his face—narrowed. "What are you doing so far north, anyway? None of your kind ever comes this far up."

"It wasn't intentional," Vehel continued, taking charge. He out of all of them had the most in common with the Fae, though they were very, very distant relatives. "We were in a difficult situation, and I was forced to use magic …"

"Magic! Magic!" the Fae exclaimed. "You're not allowed to use magic. You've broken the Treaty."

"Yes, we're aware of that," Orergon said, stepping forward. "That's why we're trying to get back, to make things right again."

The Fae waved a long, pointed finger in their direction. "Once it's broken, it can't be put back together again."

"We're hoping people might not learn it's been broken," Warsgra growled.

"No, no. People always learn about these things. It's like the earth itself has a mouth and can spread the truth of what's happened on its surface."

Debating this wasn't important right now.

Warsgra wasn't used to having to beg for anything, but these Fae might be able to help Dela, and if they could, he'd get on his knees and grovel. "Please, our friend does need help. She's been paralyzed by a venom. Is there anything you can do to help? We have Elvish steel we can trade you if you're willing."

His eyes narrowed again. "Since when do the likes of Norcs, and Elvish, and Moerians give up their things in order to help a human?"

"Since now," he insisted.

The Fae's long fingers went to his mouth, tapping on his lips as he considered their offer. "Hmm. I can't make this decision alone. I have to consult with the rest of my family."

He turned from them, and Warsgra saw twin diaphanous wings protruding from slits cut in the back of the little jacket he wore. Then the Fae placed his fingers between his lips and let out a shrill whistle.

Others came out to join him, heads peeping around from corners and out of windows. So they'd been here all along, they just hadn't wanted to make themselves known, trusting in the protection of the force field they'd created around themselves.

The male Fae beckoned them. "Come, come. You heard what they said. What do you think we should do?"

"I don't trust them," someone said.

"That one is too big!" called out another.

"No, no, Cirrus," the original Fae replied. "That's just the way the Norcs come. They all look like that."

"Ugly as sin," the Fae called Cirrus muttered under his breath.

Warsgra felt himself bristle, but he clamped his jaw down on his anger. They needed the Fae more than the Fae needed them.

"They have Elvish steel, though," another pointed out. "Think of all the lovely things we could make with that."

There was lots of hmming, and chin rubbing in consideration of that fact.

"Very well," the leader said eventually. "We'll let you in and try to help the woman, but you must leave all your weapons outside of our shield."

Warsgra exchanged looks with Orergon and Vehel. Both nodded their agreement.

"Agreed." Warsgra pulled his axe from where it was wedged

into his belt and dropped it to the ground. He didn't like the thought of not being armed, but these creatures were a fraction of his size, and he couldn't really see what harm they could do. Besides, he needed them to help Dela. The Fae were known for their magical abilities, though it was thought the race had died out years ago. Maybe they'd be able to stop the effect of the venom.

Vehel dropped his bow and quiver of arrows to the ground, and Orergon handed Dela back to Warsgra. He pulled his spear from its holder slung across his back and threw that down, too.

The Fae leader closed his eyes briefly, muttered something under his breath, and swirled his hand in a circle. His eyes opened again. "It is done. You may enter now."

Despite being told the force field was down, Warsgra still didn't fully trust it. He put out his hand as he stepped forward, tentatively feeling for the thing he'd bashed his nose on. But the Fae leader was right. The shield had gone.

"What's your name?" Warsgra asked the little person.

The Fae straightened, his hands on his hips, his chin lifted. "Nimbus Darkbriar."

"I'm Warsgra Tuskeye," he said, tapping his chest. "This is Orergon Ortiz, and Vehel Dawngleam. The woman is called Dela Stonebridge."

Nimbus sniffed. "Yes, yes. I'd say I was pleased to meet you, but I guess we'll see about that. Now bring the young woman this way, and we'll see what we can do."

"You won't get the armor if you can't help her," Warsgra warned.

"Understood, understood."

Nimbus ran off toward his house. Warsgra eyed up the size of the doorway. That was definitely going to be a squeeze. But he needed to get Dela inside, so he was going to do it, even if his shoulders took off the doorframe.

Bending at the knees, he huddled over the top of Dela, making himself as small as possible without crushing her. Then he pushed his way through the door to find himself in an equally tiny kitchen. It had a country cottage style, completely unlike any home a Norc had ever occupied. Luckily, the ceiling was higher than the door, so he got to his knees so he was at least able to straighten the rest of his torso. The others followed him in, Orergon struggling almost as much as he had, and Vehel only a little less. The compact kitchen had quickly become crammed with people, and to make matters worse, a number of the Fae followed them in as well.

"Put her on the table," Nimbus said. "I can get a better look at her there."

Warsgra did as he instructed and laid Dela across the wooden surface. Her legs hung off one end, and her hair the other. She looked so peaceful resting there, her eyes still shut, like a fairytale princess in a storybook. Would those eyes ever open again?

"You said she was stung?"

"Yes, by a huge yellow and black fly. It lives in tunnels dug into the river bank."

"Ah, the Hunter fly. Yes, yes, we know of it."

"Can you help?"

He nodded. "First we must find the sting. It will still be embedded in her body somewhere. The reason she hasn't woken is because the sting continues to release new venom long after the initial attack."

Warsgra felt wrong checking her over, as though he was invading her personal space. It wasn't that he hadn't pictured how she looked beneath that tunic, but he'd imagined her being a little more conscious when the time came.

But there was nothing sexual in what they were doing. Methodically, they pulled aside her clothing, rolling up sleeves and checking any exposed parts of her skin.

Nimbus pulled down the front of her tunic to expose her collarbone and froze. "What is this?"

At first Warsgra thought he'd found the sting, but then he realized Nimbus was talking about something else entirely. He was pointing to the ring Dela wore on a piece of leather around her throat.

"It's a ring," Orergon said from behind them. "I think someone special from home gave it to her."

"It's a Dragonstone ring," Nimbus replied.

Warsgra frowned. "A what?"

"Dragonstone. They should only ever be worn by certain people, and those people were supposed to have died off hundreds of years ago."

"Like the Fae, you mean," Vehel quipped.

Nimbus frowned at him. "You should not laugh, no, no. Those who are able to wear the Dragonstone ring are destined to be the most powerful of them all. They have the sight."

"The what?"

Nimbus sighed as though his lack of knowledge was frustrating. "The ability to project through the eyes of the most powerful creature Xantearos has ever known."

"Which is?"

"The dragon."

Warsgra burst into laughter. "There aren't any dragons anymore. There haven't been since before the Treaty."

"You're wrong, you're wrong. They've simply learned to go unseen. Has she found her ability yet?"

Warsgra shook his head, frowning. "We don't know anything about her. She's just a woman we got caught up with in the Southern Pass. She looked to be leading the human convoy, but otherwise she hasn't spoken much about her home. She definitely hasn't mentioned anything about dragons."

"She didn't want to give up that ring, though," Orergon pointed out. "Remember her reaction when it was suggested that we use it as barter for horses or food?"

The Fae crossed his arms across his chest. "You need to take her to Drusga."

"Drusga?" Vehel asked. "The Valley of the Dragons?"

"Yes, yes. You're Elvish, and you used magic. You broke the Treaty, and a second Great War may be starting. If war is coming, she might be the only one who can put an end to it before the races destroy each other for good."

Vehel's lips pressed together, lines appearing across his normally smooth brow. "Drusga is at the farthest point north of Xantearos. We'd be going in the wrong direction."

Nimbus shrugged. "So you continue to head south, and when you get there you discover war has broken out because of what you did, and then how will you stop it? By using your axes and spears? Or do you travel north and discover if this woman with the Dragonstone ring is able to project through the dragons, and use them to stop the war?"

Warsgra stared around at the others, unsure what to do. They looked as baffled as he was at this new development. He was a practical man. He dealt with food, and fighting, and fucking—not the likes of magic and dragons, and mystic stones. The idea of making decisions about girls who might or might not be wearing magical stones and could control dragons that were believed long dead was way out of his comfort zone.

"How are we supposed to believe all of this simply because the woman is wearing something called a Dragonstone?" he said.

"You don't, you don't. I suppose we had better wake her up and find out." Nimbus continued to check her over. He rolled Dela to her side, and lifted up her hair. "Ah, here we are."

There, right at the base of her neck, was the sting. It was embedded into her flesh, only the bulbous tip, which Warsgra assumed contained the venom, protruding.

"We must be very careful," said Nimbus. "If we accidentally squeeze all the venom into her body, she will die."

Warsgra's mouth grew dry at the thought. "Please, do whatever you can."

The Fae closed his eyes and waved his hand over the place of the sting. He muttered in a language Warsgra didn't understand, and slowly the sting began to retract from Dela's flesh, until it eventually popped out and dropped to the table.

Warsgra knocked it to the floor with his hand, and then stomped on it with his booted foot.

"What now?" he asked.

The Fae's lips twisted. "Now, we wait."

CHAPTER 24

DELA

Something was pulling her from the skies, and she didn't want to go. Why would she? Wasn't this where she was meant to be?

But she had no choice. The pull was too strong, and she was sucked downward, as though trapped in a whirlpool. The blue sky and cloud vanished into darkness, and suddenly that was all she was aware of, a spinning, dizzying darkness…

* * *

Dela burst from her dream, sitting upright and gasping for breath.

She had no idea where she was, her mind still spinning. Her vision was fuzzy, and she could only make out blurred shapes around her. A hard surface lay beneath her body, and the air no longer smelled of wet mud and rotting foliage, which was the last thing she remembered. She blinked a couple of times and then rubbed her hand over her eyes. When she brought it away again, things became clearer, and she found herself inside a quaint little kitchen. She wasn't alone. Warsgra, Orergon, and Vehel were all standing over her, watching her with matching expressions of concern. They weren't alone either, as she spotted a number of tiny people dotted among them—people with red hair and pointy ears, and hideously sharp teeth when they smiled.

"What happened?" she said, finding her voice. "Where am I?"

Orergon stepped forward, coming to a halt at her shoulder. "You were stung by a Hunter fly and it paralyzed you. The Fae here were able to remove the sting, so you woke up."

"Fae?" She frowned.

"Yes, this is Nimbus Darkbriar. He was the one who helped us."

"Thank you," she managed. She'd believed the Fae no longer existed, but she'd clearly been wrong about that. Just as she'd been wrong that the Norcs were uncouth animals, and the Elvish were standoffish, and the Moerians were savages. She'd been wrong about a lot of things. "Thank you to all of you, too, for coming after me. You didn't need to do that."

Warsgra frowned at her. "We weren't going to just leave you."

"I wouldn't have blamed you if you'd given up."

She spotted Vehel standing a little way back and caught his eye. "You went into the tunnel for me," she said, remembering him being there, even though she'd been trapped inside her own body and unable to communicate with him. "That was incredibly brave of you."

Her words brought a tinge of pink to his pale cheeks, and he nodded at her, refined as always. "You'd have done the same for me, I'm sure."

A small smile tweaked her lips. "Let's hope we don't ever have to find out."

They were all staring at her, but there was something different in their eyes, something she couldn't quite place.

"What? What is it?"

The male Fae jumped up and down, clapping. "Oh, tell her! Go on, tell her."

She frowned in confusion. "Tell me what?"

Orergon touched the back of her hand, and she glanced down at where their skin met, and then back up into his dark eyes. "Where did you get the ring you wear around your neck?"

She reached up and touched it, as she often did. "My brother gave it to me to take care of, right before he left as part of the Chosen three years ago. I assumed I'd give it back to him when he returned, but he never came back."

"Do you know what that ring is made from?"

Her confusion deepened. "I don't know. It's just a ring, isn't it? Metal, with a pretty stone in the middle. It isn't anything precious. Our family could never afford anything like the gold and diamonds you exchange during the Passover."

"You're wrong," Nimbus said. "Only someone with the sight is able to have that ring anywhere near their skin."

She gestured to its place at her throat. "But I'm not even wearing it. It's just around my neck."

"It doesn't matter. Having it that close to your skin would be impossible unless you have something of a Dragonsayer in you. Watch." He turned to the nearest person to him, Orergon. "Try to take the ring from around her neck."

Orergon frowned but did as instructed. He reached out, his fingers closing around the metal. But then he let out a yell and pulled back his hand.

Dela stared in amazement as smoke rose from the ring, and Orergon held out his hand to show red marks on his fingertips, the skin already rising in a blister.

Nimbus couldn't contain his excitement. "See, see! It will burn anyone who isn't a Dragonsayer."

She lifted her eyebrows. "A what?"

"You're a Dragonsayer," Nimbus continued, "and that ring is Dragonstone. You have the sight."

"I don't have anything," she protested. "I'm just a regular human."

"Then how do you explain the ring?"

"I don't know. Maybe it's enchanted."

Vehel shook his head. "It's isn't, Dela. I'd be able to tell. The Fae is right."

"You must have seen something already," Nimbus said. "Even if it's just glimpses through the dragon's eyes. The volcanoes and hot pools of Drusga, perhaps."

"No, nothing like that." But then she remembered her reoccurring dream. But that was normal, wasn't it? Everyone had dreams like that. People always dreamed they were flying.

But all the time? A little voice whispered in her head. *Every time they close their eyes?*

She shook her head. "This is madness. And anyway, all the dragons are dead, and they have been for hundreds of years. Everyone knows that."

"Just like everyone knows the Fae don't exist anymore," Nimbus muttered, rolling his eyes. "When are you people going to learn? You each have your own lands, laid out by the Treaty, and none of you ever venture any farther. Xantearos is a vast country, and there are plenty of places to hide for the creatures who no longer wish to be known to exist."

She couldn't get her head around it. If this was the truth, what did it mean for her? And did it mean her brother had been the same way? She tried to recall if he'd ever talked about dreaming of flying. They'd spoken of many things, but she wasn't sure if that had been one of them. Years had passed since he'd died, and her memories of him felt faded, like a painting left hung too long directly in the sun. There were certain things she was able to pick out clearly—such as the day he'd found a silver coin on the street, and they'd been able to buy enough food to last them a week, and had gone laughing and running down the street, their arms full of paper bags—but most times had blurred together. But she remembered how he used to wear the ring. Remembered it clearly. Perhaps he didn't talk of his dreams, but the ring had certainly never caused him any harm.

"My brother must not have known what it was," she said. "I'm not even sure where he got it, only that he always wore it."

"That doesn't matter for the moment. But what you have inside you is a great power. It's not to be pushed to one side."

"What do you mean?"

"This isn't a coincidence. This has been destined, I'm sure." The Fae turned his attention to the men. "I can tell by the way each of you hold yourselves that you're important men among your own people."

"I'm the leader of my clan," Warsgra said.

Orergon nodded. "And I of my tribe." He gestured to one side of him, where Vehel was standing. "And Vehel Dawngleam is the son of the Elvish king."

Nimbus nodded. "So, a prince." He looked back to Dela. "It isn't coincidence that you've ended up here with the leaders of each of the races. With the strength of the dragons behind you, the four races will have no choice but to listen to you."

Vehel lifted his hand. "They won't listen to me. My father and brothers think little of me. They know I'm a natural mage, and they despise me for it."

Nimbus looked to him. "With a Dragonsayer behind you, they'd have no choice but to listen."

Vehel chewed on his lower lip but did not reply.

Dela's mind was spinning. The idea that her brother's ring meant something other than a simple keepsake was crazy. Even more crazy was that she was anything more than just a girl. She felt as though she was caught in a dream, or perhaps still trapped in the effects of the poison of the Hunter fly.

"We can't just go to Drusga," she said, half to herself.

The little Fae spoke up. "With everything that's happened, I don't think you can afford not to. What are you going to do if you go back home and discover a war has already broken out because of what you did?"

Responsibility pressed down heavily on her shoulders. She'd

never asked for any of this. She wasn't even sure she completely believed it. If it wasn't for the prevalence of her dreams, she'd have rebelled against the possibility immediately, but how vivid those dreams were danced in her mind, refusing to leave her alone.

Nimbus wasn't finished with his lecture. He lifted his hand, pointing one long finger.

"This country has been divided for too many years," he said. "We think we live in peace, but do we? Each race despising the next one? Several hundred years ago, we all lived side by side, but then humans got greedy and wanted everything for themselves. The other races fought back, and humans weren't expecting them to be such skilled foes. They regretted what they'd started, but not enough to view the other races as equals again, so they set up the Treaty and forced the other races to sign it. It was that, or everyone would end up wiped out, so they did. But you have to admit, it isn't exactly fair. The Elvish, and Moerians, and Norcs are forced to go hungry, while the humans store up the grain, and then take gold and diamonds for themselves in exchange."

Dela raised her hand. "We go hungry, too. Before the Passover, the normal people of Anthoinia are starving. The prices shoot up when the quantity available is so much less, and most can't afford it."

"And in the meantime, your king and queen watch over you, with their royal cellars filled with bags of grain."

"But that grain is needed to feed the other races. It's not purely selfish on their part."

His eyebrows lifted in skepticism. "The other races would be able to feed themselves if they were allowed to colonize the eastern coasts as well. You've been outside of the walls of Anthoinia. Is there not plenty of spaces for others to reside and farm, should they want to?"

She thought back to the seemingly endless stretches of countryside. Now he mentioned it, there was a lot of space with no one in it.

"But don't the other races like where they live? The Elvish love the Inverlands, the Moerians the Vast Plains. And what about you, Warsgra? I thought you loved the ruggedness of the mountains."

Warsgra nodded. "Aye, we do, but we'd also like the choice to be able to move if we wanted or needed to."

"That's what was taken away during the Treaty," Nimbus continued. "Free choice. Everyone looks like they're living free lives, but actually we're all living in our own prisons."

She'd never thought of things this way before. A part of her had always felt the wealth of the king and queen was a little unfair, exchanging food they needed for yet more wealth, but that was just how it was done, and they were always told it was so the other races were able to feed their families. It was practically a kindness. Yet the Fae was right in saying it was the Treaty that had created this situation, and that if the other races were simply allowed to farm some of the land on the eastern coast, the Passover wouldn't need to happen. They wouldn't have The Choosing every six months, and none of them would become part of the Chosen. Her brother would still be alive now, and so would Layla and Norton and Brer.

They'd been so worried about breaking the Treaty, when actually the Treaty was the thing responsible for all of this in the first place.

"If the Treaty is broken," she said finally, "we'll go back to a time of war."

His small face was serious. "The Treaty is already broken, and *you* can stop the war."

She shook her head. "No, I can't. I'm just a human woman."

"No, you're a Dragonsayer. With the power of dragons behind you, you can bring peace and unity back to Xantearos."

CHAPTER 25

VEHEL

Vehel had the sudden feeling the world had just gotten to be a much larger place.

"What do we do now?" he asked.

"You have a responsibility to make sure she gets to Drusga," Nimbus said. "I will feed you now, and give you what you need to reach the place, but you can't ignore this."

"Dela?" Vehel turned to her. "What do you think?" None of them could make this decision without her buy-in first.

She had a distant look in her brown eyes, as though she was seeing something they couldn't. "Since I was a child, I've had a dream that I was flying. Not just flying, but soaring above and through the clouds. I always thought it was a normal thing to dream about, but now I'm starting to wonder …"

"Do you think we should do this?" Vehel asked.

She looked around at them all. "It's not only me who's doing it. If we all go, it'll mean your family and friends will spend more time believing you're all dead."

"If we go north," Orergon said, "we might not make it there alive."

"We may not make it to the south alive either," Vehel pointed out.

Warsgra beat his chest with his fist. "But at least this way we'll die on a quest."

Dela sighed. "No one is dying." She put her head in her hands. "I can't believe all of you would do this for me."

"It's not just for you," Vehel said. "I started this. I used magic in the Southern Pass, even before you came along. If what I did broke the Treaty and has started a second Great War, then this is more on my shoulders than it is yours."

"I think you're looking at the smaller picture," said Orergon. "This whole situation has been messed up since before the Treaty was signed. Xantearos has been divided for too long. The Elvish should be free to use magic if they so wish. And the Norcs should be allowed down from the mountainside. Perhaps we need things to change, and Dela being a Dragonsayer will do that."

She looked up at Orergon. "I'm no ruler. I'm just a girl."

"No, but each of us is a leader of our own race," said Vehel. "We can help you."

She fixed her gaze on his. "I'm frightened I'm going to let everyone down."

"If we do nothing, we've already let everyone down."

Tears shimmered in her dark eyes, and she turned her face as though she didn't want anyone else to see them. There was so much pressure on her shoulders, yet she was still doing her best to appear strong in front of them all.

Nimbus interrupted. "You can take your pick of ponies from the paddock. Call it our contribution toward the cause. I'll get some of the other Fae to pack you up some food and water, too."

Vehel nodded in his direction. "Thank you, Nimbus."

"So, it looks like we're doing this." Dela got to her feet. "I feel like this is the dream instead of the reality."

Orergon touched her arm. "Are you sure you're ready to move around? You've been through a lot."

She nodded. "I'm all right. It's my head that feels more messed up than my body right now." She reached to the back of her neck where the sting had been removed. "My neck does ache, though."

"We'll keep an eye on it," Vehel said, "and make sure it doesn't get infected."

"Thanks."

Orergon turned toward the tiny front door, forced to bend almost in half as he went. "I'll go and check out the ponies. Pick which ones look like they'll be a good fit for us."

Warsgra followed him out. "I'll come. I want to make sure I get whichever is the largest."

"And the meanest," Dela added, but there was a twinkle in her eye now, and Vehel found himself smiling. Sure, they were a strange group, and if someone had told him a week ago that these would be his traveling companions, and he was rather enjoying their company, he'd have laughed them off. But when he compared these people to the other Elvish he'd traveled to the Southern Pass with—his father's men—he wouldn't have swapped any of them for a single one of these folk.

He trusted them, he realized. He'd never trusted his previous companions. He'd always felt as though they were only looking out for him so they could report back to his father. But with Orergon and Warsgra—and Dela, too—he felt as though he could lay his life in their hands and they'd do everything in their power to protect it.

"When was the last time you people ate?" Nimbus asked them, his brow furrowing disapprovingly and looking them up and down.

Vehel exchanged a glance with Dela. "We managed to eat along the way, but Dela hasn't eaten anything since last night." He mentally kicked himself. Why hadn't he thought of that? Of course, she would be hungry. All they'd managed to get down her was a few dribbles of water.

Dela lifted her hand. "I'm okay, honest."

He frowned at her. "No, you need to eat. We've got a long journey ahead of us, and you need to keep up your strength."

Nimbus hopped from foot to foot. "He's right, he's right. I'll get my people to put a meal together. Everyone can contribute."

"You don't need to make a fuss," Dela insisted. "Something simple will do."

"No, no. It's no fuss. Not often we get visitors here, especially not ones of any importance."

Vehel watched the emotions change across her face—disbelief, awkwardness, and then gratitude.

"I'm still having a hard time believing I'm anyone important," she said.

"In time, you will have no choice but to believe." He clapped his abnormally long-fingered hands together. "Now, let me go and get everyone organized. We'll set up a table outside so you won't all have to crouch."

"Thank you, Nimbus. This is all incredibly kind of you."

He flapped away her compliments with his hand. "You can think of me when we're all living in a happier and unified Xantearos."

Nimbus left the small house, leaving Vehel and Dela alone.

"How are you feeling?" he asked her.

"Confused, and shocked." She touched her fingers to the ring at her throat. "I can't believe I've had this around my neck for three years and I've never known what it was."

"None of us did. The dragons were supposed to have died out hundreds of years ago, together with their magic. No one had any reason to think someone might still have a connection with them."

"And my brother? Did he have the same connection?"

"I have no idea. If he was able to wear the ring, I guess he must have."

She exhaled a long, deep sigh.

"What's wrong?" he asked her with a frown.

"I just wish he was here today. I wish I could ask him some of the hundreds of questions going through my head. Maybe then I wouldn't feel so alone."

"You're not alone, Dela. Surely you must see that? You have us now."

She lifted her head and smiled at him. "You're right, I do. And I'm eternally grateful for everything you've done for me. All of you."

A commotion came from outside, and they both rose to their feet to peer out of the tiny window. Warsgra had taken a long table from six of the Fae who'd been carrying it, and had now lifted it above his head to set down in the small square in the center of the little group of cottages. The Fae scattered away from his feet as he strode, and then had to duck as he swung the table around to the position he wanted.

Orergon appeared with a second table, which he carried with a little more grace and care than Warsgra, and set it down so the tables were end on end. The Fae brought out tiny stools and chairs, but it was unlikely either Orergon or Warsgra would be able to sit on them without crushing them flat. Not to mind. They'd be content enough with the floor.

"I guess we should get out there," Vehel said, looking down at the top of Dela's strawberry blonde head.

"Yes. I feel bad not helping."

Before they'd even made it outside, the Fae had already started to bring out bowls of fruits Vehel didn't recognize, and jugs of sparkling drink. Tiny cakes and pastries were produced on silver platters, followed by breads, and cheeses, and cold meats to accompany them.

Vehel laughed at the opulence. "They look like they've been planning for a party this whole time."

Dela's face had lit up at the selection of foods as well. "Yes, it does."

Nimbus appeared at the front door, his head sticking through the gap. "Come, come. Sit. Eat your fill."

Dela and Vehel exchanged a smile and followed Nimbus out, both of them having to duck their heads through the door before they stepped outside into the bright sunshine.

Warsgra had seated himself, cross legged on the ground at one end of the table, and Orergon the other. Dela was able to sit on one of the larger chairs, but Vehel chose the ground beside her. It wouldn't look good to start breaking the Fae's furniture when they'd gone to such effort.

Warsgra didn't wait for any more encouragement. He reached across the table and helped himself to meat and bread. With the Norc making the first move, Dela, too, started to pick items of food for herself—bread and cheese and fruit. She picked up one of the pastries, and to Vehel's surprise, tears filled her eyes.

"What's wrong?" he asked. "Don't you like them?"

She nodded. "Yes, I do. They just remind me of home. I bought my mother similar pastries the same morning I left for the Passover. I told her I'd be back, but now she believes she's lost both her children. I hate to think of her in such pain, and I miss her and my father terribly."

He put his arm around her shoulders and squeezed her tight. "You'll see them again."

She sniffed and nodded. "Yes, I hope so."

Vehel released her, and helped himself to the food on the table. He avoided the meat, but ate and drank his fill of everything else. The fruit was ripe, juice dribbling down his chin the moment he sank his teeth into its shiny skin, and though they were nowhere near the ocean, there was also a selection of different fishes, both smoked and dried, which he was able to eat with the bread. He didn't want to look as though he was being greedy, but everyone else was piling their plates high, and it didn't appear as though the Fae were on any kind of rations. So this must be how it was to live without needing to worry about the Passover, he mused. A life where there was plenty for everyone.

The Fae sat around them, chattering to each other in between staring unabashedly at their new companions. Vehel noticed them gesture toward his pointed ears, and then back at their own. Perhaps this was the first time many of them had even seen an Elvish person.

With the table cleared, and everyone seeming to be in a far better mood, Warsgra got to his feet. "Thank you for your hospitality, Nimbus, but if we're going to cover any miles before nightfall, we really should be going."

The Fae jumped to his feet as well. "Yes, yes. Of course. Let us gather supplies ready for your journey. You'll not be leaving empty handed."

The remains of the feast were cleared away as quickly as it had been set up, and they got to work to ready themselves for their trip. How long would it take to reach Drusga from here? Days? Weeks? Or even longer? At least they wouldn't be on foot.

Vehel busied himself, helping the Fae to pack bags of food and blankets, and fill containers with fresh water. He ended up side by side with Nimbus, back in the little cottage, while Warsgra and Orergon got the ponies ready. The Fae was a strange looking little creature, but he certainly seemed to know what he was talking about. He wondered how old the Fae were. They lived even longer than the Elvish, so this one might be several hundred years old, though it felt rude to ask.

"You can help her, you know," Nimbus said from beside him, "if you just stop being so afraid."

Vehel straightened at his words. "I'm not afraid!"

"Yes, you are. You're afraid of your magic. You're afraid of your family's reaction to your magic. If you learn to embrace it, you could be very powerful. Dela the Dragonsayer is going to need someone like you by her side in the very near future."

Vehel didn't want to admit it, but the Fae was right. The more he'd used his magic, the more he'd become fearful of its power and what it might do. It had brought the four of them here, after all, and he hadn't planned for that to happen. He could have helped Dela with the Hunter fly sting, but he hadn't been able to bring himself to do it, worried that something would go wrong and he'd end up hurting her.

"I don't know how to embrace it," he admitted eventually. "No one has ever taught me. My magic was always something to be ashamed of, and even feared."

"It's a part of who you are. You need to learn to trust yourself."

Vehel nodded. "Yes, perhaps you're right."

He'd doubted himself his whole life. The idea of trying to trust himself and the power within him that he'd spent most of his life trying to suppress was almost as overwhelming as the incredible journey they had ahead.

They finished filling the water bags and went outside to join the others.

Four ponies had been selected and were already loaded with the items they needed for their journey. The piebald was the biggest of the animals and would clearly be Warsgra's. Dela stood beside a white pony, the smallest of them all, and was stroking its nose and talking to the animal as though it were an old friend. Orergon had a chestnut pony that was similar in color to the horse he'd ridden to the Southern Pass. The fourth and final animal was a dappled grey, and he assumed that pony was meant for him.

"How long will it take us to reach Drusga?" Orergon asked Nimbus.

"That depends very much on yourselves." He shot Vehel a look that Vehel was sure was supposed to mean something. "It may take days, or it may take weeks. There are too many variants to be sure."

"How about you tell us how many miles we have to travel, then," Warsgra said gruffly.

"I've never been there myself, but I would take a guess at one hundred and fifty, at least."

"But it could be more?" he prompted.

Nimbus shrugged his narrow shoulders. "Or it could be less."

Warsgra glanced over at Vehel and widened his eyes, as though to say, 'what does he know?' Vehel thought the Fae knew far more than he was letting on, however.

"Thank you for all your help, Nimbus," Vehel said. "Perhaps we'll see you on our way back down."

Nimbus chuckled. "Or perhaps not, though I appreciate the sentiment. I hope to hear great tales of your achievements coming from the south in the months to come."

"I hope so, too."

The four of them caught up the rope harnesses that were around the ponies' noses and led them back to where they'd thrown down their weapons upon entering the Fae's village. Dela didn't have anything to retrieve, as she'd been paralyzed when they'd brought her in and the Fae hadn't noticed the dagger at her waist, so she pulled herself up on her pony's back. She didn't seem any worse for wear after her ordeal with the Hunter fly sting, though she was still, understandably, a little shocked with the news of what she apparently was.

Vehel was happy to retrieve his bow and quiver of arrows. His back had felt bare and exposed without it. From the look on Warsgra's face, he felt the same way about getting his axe back. Orergon also smiled when he slid his spear into the holder on his back.

They mounted the ponies and looked back to where the Fae had all gathered to see them off. They were a strange looking group of folk, but, despite their initial resistance, they'd been welcoming and more than helpful. Vehel hoped that if they met any others on this next leg of their journey that they would be equally as hospitable.

He kicked his mount's rotund belly, and they got moving, heading toward Drusga and whatever lay between.

CHAPTER 26

DELA

As they left the Fae village far behind, Dela found herself constantly glancing over at Warsgra riding the piebald pony, and having to clamp a smile behind her lips each time. It wasn't only that his feet practically dragged on the ground; it was the sullen expression on his face as he urged the animal forward. His muscular thighs were spread across the pony's wide back, and the whole setup simply looked ludicrous, and Warsgra knew it. Orergon didn't look much better, but he held himself with a certain poise that Warsgra was lacking. Only Vehel barely had his feet above the ground, and even he was too tall for the ride.

She leaned forward and scratched her pony between the ears. "What shall we call you, huh?" she said, half to herself. "Well, you're white, so we could go with something to do with that. Snowy doesn't seem right. What about Ghost? Yes, I like that. Ghost, it is."

"Are you talking to your ride?" Warsgra called over to her.

"Yes, he makes a better conversationalist than you," she teased in return.

Warsgra rolled his eyes at her, but she saw him holding back a smile.

It was true, she couldn't remember the last part of their journey, but she was still thankful they were no longer on foot, and that they had basic supplies as well. A canvas to sleep beneath. Blankets for comfort. Containers to carry water. They were simple things, but they made everything else far more bearable. She still hadn't fully processed the idea that she had some kind of connection with dragons, but she couldn't deny what she'd seen when Orergon touched the ring, or the feeling of flying she'd experienced most of her life. Something must have rung true to her, or she wouldn't be doing this, would she?

Night would be creeping in soon. Maybe they should have spent the night at the Fae village, but it made sense for them to cover as many miles as possible before they were forced to stop. At least now they had blankets and a canvas to sleep beneath. It would make for a far more peaceful night than sleeping beneath the stars with only Warsgra's shoulder protector as a pillow.

They were heading in a different direction to how they'd traveled here. Though they'd always been going south previously, and they were now riding back north, they no longer had the river to follow. Their previous route had brought them more south-west than directly south, but now they were definitely heading directly north.

Dela couldn't stop her thoughts from going to what Nimbus had told her about the ring around her throat. Had she always dreamed of flying, or had the dreams only gotten more powerful once she'd been in possession of the ring? She wanted to take the ring off the leather cord and put it on her finger, but her fingers were far smaller than the ring, and she was sure she would lose it. She wished there was a way she could wear it properly, however. Maybe that would help give her more of an insight into what she was supposed to be able to do.

They traveled in good-natured silence, each of them lost in thought. The ponies plodded on, seemingly unaware of the massive difference in size between their usual riders and their new ones.

The river and trees they'd passed through before reaching the Fae village were replaced with rolling hills and grasslands. A herd of hooved animals Dela had never seen before, with long necks, stripes, and curled horns protruding from the tops of their heads, stampeded across the plain ahead of them. The animals paid them no attention, though Orergon made comments about them being good hunting stock.

The birds that circled overhead were also like none Dela had ever seen. They were huge, with a wingspan as large as her outstretched arms, orange heads, and blue feet. They circled in the warm eddies, dipping lower and lower, before suddenly soaring back up again. Their movements reminded Dela of her dreams, and she experienced a strange combination of jealousy and nostalgia.

They continued for another hour or so. The sun began to drop in the sky, and at some point soon they would need to stop for the night. Dela's stomach was still comfortably full from the splendid meal the Fae had provided, but she was unused to riding, and already her thighs and rear end ached from the steady motion of the pony. She'd have to get used to it. They might have another week or more of riding, and she wouldn't be able to walk at this rate. She wanted to reach Drusga and find out the truth about what Nimbus claimed about her as soon as possible, but the last few days—few weeks, even—had been taxing, and she was exhausted.

Dela thought of what she knew about Drusga. The place existed, but, because of its heritage, it had almost mystical qualities. It wasn't an area of Xantearos anyone would ever want to visit. The landscape was volcanic, and though the area's fire mountains weren't believed to be active, it wasn't as though anyone went there to confirm. Sometimes, down in Anthoinia, the ground trembled beneath their feet, and people would whisper how a fire mountain had blown in Drusga, but none of them knew if such a thing was actually true or not. It was just something they said.

If nothing else, Drusga was an inhospitable land. It wouldn't be easy to reach.

Through the tall grass, Dela spotted something up ahead. She narrowed her eyes in that direction, trying to make out what it was, and lifted her hand from Ghost's reins to point. "What's that?"

In a small clearing in the grass, a large lump appeared to be twitching. A moving black line ran to and from the lump, cutting its way through the meadow.

Warsgra frowned. "I'm not sure."

They slowed, pulling the ponies to a halt so they could get a better look. Dela's fingers tightened around the reins, and her heartbeat tripped in her chest. She was ever conscious of her experience with the Hunter fly, and she didn't want to go anywhere near whatever that was.

Her teeth dug into her lower lip. "We can go around it, right?"

Orergon sat up taller on his pony, craning his neck to get a better look. "I think so. It depends on how far those lines reach out."

"What are they?" she asked.

Orergon shook his head. "I'm not sure, but because of the grass, it's hard to tell how far out they run."

They had no choice but to kick their ponies on and get a little closer to see what they might have to deal with. As they did, the black blobs took on the definition of giant ants, each one the size of a small dog. The creatures moved with military efficiency. They crawled over the larger lump, and, as a small area cleared, she saw the lump was one of the birds she'd seen circling. As she watched, the bird feebly flapped a wing.

Dela shuddered right down to her core and turned her face. She didn't want to look at the poor creature. There was nothing they could do for it. They couldn't risk attracting the ants to them. They might be able to fight one or two of the giant ants, but not a whole colony.

"This way," Warsgra said, jerking his head to their right and pulling his pony's head in the same direction. "We should be able to avoid them."

The thought of that bird being eaten by the ants made her skin crawl. Something similar had almost been her fate, too. If Vehel, Warsgra, and Orergon hadn't come after her, she'd be dead now instead of on a crazy quest to unite Xantearos. She didn't even know how that was going to work. Even if she was able to somehow connect with dragons, and the dragons were actually alive, she had no idea how she was able to use that ability to prevent a war and bring the four races together.

They gave the ants and their meal a wide berth, and put some distance between themselves and the critters before stopping for the night. Out in the open, with only wilderness surrounding them, it was impossible to find somewhere they'd be completely safe from all local wildlife. All they could do was get a fire going, set someone to keep watch, and hope that was enough to keep any monsters away.

Vehel and Dela set about putting up the canvas shelter, while Orergon got a fire started and Warsgra sorted out the food. Now they'd been provided with equipment, they no longer needed Vehel's magical abilities to start a fire. A flint and steel would do.

As night fell, Dela and Vehel worked together with easy grace. Even though Vehel was an Elvish prince, he didn't have any of the airs and graces she'd assumed someone of stature to possess. When they'd first met, he'd clearly looked down on humans, but she definitely didn't get that impression from him now. If anything, they'd almost gone the opposite way, and he treated her with a kind of reverence. She didn't want this news about the Dragonstone to change anything between them, though. She wanted him to see her only for who she was, nothing more.

With the shelter erected, they moved beneath it, rolling out the bedding rolls. When they were finished, they dropped down to sit side by side.

Vehel spoke up. "I owe you an apology, Dela."

"No, you don't."

He nodded but wouldn't meet her eye. "Yes, I do. Warsgra and Orergon asked me to use my magic to try to bring you around when you were paralyzed, but I refused. I could have done something to help, but instead I was too frightened of what might happen to even try."

She reached out and placed a hand on his arm. He was so intense, so serious. His light blue eyes looked silver in the moonlight, and the tips of his white-blond hair were still stained red with mud.

"Vehel, you climbed into a fly's burrow to save me. You've got nothing to apologize for."

"I could have done more …" His teeth caught his lower lip, and he glanced away.

She reached out and touched his chin, drawing his face back to hers. "Stop it. You did more than enough."

"No, I—"

She quieted his protest by leaning in and placing her lips to his. The kiss surprised him into silence. Her fingers remained against his skin, and she leaned in closer. He responded, his lips parting, and their tongues touching.

Dela hadn't been planning this; it had just happened. She didn't want Vehel to think she liked him any more than she liked any of the others. Up until this point, she hadn't really thought of any of them that way, had she? Okay, she might have admired Warsgra's muscles, of Orergon's dark eyes and protective nature, but not romantically. They were all different races. This wasn't how it was supposed to work.

She broke the kiss and turned her face away. "I'm sorry, I didn't mean to do that."

"No, don't be sorry."

She glanced around to see where the others were. Warsgra was spearing food onto a stick, and Orergon was seeing to the ponies, making sure they were all secured, with fresh water and plenty of grass underfoot for them to eat. She didn't know why the thought of either of them seeing her kiss Vehel bothered her. Was it because they were different races, or was it that she didn't want either of them to assume she'd chosen Vehel over them? It wasn't as though she would ever want to turn Vehel away. She just didn't want to have to turn *any* of them down. They'd protected her and cared for her in a way she'd never experienced before, and she found she liked that feeling. She liked having all of them around and couldn't imagine a time when they'd all have to go their separate ways. But they would have to at some point, wouldn't they? They'd each have to return to their people. If a second Great War began, they might even find themselves on opposite sides, forced to fight each other. Such a thing would be unbearable.

"Are you all right?" Vehel touched the back of her hand and ducked his head to look at her in concern.

"I was thinking about the future, and what will happen to each of us. I could never bear it if I was forced to think of any of you as my enemy."

Vehel nodded. "I feel the same way, and that's why we're doing this, isn't it? Because we should all be united, no matter what our races. The whole of Xantearos should be like we are now."

She grasped his hand like a lifeline. "You're right. This is what we'll be fighting for. I'm just frightened I'm going to let everyone down."

"You won't. We'll all be here for you. I won't let you down again either, Dela. I promise you that."

Footsteps approached, and they released hands.

The Moerian and Norc appeared in the gap, holding chunks of cheese and cured meat and loaves of bread in their hands.

"What are you two gossiping about?" Warsgra slid under the canvas to join them. "Like a couple of old maids."

"Just discussing your cooking, Warsgra," said Vehel. "Wondering if we'll make it through the night."

"If anyone knows how to cook meat, it's me," he replied.

"Vehel doesn't eat meat." Dela smiled.

Orergon sat down beside him. "More fool, him."

Vehel laughed. "I can make do. There's plenty of bread to eat, and a hunk of cheese."

"Maybe we'll come across another river soon, and then we can catch more fish for you," she suggested, reaching across to help herself to some of the bread and meat. Though she'd been full from the Fae's meal not so long ago, she was surprised to discover a hollow place in her stomach that was grateful for more food.

"Maybe, but the bread and cheese will keep me alive just fine." Vehel took a big bite out of a chunk of bread, as though to make a point.

"We'll reach the coast eventually," Warsgra said. "We can't keep traveling north and not expect to hit the sea."

"That's true."

Dela chewed and swallowed, half covering her mouth with her hand when she spoke. "What sort of creatures do you think live in the waters of The Lonely Strait? The seas are far warmer up there. I imagine things could grow to extraordinary sizes."

Vehel shuddered. "The sea creatures of the south are bad enough. We Elvish have been losing more and more people to them over the last hundred years or so. I can't imagine them being any bigger, or meaner."

"Hopefully, we won't have to find out," Dela said.

With the meal finished, they cleared everything away and settled down to sleep. Dela slept in the middle, with Vehel on her right, and Orergon on her left. Warsgra had taken up position right at the entrance, lying across it to protect them from anything that may come sniffing around them while they slept.

The soft snorts and whinnies of the ponies not far away gave Dela a strange comfort, too. Should anything try to approach them, she was sure Ghost and his friends would let them know.

* * *

Dela dreamed of flying again. Her arms were spread wide, the wind blowing in her face. Her heart beat fast with excitement, and she held back the urge to whoop for joy. It was a freedom like nothing she'd ever experienced when her feet were firmly on the ground. She could cover a hundred miles in mere minutes, her speed incredible, causing the world below her to blur.

But a heaviness lay at her heart that hadn't been present before. Though exhilarated by the flight, a part of her knew it was a mistake. She'd left them behind, and it felt wrong. Terribly wrong. They would never do that to her, and yet she'd abandoned them for something else.

Her euphoria turned to turmoil. She didn't want to leave them behind. They'd become everything to her, and if continuing alone was what this required, she didn't think she wanted it any longer. Already she ached with their loss and wanted to turn back. What had been a moment of excitement now became anguish.

No, stop. Go back.

But she didn't have any control. She was merely an observer.

She had no choice but to be taken farther and farther away, until she knew there was no chance of seeing Warsgra, Orergon, and Vehel ever again…

CHAPTER 27

ORERGON

The days passed by in a routine of sorts. They rose when the sun did, and settled down again for the night when it fell. The ponies the Fae had given them were sturdy beasts, and while they weren't going to break any land speed records, they plodded onward without tiring.

Orergon did find himself missing his old horse, Corazon, who he'd ridden across the Vast Plains and into the Southern Pass. That horse had been his for the past couple of years, ever since he took his place as tribe leader, and he hoped Corazon had managed to get out of the Southern Pass unharmed. The horse would have known his way home, even without Orergon on his back. That might even be the first way his tribe realized things hadn't gone to plan—if the horses turned up on the Vast Plains with no riders. What would they do when they realized their leaders weren't coming home? Who would step up to try to take his place, or would neighboring tribes attempt to take over? He hoped his people had enough strength to stand united. The thought of returning to the Vast Plains, only to discover his tribe absorbed into another, would feel like the deepest blow.

He released the pony's reins with one hand, and took out the bands holding his twin braids in place, and raked his fingers down through the middle, separating the hair. He shook it out, letting the hair fall loose over his back and shoulders. It was tradition in his tribe for its leader to wear his hair as long as possible, and to keep it braided, but he supposed tradition didn't matter so much now.

As they'd moved farther north, the hotter the temperatures became. The vegetation began to change, too, the trees growing short and stubby, the grass drying to yellow, making it harder to graze the ponies.

In the distance, tall peaks rose into the sky, but these weren't topped with snow. No, instead of snow, plumes of white and grey smoke rose into the sky, creating a cloud above.

"We're running low on water," Warsgra called back over his shoulder, from where he rode up front on the largest of the ponies, which the Norc had affectionately nicknamed Giant. "If we see anywhere we can refill the water pouches, we're going to need to stop."

"We're getting close now," Dela said. "Those are the fire mountains of Drusga up ahead."

"And it's only going to get hotter." Sweat beaded on Orergon's brow, and he was used to warmer climes. "We won't make it unless we stop and get more water. We don't want to get caught up there with nothing."

"Okay, let's stop for a while as soon as we see somewhere."

Trouble was, they hadn't come across any running water for some time. The hotter the temperature, the drier the land. What if they went too far, and ran out of water completely, and couldn't make it back again? They would die of thirst out here, and it would be a horrible and painful death.

Vehel's lips pressed together in concern. "What if we can't find any water? What do we do then?"

"We're too far into this now," Orergon said, sitting straighter on the pony's back. "We have to keep going. If death is our fate, then so be it."

Dela glanced over at him. "No one is dying."

"Can't you conjure us up some water, Vehel?" Warsgra called over to the Elvish prince. "That would be handy right now."

"The day I have the ability to control the rain will be the day I become ruler of Xantearos." He laughed, and the others joined in.

Vehel, out of all of them, was struggling the most with the heat. He'd left his armor with the Fae, though they'd insisted they hadn't needed to take it for payment. But there was no point in him wearing the heavy armor all this way in the heat, so now he only wore the lightweight tunic and pants beneath. At least it covered his pale skin, though his nose and the tips of his ears, where they protruded from his fair hair, were tinged pink.

They continued on their way, keeping the volcanic peaks in front of them. At times, they dismounted the ponies and walked alongside them to give the animals a break.

Warsgra took a mouthful from one of the water pouches and handed it over to Dela. "That's the last of the water."

She took a small swig, and then handed it on to Orergon. Only a small amount sloshed at the bottom of the pouch. The thought of being out of water concerned him more than anything right now. When they were on the Vast Plains, they often went miles between water sources, but they always knew where the next one was located. They were nearing the fire mountains now, and had no idea what lay ahead.

He drank from the pouch, the water now warm and doing little to quench his thirst, and then passed it on to Vehel.

"Finish it," he told Vehel.

Dela put her hand over her nose. "What's that smell? It's like eggs gone bad."

Orergon lifted his nose to the air and inhaled. She was right. There was a strange aroma on the air, and it was getting stronger.

"It's not eggs," Warsgra grunted. "It's sulfur."

Vehel's eyebrows raised. "Sulfur? From the fire mountains?"

"Aye. And the ground around them. I've smelled it before in some parts of the Great Dividing Range. It doesn't happen often, but if the ground moves and opens up a fissure, the smell is the same."

Alarm jarred through Orergon. "Is the ground likely to move now?"

Warsgra shrugged his massive shoulders. "No way of knowing."

With their approach to Drusga on the horizon, Orergon had the strange feeling the land itself was going to work to keep them away. If they were unable to find water, and then the ground itself began to shake, it wouldn't matter how much they cared for Dela or tried to protect her. There were some things they couldn't protect against.

They continued, the temperatures soaring. The sun beat down on their heads and shoulders, and even the ponies had slowed, their hooves dragging against the dirt. How much longer could they go on like this? They would be forced to kill one of the animals and use their blood to rehydrate. It would be salty and would do little to quench their thirst, but it would be better than dying. Still, he'd grown fond of the sturdy little ponies, and didn't want them to meet such an end. If it was the choice between their lives or Dela's, however, he wouldn't have much of a choice.

No matter how many steps they took, the fire mountains never appeared to get any closer.

"Is this what Nimbus was talking about?" Vehel said suddenly. His nose had burned, as had his shoulders. He'd wrapped a piece of material around the top of his head to keep off the worst of the sun, but the rest of his clothing was damp with sweat.

Orergon frowned at him. "What do you mean?"

He shook his head. "I'm not totally sure, but the Fae said something about how long it took to get to Drusga being very much dependent on ourselves. Something about it niggled at me at the time, and now it's got me thinking."

"We don't seem to be getting any closer," Warsgra growled.

Dela spoke up. "Could it just be a mirage? A trick of the light?"

Vehel's lips twisted. "Honestly, I'm not sure. Maybe it's something about this place …"

Warsgra suddenly straightened and pointed ahead. "What's over there? I can see trees."

Orergon looked in the direction he was gesturing. After what had felt like miles of dried out grassland and black dirt, there was a hint of green on the horizon.

"There might be water!" Dela exclaimed.

They exchanged wide smiles of hope and climbed back on the ponies, kicking them into a gallop. The greenery quickly took shape in the form of an oasis of trees and bushes, and through the tree trunks, Orergon glimpsed blue. "Looks like a pool of some sort."

"Not just one," Vehel said as they broke through the tree line.

No, there were a number of pools dotted around the main one in the center of the oasis. The trees offered welcome shade, and Orergon closed his eyes briefly with bliss. He was used to the sun, but the intense relentlessness of the last few days had been draining. He heard the others moan in pleasure at the cool shade as well, but the priority was water, and, by the looks of the lush pool in front of them, it seemed that need was being taken care of, too. Where only a few hours ago, it had felt as though Xantearos itself was working against them, now they had been blessed.

"The Gods are smiling down on us today," he said.

Dela turned to him with a smile that lit her eyes. "You think this is a good sign?"

He nodded. "Yes, I'd say so."

This would be the last comfort they'd see before they started the hike up the volcanic region. The fire mountains and valley of

Drusga were ahead, and beyond that lay the rough waters of The Lonely Strait.

The smell of the sulfur was still strong, but Orergon didn't care. As long as the water was drinkable, he could handle the stench.

Dela appeared to be thinking the same. "Is the water fresh?"

"Seems to be. Must be coming from an underground source."

He jumped off his ride and gave his pony a gentle smack on the rear. The pony snorted and trotted over to the first pool. The animal lowered his head and drank.

Warsgra shrugged. "The pony seems to think it's good to drink. If it's good enough for them …"

Dela's lips twisted. "Plus, I don't think we can exactly be fussy right now."

Vehel lifted his eyebrows. "She's got a point."

Orergon moved around the edge of the pool, putting some space between himself and the drinking ponies. He got to his knee, and scooped his hand into the water, but instead of a refreshing cool liquid against his skin, he discovered the water was warm. "What, by the Gods …?"

"What is it?" Dela called over.

"The water's warm. I've never known anything like it."

Vehel came to join him. "If the water's coming from an underground source, it must be passing volcanic rock, which is what is heating it."

Warsgra let out a whoop and started to pull off his shoulder protectors. "It's gonna be like taking a warm bath."

"Wait one minute," Dela said, raising a finger. "We need fresh water. Not water everyone has been swimming in."

Warsgra waved a hand dismissively. "There are other pools. Try them."

Orergon shook his head. "We know this water is good from the ponies drinking from it. How about you try one of the other pools?"

"Fine," Warsgra grumbled, wandering off to test out the next one. He dipped down and put his hand in. When he lifted his head, his wide grin had returned. "Aye, this one is warm, too."

"There's nothing we can do about the drinking water being warm," Dela said. "We have water now, and the ponies can drink their fill, which is the important thing. Let's fill up the water pouches," she smiled, "and then, I say we swim."

Orergon returned her smile. "Yes, let's do that."

They'd been traveling for so long, they all had sweat-covered bodies and filthy clothes.

First they kneeled at the waterside, drinking their fill using their hands. Then the group set to work, filling up each of the water pouches, and placing the stoppers back in them. When that was done, they looked back to the second pool.

"I'm going in." Warsgra had already thrown aside his shoulder guards, and now bent to pull off his boots. He didn't wear much normally, and the long ride in the sun had tanned his skin to a deep brown. He removed the loincloth from around his waist, exposing a rear end numerous shades whiter than his back. With a hoot, he ran a few steps and then jumped, landing with an almighty splash in the middle of the water. He burst from the surface, using both hands to push his long, soaking wet hair out of his face.

Beside Orergon, Dela laughed at Warsgra's antics. It felt like it had been some time since he'd heard her laugh.

"If you can't beat them," she said, already walking over.

Orergon watched as she pulled her tunic over her head and dropped it to the ground, and then toed off her boots. Her hands went to the front of her pants, and she undid the belt holding them together, leaving both of them, together with her rope belt and her dagger, in a pile. She wore only her underwear now, and she hesitated for a moment before pulling her vest over her head, and, using her arm to cover her breasts, ran into the water to join Warsgra.

Orergon glanced over at Vehel, who'd also been watching, mesmerized. It wasn't only that she was a human woman, practically naked, it was that it was Dela. She was special, and he knew the others felt that pull of her, the same as he did. They'd been brought together for a reason, and he felt sure the future of Xantearos lay in the hands of the beautiful young woman who was now dipping her shoulders beneath the warm waters of the volcanic pool.

She turned and looked over her shoulder, catching his eye and jerking her head to tell him to join them.

He stepped forward, removing his own traditional clothing and leaving it on the ground. The sun hit his bare skin, but he didn't burn. This was the first time he'd exposed the tattoos of his tribe, the black lines and swirls across his chest that told other tribes which one he belonged to and what his position was within the tribe. He caught Dela looking but made no move to cover himself.

Instead, he walked forward to the pool's edge and dived in.

The warm water engulfed his arms and head, followed by the rest of his body. He plunged beneath the surface, swam a couple of strokes, and then emerged close to the opposite side.

Both Dela and Warsgra laughed and clapped, and a bubble of something he couldn't quite place swelled inside his chest. It had been a long time since he'd felt this way, not since he'd lost his family. It was a sense of belonging, of being bigger than just himself. He'd always felt that way with his tribe, but it was different being so close to others. How strange to feel this way with folk who were so utterly different from him and knew nothing of his ways and customs. And yet he did feel that way—as though they were family.

Vehel was the last to get into the water, peeling off the shirt and pants he'd been wearing beneath the armor he'd left with the Fae. His pale skin, hair, and eyes were a strange sight in the heat and sunlight, and he entered the water with more caution than the others.

Orergon glanced over at Dela and saw a mischievous glint in her eye. As Vehel made his way in, she plunged both hands beneath the surface of the pool and then pushed them forward, sending a rush of water over the top of Vehel, soaking him from the top of his head.

Vehel's mouth dropped as he stood, thigh deep in the water, but soaking wet. The same wicked glint lit his blue eyes. "I believe you're asking for trouble."

A grin split Dela's face, and she let out a shriek before turning and plunging through the water to get away.

"I've got her, Vehel," Warsgra called and lunged forward, catching her around the waist. He was fearsomely strong and lifted her with both hands above his head.

She let out another shriek of laughter and struggled, kicking her legs in the air.

"What's her punishment?" Warsgra said, humor of his own dancing behind his voice.

"Throw her in!" Vehel called back.

"Very well." And he did, throwing her into the pool so she landed with a huge splash. She submerged momentarily before bursting back to the surface, gasping and holding back laughter.

"Right, this means war," she threatened and took after Warsgra.

Orergon joined in. "Not if I get you first."

He copied the movement she had used, splashing a wave of water into her face. She screamed and turned her attention on him and splashed him back, until they created a torrent of water between them.

"Okay, okay," she managed between gulped breaths. "You win."

Orergon quit his splashing, but Vehel was creeping up behind her. He was right behind her before she even noticed, and he leaned in and said, "But you lose," right before plunging beneath the surface and pulling her under with him.

Dela surfaced again, twisting one way and then the other until she spotted Vehel. "Oh, you are so dead." She looked around at all of them. "You are all so dead."

They played that way for the longest of times, laughing together and simply enjoying each other's company. Though none of them said as much, Orergon knew they were all thinking the same thing. This might be their last time together. Once they crossed the fire mountain to Drusga, everything would change.

CHAPTER 28

DELA

However much she would have liked to stay in this place and not continue to Drusga, Dela knew they had to keep moving.

They washed their clothes in the pool and left them out to dry. In this heat, which came from both the sun and beneath the ground, their clothes and bodies were dry in no time. She'd spent so much time with Warsgra, Orergon, and Vehel, that being practically naked around them didn't bother her. She caught them watching her, curious eyes on her skin, but she assumed it was because she was human. She must look different than the females of their own kinds—Warsgra must think her skinny and weak. Orergon probably thought her to be too pale, and she imagined the Elvish females as exotic creatures with their long white-blonde hair and pale blue eyes and pointed ears. Okay, so she'd kissed Vehel, but that had been done on the spur of the moment, and it didn't mean anything. They were all here for one reason only, and that was to get her to Drusga and see if the Fae had been speaking the truth about her connection with the dragons.

She kept glancing up at the sky, wondering if she'd see one circling high above them. Surely they should have seen one by now, if this was where the dragons still lived. Rumor was that they'd died out long ago, yet Nimbus said that was wrong. But if they still existed, why hadn't they seen any? Drusga was so close now. Yes, the dragons were always supposed to fly high and fast, staying out of reach of the human eye, but it still niggled at her.

"We need to keep moving," she said. "The ponies are rested now. We still have a few hours of light left."

"We can't convince you to stay here forever?" Warsgra asked.

She gave him a regretful smile. "Yes, you probably could, but we all know there are bigger things resting on our shoulders. Every day that passes might be bringing us closer to war. We need to think of our people."

He pushed his hand through his hair, which was still wet and straggly at the ends. "Of course."

They finished attaching the water pouches to the ponies' packs and gathered up the rest of their belongings. They were down to the final rations of food now, but though it wasn't luxurious, it would be enough to get them the rest of the way. Dela didn't know what they'd do on the journey back, but she figured they'd work that out once they knew their next steps.

"Are you ready, Ghost?" she said to the pony, stroking his velvet-soft nose. "This next part is going to be tough."

The pony whinnied as though he understood her, and she gave him a final pat, before pulling herself up on his broad back. Her stomach churned with nerves, a tight knot of anticipation. She glanced at the men around her, each of them strong in their own way, and prayed to the Gods she wouldn't let them down.

They left the sanctuary and shade of the pools behind them. Dela led the way, Ghost picking between the scrubland and increasingly rocky terrain. She'd grown used to the faint aroma of sulfur on the air when they'd been at the pool, but as they covered more miles, the stench grew stronger.

Dela's mood was brighter now they had refilled the water pouches, and they'd refreshed themselves in the pool. The warm water had even soothed away some of the aches and pains that had been plaguing her ever since she'd set out from Anthoinia. She'd grown used to being on Ghost's back, and even took comfort in the rocking, rolling motion of his body beneath her. The others seemed happier, too, telling stories of different journeys they'd been on, or funny tales from back home. It was good that they'd had this small respite. She had the feeling they were going to need every ounce of strength over the next few days.

After the lushness of the oasis, the land they traveled now felt even harsher. Ahead, the summits of the fire mountains, which led to the Valley of the Dragons, dominated the landscape. The ground grew noticeably warm, even through the soles of their boots, and the brown dirt began to turn black.

"We're going to need to stop soon," Warsgra called over his shoulder. "Night will fall within the hour."

Dela gritted her teeth in frustration. Being able to see the fire mountains made her want to keep going, but she couldn't ask the others to walk through the night. Though they'd taken some respite at the oasis, they still had a distance to travel, and they'd make better time rested.

She took in the expanse of nothingness. "Where should we stop?"

"I can't see it making much difference where we decide," said Orergon.

Vehel looked around, as though something might just appear. "This is as good a spot as any."

Normally, they'd have chosen something that offered natural shelter—a small copse of trees, or an outcropping of rock—anything to make them feel protected from one side or the other. If they didn't have that, they'd at least have camped out near a river for water and food. But out here there was only desolate waste. They had no choice but to simply pick a spot and set up for the night.

Dela slid down off Ghost's back and put her hands on her hips.

The sun had dipped low in the sky, sending a red glow over the land. She stared across it, toward the place they were headed. It felt as though they'd been traveling forever, but even though the scenery had changed, the fire mountains never appeared to get any closer.

She let out a sigh and turned to the pony's pack to take out what they needed for the night.

"What's wrong?" Warsgra asked. He glanced over at her as he did the same, working the canvas shelter out from his own pony's bags.

"It just seems like we're never going to get there. We keep going and going and going, but Drusga never feels like it's getting any closer."

Vehel came to stand beside her, looking out across the landscape with her. "I know what you mean, but there's nothing between us and the fire mountains now. Tomorrow, we'll have to see that we're getting there."

She nodded and released a heavy breath through her nostrils. "I hope you're right."

They finished unpacking what they needed for the night. The canvas and wooden poles they used as a shelter only offered the impression of security. It wasn't needed for warmth, and the likelihood of rain was slim to none.

"Do we even need to light a fire?" she said. "It's so hot anyway, and it's not as though we have any fresh meat or fish that needs to be cooked."

"Even if we did," said Orergon, "we could probably cook it just by putting it on one of those rocks."

"Aye, it's certainly hot enough," Warsgra agreed. "But we don't know what kinds of creatures live out here. A fire might keep them away."

Dela lifted her eyebrows. "I'm not sure anything that lives out here is going to be scared of a little fire, but I guess it's best not to take the risk."

Trouble was, there weren't many trees out here either, and wood was in short supply. Scavenging around, they found moss clinging to the sides of some large rocks, and a fibrous, silvery-green plant which grew in spiky leaves from a bulb in the ground. None of these things would burn for very long, but the group gathered what they could, trying not to prick their fingers on the sharp leaves of the plant.

With the fire crackling, they took their seats around it and divided up the food. They were down to basic rations of stale bread and cheese now. The luxurious food of the Faes' meal felt like a long time ago, and Dela's mouth watered at the memory of the succulent fruits they'd eaten, the sweet tartness of the flesh, and the juice dribbling down her chin.

"Do any of you wonder if this whole thing is crazy?" she blurted.

Warsgra chuckled. "It is a little crazy."

She touched the ring at her throat. "I know, but I mean, what if we get there and discover this was all some trick created by the Fae? We don't know that he didn't somehow enchant the ring so Orergon burned his fingers on it. The Fae have no reason to help us. I doubt they even like us."

Orergon shrugged. "They seemed pretty friendly back at the village."

She sighed and rubbed both hands over her face. "Maybe, but it still might have been some kind of ploy to trick us."

"To do what?" Orergon insisted.

"I don't know. Just leave them alone, I guess."

Vehel spoke up. "I believe what Nimbus told us. He seemed sincere. I don't believe he's sent us off on a wild goose chase."

Dela chewed her lower lip. "I don't know if I'm going to be relieved or furious if we get to Drusga and discover this was no more than a crazy story."

Warsgra fixed her with his green gaze, looking at her from

beneath his bushy eyebrows. "Whatever happens, we'll be there for you."

Oregron nodded in agreement. "Yes, we'll be there for you."

The fire crackled, the final remnants of the foliage they'd collected burning out.

And the last of the sun dipped beneath the horizon, casting them into darkness.

CHAPTER 29

WARSGRA

Each day had started to feel the same as the last. They packed up the remains of their camp and mounted their rides. Warsgra had been annoyed at having to ride the pony at first, but he'd become surprisingly fond of Giant.

He glanced over at Dela riding Ghost beside him. That was someone else he'd also become surprisingly fond of. He'd never for a moment thought he'd have feelings for a human—in fact, feelings in general were foreign to him—yet he found himself worrying about what they'd discover when they reached Drusga. He didn't want her to be disappointed, but he also worried about what lay ahead if the Fae had been telling the truth. He'd lived a simple life so far, and he realized supporting Dela in this quest would mean he'd be diving into the politics of four different races. Did he have the sort of mind that would be able to understand such things? Even if he didn't, he would still be Dela's strength, if she said she needed him. He would protect her with his body and his axe. Though if she had a dragon, it might end up being Dela who did the protecting.

The journey felt relentless. It was an onward trudge, with nothing to break it up. The ponies walked with their heads hung.

Though they took regular breaks to give them water, the supply wasn't endless, and they'd eventually have to prioritize themselves before their mounts. The lack of foliage didn't help either, as there was little for them to graze upon.

The sun reached the highest point in the sky and began to descend again.

Dela suddenly let out a growl of frustration.

He narrowed his eyes at her as they rode, side by side. "What's wrong?"

Her lips pressed together, her nostrils flared. "How many miles have we traveled since leaving the pools? Twenty? Thirty?"

He nodded. "Yes, at least."

She gestured ahead. "So why aren't the fire mountains getting any closer? The scenery around us is changing, but the fire mountains look exactly the same."

He exchanged a glance with Orergon, who also nodded to say he agreed with her.

"Could it be some kind of mirage?" the Moerian suggested.

Warsgra's frown deepened. "You mean being able to see the fire mountains could be a trick of the eye?"

Sudden panic flitted across Dela's face. "Are we even heading in the right direction?"

"Yes," he reassured her. "I'm sure we are. North is north. Nothing can change that."

"Then why aren't the fire mountains getting any closer?"

"Maybe they are," Vehel said. "They just don't look like they are."

Warsgra scowled at him. "That doesn't make any sense."

"I'm not sure what I mean, but I wonder if it's a way of keeping people away. Some kind of magic to make people think they're nowhere near and make them give up, when actually, they're closer than they think."

Dela's eyes widened. "You think this is magic?"

The Elvish prince nodded. "I think it could be. Before we left the Fae village, I asked Nimbus how long it would take for us to reach Drusga, and he told me that depended on us. I thought he was talking about how fast we were able to move, but now I wonder if it's something else."

"Like what?" she asked.

"I'm not sure. Maybe we're just not looking at things right."

Warsgra shook his head. "That's nonsense. There's only one way to look at things."

"No, there isn't," Vehel replied. "When you see the reflection of the mountains in the stillness of a lake, you still see them, don't you? You might not be looking directly at them, but you can still see them."

Lines appeared across Dela's brow. "You think we need to not look at them directly?"

"I'm not sure. I'm just thinking out loud."

Warsgra didn't like things like this. He liked things to be exactly as they should be. "No. We just need to cover more miles. Distance is distance."

With that, he kicked his heels into Giant's belly. "Yah!" he yelled, pushing the pony into a gallop.

Giant took a moment to get going, but then fell into a steady canter, his sturdy legs covering ground, kicking up dust behind them. The pounding of the pony's hooves against the dirt was joined by several others, as his traveling companions followed suit and joined him. They'd all had enough now. They just wanted to get there and figure out what they needed to do next, and having a bunch of damned rocks playing mind tricks on them wasn't helping matters.

Soon, both his own breathing and that of Giant's became labored, snorting hard against the hot air. Not wanting to run the pony to the point of collapse, he pulled Giant to a halt and jumped down from his back.

Warsgra stared into the distance. "What, by the Gods …?"

He locked his hand in his long hair and shook his head in

disbelief. They'd covered more miles, but the mountains looked exactly the same. Dela was right in her frustrations. This had to be some kind of magic.

The others galloped up beside him and also pulled their rides to a stop. They climbed off to join him.

Vehel shook his head, his eyes narrowing. "So, nothing has changed."

"We're just not getting any closer," Dela cried, her eyes shiny with frustration. "It doesn't matter how far we go. We might as well turn back, or we'll end up killing ourselves trying to reach them."

Vehel shook his head. "No, it's some kind of trick."

"Can't you use your magic to reveal it?" Orergon asked.

His teeth dug into his lower lip. "I have no idea where to start."

Vehel's words about seeing a reflection in a lake played through his mind. He wasn't the kind to normally think on such things, but it was worth a try.

He lifted the huge blade of his axe, and turned so his back was to the direction they'd been heading. The others had all dismounted, and crowded around him, their bodies pressed in close. He was taller than each of them, and lifted his axe blade high, allowing the others to see.

They staggered back with cries of surprise.

Beside him, Dela gasped.

The tall slopes of the fire mountain that lead to Drusga was right there, towering over them, only a matter of a few miles away. They were looking at a reflection, but as they turned around they discovered the blackened sides of the fire mountain only a matter of a few miles away.

Vehel shook his head in wonder. "Viewing the fire mountain through Warsgra's axe must have broken the illusion."

Warsgra exchanged glances with his companions. They'd believed they still had a long way to go, but that was incorrect.

They'd already arrived.

CHAPTER 30

DELA

Dela's stomach flipped with nerves. She'd thought she had more time, but all of a sudden, they were already here. All they had to do was climb a part of the fire mountain to reach the opposite side and look down onto the valley beyond. Then she would learn the truth of what she was.

She exchanged a nervous smile with the others. "I guess we should keep moving, then?"

Warsgra nodded. "Aye. Let's do this."

They mounted the ponies for the final part of their journey.

Her breathing grew shallow with nerves, but also because the stink of sulfur grew strong enough for her to want to cover her nose. Now that they were so close, she could see smoke rising from the surface of the volcano.

Had the magic been created by the volcano itself, or was something else responsible? The dragons, perhaps? Her heart lifted with hope. Was it possible that the same magic that made them think Drusgra was almost unreachable was the same magic that had kept the secret that dragons still lived for so long?

"Be careful, the ground is getting boggy," Orergon called.

He was right. Patches appeared between the rocky crags, soft ground that looked solid at first, until it was stepped upon and vanished to reveal liquid beneath. The ponies began to stumble, placing their footing on ground they thought to be solid, but then suddenly wasn't.

"We need to continue on foot," Dela said. "One of the ponies is going to end up with a broken leg, if we're not careful."

They all did as she suggested, sliding from their backs and leading them forward with the rope harnesses.

The areas of bog started to spread, becoming larger than the areas of rock. As they climbed, picking their way around the loose areas, the smoke in the air increased, and the remaining air grew thin. Dela found her lungs tightening in protest, and she coughed often, covering her mouth with the back of her hand. The others were coughing, too, and she hoped the air quality wasn't going to get much worse. The route they followed was taking them higher, but they wouldn't need to go right to the summit of the fire mountain. Sweat poured down her back and ran from her hairline. The heat continued to increase, and she could see the ponies starting to struggle, too.

"Come on, Ghost," she encouraged her pony. "You can do it." The pony snorted in response, but his breathing was labored, and guilt speared through her. "We should have left them at the pools," she called to the others. "I don't know how much more of this they can take."

"We can't go back now," Warsgra replied. "We have to keep going."

She nodded and coughed again, her throat burning. Her chest felt tight, too, as though she couldn't draw enough air into her lungs, but she didn't know if it was from the smoke or the altitude.

How much farther would it be? The smoke from the fire mountain made it impossible to see the ridge, but she knew it was there. Her mind went to the dragons again. How could anything survive in such an alien, inhospitable landscape?

At some point, Warsgra had overtaken her, and now he came to a halt. "We have a problem."

"What's wrong?"

"We've run out of solid ground. There's only boggy ground ahead, as far as I can see."

Her heart sank. "No, there must be another way around."

Warsgra shook his big, shaggy head. "Not that I can see."

She glanced behind them, desperate. "What if we go back and retrace our steps? Maybe we can find another route."

"We only have another hour or so of light," Orergon said. "If we go back now, we'll never make it to the ridge on time."

Vehel bit his lower lip. "I'd hate to try to get off this thing in the dark."

Dela wondered exactly what they thought they were going to find when they reached the ridge. They may have reached their destination, but that didn't mean that whatever lay next wasn't going to be equally as grueling. She wasn't imagining a city paved with gold lying beyond the ridge, though she also wasn't sure what to expect.

She focused on the route ahead. "If we can't retrace our steps, then we've got no choice but to go through it. How deep does it appear?"

Warsgra stepped forward and allowed his foot to sink into the crusty mud. It went up to his knee, but he was tall, so it would be more like her thighs. "Not deep," he said, "but that might change."

"Are you all right to go first?" she asked him. "If it gets too deep, the rest of us will know we won't be able to continue."

He nodded. "Aye. I can do that."

His pony, Giant, dug his hooves into the rock and reared back, but Warsgra pulled on the rope harness. Giant drew back at first, but then eventually gave in, and followed Warsgra into the sludge. Orergon stepped in after, also guiding his pony in behind him.

"You go next," Vehel told her. "It's safer for you between us."

She lifted her eyebrows at him. "I can take care of myself, Vehel."

"I don't care. I'm going at the end."

There was grim determination in his light eyes, and she wasn't going to argue further. Stepping forward, she grimaced as hot sludge sank up to her thighs. "You didn't warn me that it was warm," she called to the front of the group.

Warsgra looked over his shoulder at her. "I thought you'd have figured that out for yourself."

He had a point. Smoke and steam rose in billows from pockets in the sludge, and it grew worse as they moved through it, as though they were disturbing the buildup.

"I'm so glad we washed our clothes," she quipped, trying to lighten the dour situation. It was a feeble attempt, and no one laughed.

Her pony pulled back on his harness. "Come on, Ghost. You can do it." The grey mud was up to his chest, and she could see every step was a struggle. She wished again that they'd left the ponies behind and carried their supplies themselves, but wishes were empty.

Ahead of her, Orergon was suddenly sucked downward. He disappeared into the mud and vanished from view. It happened so fast, the Moerian hadn't even had time to let out a yell of shock.

"Orergon!" she cried.

Warsgra spun around. "What happened?"

"I don't know. He was right in front of me, and then he wasn't."

They looked around, frantic. A few feet away, a hand reached out from under the sludge, and then vanished again.

"Orergon!" she cried again, lunging after where she'd seen the hand appear.

Warsgra moved, too, getting there before her and plunging his arm and most of his chest down into the mud.

"Where is he?" Vehel shouted. "What's happened?"

Warsgra continued to feel around in the mud. "There must be some kind of current. He's gotten caught up in it."

"No!" Tears filled her eyes as she stared around, desperate. He wouldn't be able to spend long under there. There was no air, and it was hot. She imagined thick sludge filling Orergon's ears, nose, and mouth, how his eyes would be squeezed shut against it. Was he fighting, struggling? Was he scared? Blind panic filled one side of her mind, while the other side tried to remain calm and think rationally to try to find him. They'd seen his hand over there, which meant the current he was caught in was pulling him east.

"This way," she said. "He must be this way."

She ploughed forward, leaning into the mud to use her hands to feel in every direction. She couldn't lose Orergon, she simply couldn't. She needed all three of them, and the thought of continuing with Orergon lost was more than she could bear. Warsgra was ahead of her, mimicking her movements.

"Orergon!" he bellowed, as though the Moerian hearing him would somehow help.

Dela glanced over her shoulder. To her shock, Vehel was just standing there, unmoving.

"Help us!" she cried.

The Elvish prince spoke through a tightened jaw. "I'm trying."

CHAPTER 31

✧

VEHEL

Nimbus's words rang through Vehel's head.
You can help her if you just stop being so afraid ...
If you learn to embrace it, you could be very powerful ...
It's part of who you are. You need to trust yourself ...

He couldn't allow Orergon to be lost in this forsaken place. Not only did the anguish on Dela's face break his heart, he'd also grown fond of the Moerian. They would be a weakened group without Orergon, and they needed him. If there was ever a time to trust in his magic, it was now.

He reached deep inside himself, searching for the swirling ball of energy that lived in the very center of his chest. It still went against everything he'd spent his whole life trying to restrain, but now he needed to fight against the things he'd been taught. He didn't need to repress his natural abilities any longer. The damage had been done—though he'd only ever used his magic trying to save lives—and now he needed to do everything in his ability to put things right.

The ball of energy expanded, spreading throughout his entire chest. He needed to channel it and push it out, to take the energy inside him and deliver it to the world instead. To make the world react to his force.

But he could feel himself failing.

He couldn't do it. Every part of himself fought against it, his mind rebelling. But he had to be stronger than that. Orergon's life depending on it, and he couldn't let Dela down. Nimbus had told him to trust himself—that Dela had needed his strength—and right now she needed it more than ever.

Power flooded through his arm and out to the place where he'd seen Orergon's hand. The thick sludge wobbled on top, and then parted, pushing to the sides to reveal a space between and the rocky face of the fire mountain beneath. Orergon wasn't there, but Dela and Warsgra both saw what Vehel was doing. Warsgra grabbed Dela's arm and pulled her out of the way, giving Vehel the space to do what he needed.

He refocused his attention, sweeping farther down the rocky face, clearing more of the sludge. Time was running out. How much longer could Orergon survive under there?

He swept his palm to one side, and the area he focused on cleared, revealing more black rock beneath. But there was still no Orergon. Vehel changed tactics, directing his energy in another route. The mud parted, clearing a space, and there, lying on the rock, was Orergon, face down and unmoving.

"Hold it back, Vehel!" Warsgra yelled, running into the cleared space. He reached Orergon and bent down, scooping the other man into his arms. Orergon was tall, but Warsgra was fearsomely strong, and he held Orergon against his chest as he turned.

"We need to get out of here," Warsgra yelled. "Back onto solid ground. Vehel, can you clear the rest of the way?"

His strength was draining from him, but he nodded. He'd keep this going until they all reached safety. The ridge they were aiming for was in sight now. Drusga, The Valley of the Dragons, was right over that peak. They were almost there. They'd almost made it.

"Is he alive?" Dela cried.

"I don't know, but we need to move. He's struggling."

She glanced over at Vehel, and Vehel realized Warsgra had been talking about him. Yes, he was starting to struggle to hold back the sludge. It was trickling in, like puncture holes in a dam.

"Go," he tried to yell, but his voice came out hoarse. All of his energy was going into controlling the matter threatening to suck them under and drown them, and now he barely had the ability to speak.

"You need to come with us!" Dela reached for him.

But he shook his head. He only wanted them to get across, and he would figure out his next move after.

The ponies snorted and kicked up their heels, not needing any encouragement to cross. Vehel released the reins of his ride, allowing the animal to follow the others across to solid ground.

"We're here, Vehel," Warsgra called back. "We made it."

Warsgra laid Orergon back on the rock and started to wipe the mud away from his face, clearing his airways. The Moerian was motionless.

Vehel started to walk across the bedrock, through the cleared space, to join them.

With every step, he lost a little more control and the sludge started to creep back in. First it was at his feet, then creeping up to his ankles, then his shins.

Dela must have seen him from where she was trying to help Orergon. "Come on, Vehel. You can do it. Move quicker! Just run!"

If he ran, he'd lose all power he had over the matter. Would he reach the other side before the mud all crashed in on him? He didn't know, but it was already up to his knees. Could he even run with his legs already thick with the sludge? He was losing control either way, and if the two sides joined fully again, he could easily be pulled under by whatever force had caught Orergon. The Moerian was a bigger man than he was, and would have been harder to pull under. If it caught Vehel, he wouldn't stand a chance.

With no choice, he broke his concentration, feeling the magic drain from his soul, and burst into movement.

He threw himself forward, hitting the rock, his momentum propelling him so he landed with no choice but to go into a roll and bring himself back up on his feet. Right behind him, the sludge crashed back together with waves clashing. His breath burst from his lungs, and he sucked it back in again, gathering himself. Gradually, his pulse began to slow. He wanted nothing more than to lie down and process what had just happened, but Orergon needed his help.

Both Dela and Warsgra were leaning over the motionless Moerian. Had he been submerged too long? Were they too late?

"Move," he rasped, barging the much larger Warsgra out of the way. He dropped to his knees beside Orergon. The black volcanic rock was hot beneath him, and the air was thick with sulfur. Close by, a crack in the rock released a billowing stream of grey smoke into the air. This fire mountain hadn't blown for hundreds of years, and he doubted it would go now, but the way their luck was heading, he couldn't help but glance up at the summit in worry. He didn't know what he was going to do, only that this was what his instinct told him, and Nimbus had told him to believe in himself.

Most of his magic had faded, but he still sensed a spark inside him, right in the center of his chest.

He pulled Orergon's leather vest apart, exposing the other man's smooth, brown chest. He leaned in and placed both hands at the spot directly above Orergon's heart. His chest was still, no sense of a heartbeat beneath.

"Please help him, Vehel," Dela begged, tears streaming clear tracks down her dirty face. "Please."

With both hands placed on Orergon's chest, Vehel focused once more. He only had a tiny amount of strength remaining, but he'd give Orergon everything he had if it meant the Moerian would survive.

He dug deeper, coaxing that final nugget of magic from his soul. Just as before, it swelled and surged forward. This time, he fixed the energy on his fingers right above Orergon's heart. Heat pulsed beneath his fingers, and a blue light glowed, similar to the light he'd created in the Southern Pass that had started all of this. He gritted his teeth, pushing it deeper, willing its energy into Orergon.

Something moved beneath his fingers. *Thu-thump.*

At the spark of life from Orergon, the final reserve of his energy exploded from Vehel. The power of it threw Vehel away from Orergon, so he landed on his back on the rock and the last residues of his power sapped from his body. He was vaguely aware of Dela calling his name, of the jagged black rock pressing into his back, of the smoky sky drifting across his vision…

And then he was gone.

CHAPTER 32

DELA

She couldn't believe her eyes as Orergon sat up, coughing and spluttering, and Vehel fell back, his eyes shut. Had she gained one and lost the other? She hesitated, not knowing who to go to first.

"It's okay," Warsgra growled, clearly sensing her indecision. "Vehel has only passed out. He'll come around again."

Even so, though she longed to go to Orergon and check he was all right, she'd seen how much Vehel had sacrificed for Orergon.

No, what he sacrificed for *all* of them.

She took a couple of steps to bring her to the Elvish prince's side and dropped to her knees.

Vehel let out a groan, and his eyelids flickered. She reached down and swept some of his white-blond hair from his face.

"By the Gods, Vehel, are you okay?"

He groaned again and tried to sit up. Dela moved behind him, slipping her arm around his back to help him sit.

"Orergon," he croaked. "Is he okay?"

She looked over to where Warsgra was helping Orergon to his feet. Warsgra met her gaze and nodded to show the Moerian was well.

"Yes, he's fine," she said, beaming at him. "You did it, Vehel. You saved Orergon. You used your magic, and you saved him."

Vehel nodded, still in a daze. "Yes ... Yes, I did."

"Are *you* okay?" Dela asked, trying to support him. "Do you think you can stand? Walk, even?"

"I think so."

She took his hand and helped Vehel to his feet. He felt wobbly at first, but as each minute passed, he grew stronger and more like his old self.

Orergon was also standing now. His long black hair was matted with the sludge he'd almost drowned in, and his clothes and skin were crusted in it. Orergon didn't appear to notice, however. After almost dying, Dela assumed he had more important things on his mind.

Dela quickly went to Ghost and removed a couple of the water bladders from the bags slung across the pony's rear end, and handed one to Vehel and the other to Orergon.

"Thanks." He took a couple of swigs, but didn't swallow, instead swilling the water around the inside of his mouth and then spitting. He must have swallowed some of the sludge, and from the eggy stench still rising from the volcanic mud, it must have tasted as bad as it smelled.

The Moerian looked over to Vehel.

"Thank you, Vehel." Orergon ducked his head at the Elvish prince. "I owe you my life."

Pink spots appeared in his pale cheeks at the praise, and Vehel bowed his head in return. "Of course. Dela needs all of us alive to make it the last part of the way."

She glanced across the volcanic rock, up at the point where they were headed. "We're almost at the ridge now. It isn't far at all. The smoke is clearing, and you can see it. Look." She pointed that way. The ridge fell away in the valley, which was hidden from view and would be until they reached the crest. The sun was soon to be setting and already cast an orange glow across the sky. Where it hit plumes of smoke, those, too, turned an orange red, creating what looked like a supernatural flame against the black volcanic rock.

Her heart pattered inside her chest. They were almost there. They'd nearly done it. She reached up and touched the ring at her throat. She had no idea what to expect when they got there.

Beside them, the ponies whinnied, anxious to move on. Like the rest of them, the animals were coated with mud up to their chests, and in the heat it was drying in a thick crust. Dela desperately wanted to be away from this forsaken place. She hoped what lay beyond would give them the answers they so desperately needed.

"Are we okay to keep going?" Warsgra asked, his brows pulling together.

She nodded. "I don't think we've got much choice. We can't stay here, and we can't go back now."

"Watch out for any more of those mud pools," he warned as he got moving, and the others followed. "We don't want to have to go through the same thing again."

But they appeared to be out of the worst of it. The remaining pools they came across had dried out, so the crusts on the surfaces were hard enough to stand upon. Even so, they took it cautiously, testing every footfall before placing their weight. Warsgra led the way once more, leading his pony behind him. Dela came next, pulling Ghost, who was now half white and half black from the chest down due to the sludge.

Vehel and Orergon followed, side by side, both leading their ponies. They were lucky not to have lost Orergon's mount in the sludge. Both men were unusually quiet, having been through a lot, and Dela hoped there would be no lasting consequences from what they'd experienced. She'd seen how much energy Vehel had given over to save Orergon, and she'd also seen how long Orergon hadn't been breathing. She worried about them both. She needed them, and they needed each other. At some point along this journey, the four of them had become a unit.

Her anticipation increased with every step that took her closer to the ridge. Soon they'd look down onto Drusga—The Valley of the Dragons. Would they see dragons for real, roaming around down there, content to live in the shadow of the fire mountain? Would they recognize her and somehow welcome her, or would they see her and the others as the enemy, and the group would find themselves with a far more dangerous fight on their hands?

Warsgra reached the ridge first, mounting the crest to look down onto the valley.

Dela picked up her pace, her mouth drying, her heart beating so hard she thought her chest might explode. What was he seeing? He had his back to her, so she couldn't read his face, but then he turned to her and locked his gaze on her, and she still couldn't read what he was thinking.

"What?" she cried, breaking into a trot to reach him. "What is it?"

She reached the edge and staggered to a halt. Exposed on the ridge, a wind buffeted them from the direction of the sea, and she had to push her hair away to prevent it tangling around her face. The sun was only moments from setting, sending long shadows down over the valley. The valley was huge, spreading into the distance, and, peeping through the hills on the other side of the gorge, she spotted the blue waters of the Lonely Strait.

But none of those things were the reason her heart sank.

Beside her, Orergon and Vehel also reached them and drew to a halt.

"By the Gods," Vehel exclaimed.

Dela clamped her hand to her mouth, not knowing what to say.

The valley was made of the same black volcanic rock as they'd just climbed, but it wasn't pure black. Embedded into the rock were swathes of white—lines and circles, all intricately joined together.

"Skeletons," she breathed.

They were looking down on numerous giant skeletons. From the shape of their massive heads, with their deadly, sharp teeth still in place, down to the long line of their tails. She could even make out the huge, delicate bones of their wings, the skin and tendons that held them together long since disintegrated.

A strong hand wrapped around her fingers and she managed to tear her eyes away from the scene before her to see Warsgra looking down at her. "I'm so sorry, Dela."

She'd been expecting to find live dragons, but instead she saw only skeleton after skeleton of dragons as far as the eye could see. The rumors had been right. They *had* been wiped out all those years ago.

The valley shimmered in her vision as her eyes filled with tears.

"They're all dead," she managed, speaking past the painful lump that had formed in her throat. "Just like everyone has always believed. This whole thing has been for nothing."

What had she expected? That she really was someone different, that she'd be able to change Xantearos and bring everyone together? Why? Because she had strange dreams and a ring other people couldn't touch. Because she'd been fed a pipedream by a Fae she'd only met for a matter of hours.

She tugged her fingers from Warsgra's grip and covered her face with her hands. "I can't believe I've been so stupid. All of this, it's been for nothing. I'm so sorry I put you all through this. By the Gods, we almost lost Orergon!"

"It hasn't been for nothing, Dela," Orergon said. "It's brought all of us together. You can't say that it means nothing."

She shook her head, her face still in her hands. "That's not what I meant. I thought I was going to be able to make a difference in the way everyone lives." She lifted her face from her hands and gave a cold laugh. "I thought I might somehow be able to stop The Choosing. I thought there would be no more Passovers, and that we wouldn't keep losing people the same way we lost Ridley and Layla and so many others."

"Maybe there's still a way," Vehel said, lifting his chin and looking out across the valley and the numerous dragon skeletons. "It might not be this way, but we can still try."

She shook her head. "How? Four voices among thousands. How is anyone going to notice us?"

He fixed her with those pale blue eyes. "I don't know, but we can try. It's only over if we give up."

A sob escaped her throat. "But we have so many miles to travel to get home. We were already so far away from the south, and now we have to turn around and retrace our steps. There are so many dangers. What if one of us or more doesn't make it?"

"Then we'll keep fighting," Orergon said, lifting his voice against the wind, "the same way we have on this whole journey, and we'll take care of each other. It's the only thing we can do." He reached out and swiped the tears from her face with the pad of his thumb.

She caught his hand and kissed his palm "Thank you, Orergon. Thank you, all of you. I'm sorry it was all for nothing."

"Stop saying that," he chided.

Warsgra's deep voice suddenly sounded. "Hey. What's that?"

The Norc was looking down at the ground, a frown on his face.

Dela sniffed. "What?"

"It's a rock. But it looks the same as the one in Dela's ring."

"Dragonstone?" Her interest had been piqued, and her tears dried as quickly as they had arrived.

Warsgra bent to pick up the stone, but he snatched back his hand, hissing air in over his teeth in pain. "Aye, that's the same stone." He held out his big hand to display the blisters already forming.

Dela took a couple of steps to bring her at Warsgra's side and looked down at the stone. It did look the same—black with red swirls, and shiny. She reached to the back of her neck and untied the leather cord, letting the ring drop into the palm of her hand. Then she knelt and held the ring beside the larger piece of stone on the ground. "Yes, it's definitely the same."

Her heart thumped, her pulse racing. Everything else fell away around her—Orergon, and Warsgra, and Vehel. The surrounding fire mountains and even the valley filled with the massive skeletons of the long dead dragons. Somehow she knew this would be the turning point, that when she picked up this stone and held it in her palm, everything would change.

Dizzy with fear and anticipation, she scooped up the rock and cradled it in her hand.

She held her breath, waiting, though she wasn't sure what for.

Still, nothing happened.

She turned to look at the others, and they all gave a gasp of shock,

"What?" she said. "What's wrong?"

"Dela, your eyes," Vehel said.

"They're glowing red," Orergon added.

She lifted her hand, as though placing her fingers beside them would mean she could see them.

"I don't know what's happening. I don't feel any different—"

A sudden screech came from the distance, across the other side of the valley. She'd never heard a sound like it before, somehow ancient, bloodthirsty, and beautiful, all at the same time. It echoed around the valley, bouncing from the volcanic walls, sending her heart racing. She sensed the others tense, and Warsgra pulled his axe from its holder. The others followed suit, Vehel lifting his bow from his back and pulling an arrow from his quiver, while Orergon withdrew his spear and stood, one foot forward, preparing himself for attack.

"Put the weapons away," she said. "He mustn't think we're the enemy."

She held her breath, her gaze searching the skyline.

The haunting screech came again, drawing her line of sight to the east.

The dragon appeared, rising from beyond the peaks, its great wings flapping slowly to lift its massive body higher. Its scales were an emerald green, but glinted blues and purples in the low light, like oil shining on the surface of a pond. Twin horns protruded from the top of its head, and spikes ran down the sides of its face, growing larger as they continued down its neck and back. Its long throat stretched out as it flew, its tail streaming out behind it.

In her palm, the Dragonstone grew hotter, though it didn't burn her skin. Instinctively, she knew if she handed the Dragonstone over to one of the others, their skin would rise in a blister within seconds. She could feel the others staring at her, and knew her eyes were burning bright with the power of the stone.

Suddenly, the valley and the fire mountain vanished, and she was spiraling, her mind vanishing down a black hole. She was flying again, but instinctively she knew her feet were still on the ground. This wasn't like before, where she felt like she was present in the moment. No, this time she was seeing something already gone by. These were the dragon's memories she was witnessing, rather than flying with him and seeing through his eyes.

Though they were a thousand miles away, on the other side of the country, she found herself looking down on her home city of Anthoinia. The streets were mapped out below her, a labyrinth of alleys and lanes. But the streets were not peaceful. No, it was chaos. People shouting. Families running and hiding.

And in the city square, armies were being gathered.

She saw it all from above, looking down, and understood exactly what it meant. News of what had happened in the

Southern Pass had got back to King and Queen Crowmere. They knew the treaty had been broken, and now they were preparing for war.

Dela's eyes flew open, though she hadn't even realized she'd shut them, and her fist unclenched. The Dragonstone fell from her palm and onto the blackened, rocky ground.

Warsgra, Vehel, and Orergon stared, wide-eyed, between her and the dragon now swooping across the valley.

The dragon landed in the middle of the valley, among the skeletons of his ancestors. Was he the last one, or were there more? He tucked his wings in, and then lifted his head high, stretching out his long neck, and when he opened his mouth, a billow of smoke and flames burst out.

"What did you see, Dela?" Vehel asked, his voice breathy with amazement. "We know you saw something."

She turned to them, wishing she had different news to deliver. They'd done so much to bring her to this point, but she feared it simply wasn't enough.

"We're too late to stop it," she blurted.

Orergon frowned at her. "To stop what?"

She looked between them all, taking in the sight of each of their expressions—worried, anxious, and a little hopeful, though that hope was misplaced. She cared about each of them and feared for what lay ahead.

"The Second Great War," she said eventually. "It has already begun."

AFTERWORD

Like what you've read? 'With a Dragon's Heart', book two in The Chronicles of the Four is out now and can be purchased from Amazon. Make sure you sign up to Marissa Farrar's Reverse Harem newsletter to stay updated about the new release!

https://landing.mailerlite.com/webforms/landing/e2x3e1

Cast of Characters

The Humans

The humans have the highest population of Xantearos, having taken claim to most of the Eastern coast. Their main area of residence is the capital city of Anthoinia, though some humans do live outside of the city walls.

King and Queen Crowmere: rulers of the City of Anthoinia and the Eastern Coast of Xantearos.
Philput Glod: The head of the City Guard.
Dela Stonebridge: One of the Chosen. Carries a dagger made of Elvish steel.
Ridley Stonebridge: Older brother of Dela Stonebridge.
Layla Whatley: Dela Stonebridge's best friend.
Johanna Stonebridge: Dela Stonebridge's mother.
Godfrey Stonebridge: Dela Stonebridge's father
Brer Stidrisk: Young man at school with Ridley Stonebridge.
Wayncguard Norton: Older man, bearded. Heads up the group of the Chosen.
Ellyn Rudge: Older woman who is part of the Chosen.

The Elvish

Blessed with the ability to magic, they're no longer allowed to use magic as signed in the Treaty. The Elvish live in a mountainous region in the South of the country called The Inverlands. They don't eat meat, but do eat fish.

King and Queen Dawngleam: Rulers of the Elvish Kingdom of The Inverlands

CAST OF CHARACTERS

Vehel Dawngleam: Youngest son of the king and queen of the Elvish
Vanthum Dawngleam: Middle son of the king and queen of the Elvish
Vehten Dawngleam: Oldest son of the king and queen of the Elvish
Ehlark, Folwin, Athtar, and Ivran: Elvish riders sent to accompany Vehel Dawngleam during the journey to the Southern Pass and the Passover.

The Moerians

Made up of several tribes of people, they live in the Vast Plains. Excellent hunters, skilled on horseback and with weapons of most kinds.

Orergon Ortiz: Leader of his tribe and tasked with the journey to the Southern Pass.
Aswor and Kolti: Tribesmen of Orergon, traveling with Orergon to the Passover.

The Norcs

Living along the side of the Great Diving Range in an area known as the Southern Trough, the Norcs live in clans. They are meat-eaters, and strong fighters.

Warsgra Tuskeye: Leader of his clan of the Norcs.
Jultu Leafwalker: Warsgra's right hand man.

The Fae

A race thought to be extinct, they live in the north, outside of the rules of the Treaty. They also have the ability to do magic, and continue to do so, despite the Treaty.

Nimbus Darkbriar: Leader of the Fae village in the north
Cirrus Fleetfoot: Member of the Fae village in the north

ACKNOWLEDGMENTS

I've wanted to write a fantasy novel for some time now. When I first started writing, it was in the horror and dark fantasy genre, but over time the fantasy morphed to paranormal romance, and then the paranormal romance morphed to contemporary romance. I've always loved the darker side of things, however, and when the idea came to me of combining the trope of Reverse Harem with fantasy, I couldn't wait to get stuck in!

As always, I had my team of amazing people around me to help! Thank you to Anika Willmanns of Ravenborn Covers for the amazing cover for this book. I bought it as a pre-made and it fit the story perfectly! Thank you to my editor Lori Whitwam, for being flexible toward my ever changing plans of which story to write next! And thank you to my proofreaders, Tammy of BookNookNuts, Karey McComish, Linda Helme, and my lovely mum, Glynis Elliott, who said Through a Dragon's Eyes was the best thing I'd written (I hope she was right!).

And finally, thank you to you, the reader, for continuing to read my stories.

Thanks for reading!

Marissa. XXX

ABOUT THE AUTHOR

Marissa Farrar has always been in love with being in love. But since she's been married for numerous years and has three young daughters, she's conducted her love affairs with multiple gorgeous men of the fictional persuasion.

The author of more than thirty novels, she has been a full time author for the last six years. She predominantly writes paranormal romance and fantasy, but has branched into contemporary fiction as well.

If you want to know more about Marissa, then please visit her website at www.marissa-farrar.blogspot.com. You can also find her at her facebook page, www.facebook.com/marissa.farrar.author or follow her on twitter @marissafarrar.

She loves to hear from readers and can be emailed at marissafarrar@hotmail.co.uk and to stay updated on all her new Reverse Harem books, just sign up to her newsletter! https://landing.mailerlite.com/webforms/landing/e2x3e1

ALSO BY THE AUTHOR

The Blood Courtesans Vampire Romance:
Stolen

The Serenity Series:
Alone (free first novel of the series!)
Buried
Captured
Dominion
Endless
THE COMPLETE SERIES BOXED SET

The Dhampyre Chronicles:
Twisted Dreams
Twisted Magic

The Spirit Shifters Series:
Autumn's Blood (free first novel)
Saving Autumn
Autumn Rising
Autumn's War
Avenging Autumn
Autumn's End
THE COMPLETE SERIES BOXED SET

The Monster Trilogy

Defaced

Denied

Delivered

Contemporary Fiction Novels

No Second Chances

Dirty Shots

Cut Too Deep

Survivor

The Sound of Crickets

Dark Fantasy/horror novels:

Underlife

The Dark Road

COPYRIGHT

THROUGH A DRAGON'S EYES
Chronicles of the Four
Book One

Copyright © 2018 Marissa Farrar

Warwick House Press

Edited by Lori Whitwam
Cover art by Ravenborn Designs

PUBLISHER'S NOTE

This is a work of fiction. Names, characters, places, and incidents are either the products of the author's imagination or are used fictitiously, and any resemblance to actual persons, living or dead, business establishments, events, or locales is entirely coincidental.

Printed in Dunstable, United Kingdom